Treachery in Torquay

A Sherlock Holmes Adventure

W. P. Lawler

First Edition published in 2018
Copyright © 2018
W. P. Lawler

The right of W. P. Lawler to be identified as the author of this work has been asserted by him in accordance with the Copyright, Designs and Patents Act 1998.

All rights reserved. No reproduction, copy or transmission of this publication may be made without express written permission. No paragraph of this publication may be reproduced, copied or transmitted except with express prior written permission or in accordance with the provisions of the Copyright Act 1956 (as amended). Any person who commits any unauthorised act in relation to this publication may be liable to criminal prosecution and civil claims for damage. Every effort has been made to ensure the accuracy of the information contained in this book. The opinions expressed herein are those of the author and not of MX Publishing.

Paperback ISBN 978-1-78705-301-4
ePub ISBN 978-1-78705-302-1
PDF ISBN 978-1-78705-303-8

Published in the UK by MX Publishing
335 Princess Park Manor, Royal Drive
London, N11 #GX
www.mxpublishing.co.uk
Cover design by

Some of the characters appearing in this work were historical figures. Most, however, are creations of Sir Arthur Conan Doyle and Mr. Lawler. Therefore, there may be resemblances to real persons, living or dead, but most are purely coincidental.

Table of Contents

	Dedication	iv
	Preface	v
	Map	viii
Chapter 1	And So it Begins	9
Chapter 2	Dark Days for Torquay	19
Chapter 3	A Gathering Storm	30
Chapter 4	Aggie Moves On	45
Chapter 5	Your Services Are Requested	56
Chapter 6	Torquay and Torre Abbey	68
Chapter 7	Cary's Journal	90
Chapter 8	The Plot Thickens	107
Chapter 9	Dinner for Four	138
Chapter 10	The Report	152
Chapter 11	Return to Torre Abbey	171
Chapter 12	What Holmes Discovered	196
Chapter 13	Ashfield	213
Chapter 14	Daddyhole	226
Chapter 15	Return to the Caverns	237
Chapter 16	Too Late	265
Chapter 17	All is Explained	287
Chapter 18	Heading Home	302
	Afterword	314
	Acknowledgements & Credits	316

Dedicated to My Friends, Family

&

Sherlockians Everywhere

Preface

For those of you who have not been able to find a copy of my first Conan Doyle pastiche, <u>Mystery at St Andrews</u>, you may be in luck. There are still a few copies available from MX Publishing. It's a golf mystery which takes place in the "Auld Grey Toon", St Andrews, and on the world famous Old Course.

Now to be fair, while I had a great time creating the story line and many original characters to interact with some of Conan Doyle's most famous heroes and villains, there is a lot of golf involved. Strange matches are described along with some very interesting rule interpretations that will have golfers and non-golfers alike very entertained. Still, if you don't like golf, well, this one might not be for you.

While I will acknowledge that the target audience for my first pastiche was fairly limited, I can proudly state that my latest effort, <u>Treachery in Torquay</u>, should prove to be an enjoyable read for one and all. I'm certain that it will appeal to the true Sherlockian.

As my friends and family know, I'm the type of person who likes to challenge myself. Whether it's on the golf course trying to shoot a score, composing or learning a new piece of music, or even undertaking the task of writing the history of my golf club, Fox Hill CC in Exeter, Pennsylvania, I find I enjoy projects that require major commitments of time and energy.

Well, not really. I mean if I could just turn out a pastiche just like that, it would be nice, but that's not the mark of a committed author. There are so many aspects to successful writing that need to be considered, that is, if you want to do it correctly.

Great stories require great plots and interesting characters. Locations for the tales need to be accurately portrayed so that the reader can paint scenes in his/her mind's eye. If the author is attempting to write a mystery, it's important to create clues, some necessary to help answer questions and others placed to deliberately mislead. All of these choices are there as the story comes together.
Next, the work must be checked for correct spelling, use of proper grammar, punctuation, and many, many re-writes until the author is satisfied. If you're willing to put the time and effort into your writing, you may find that you really enjoy what you've created!
Those are just some of the steps that most writers take when putting their ideas to paper.
Having read all of Conan Doyle's Sherlock Holmes and Doctor Watson tales several times over, I thought I might, once again, attempt to emulate his superb writing style in this, my latest pastiche, <u>Treachery in Torquay</u>. Of course, we get to follow Holmes and Watson on another interesting case. Like most of their mysteries, this tale includes plot twists, character development, historical detail, and clever "Holmesian" deductions to capture and hold the reader's attention.
While our favorite protagonists are busy finding clues and solving puzzles, an effort was consciously made to include real, live, historic figures in this story. We meet residents of Torquay, a resort town on the southeast coast of Britain who become involved in helping Holmes and Watson as they strive to bring criminals to justice. Action takes place in 1905, when a call for help reaches our duo as they languish through another damp winter in their 221B Baker Street dwelling.

It's a typical Holmes and Watson mystery that begins with an incident that triggers future events. The two will be required to leave London to help a famous lawyer who has received threats that could put his family in great peril. While attempting to track the culprits, Watson and Holmes find themselves helping to solve other crimes that have the citizens of Torquay terrorized. There is a touch of the macabre in the novel as well, that should add some special interest.

I invite all Sherlockians and other mystery fans who have enjoyed reading about the most famous characters in the history of fiction to give this one a try.

W. P. Lawler

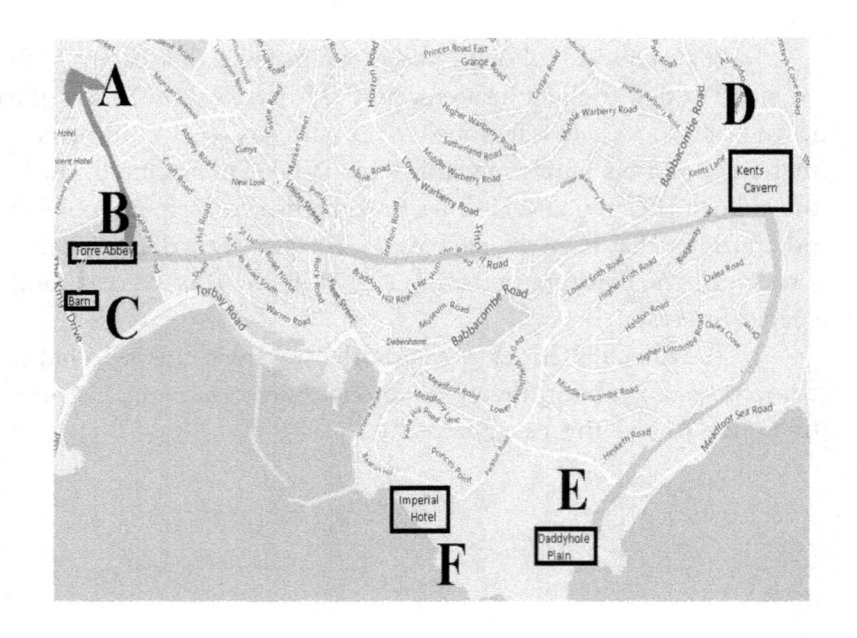

A - - Ashfield
B - - Torre Abbey
C - - Spanish Barn
D - - Kents Cavern
E - - Daddyhole Plain
F - - Imperial Hotel

Main locations for the story:
- Arrow shows the route from Torre Abbey to (**A**)Ashfield
    - Gray paths show location of tunnels

Chapter 1   And So It Begins. . .

Wednesday, October 18th, 1905

The sounds of waves breaking over the stony shoreline shattered the evening's silence along an isolated byway on the outskirts of the peaceful seaside village of Torquay. Peeking through the racing clouds, a gibbous moon shone overhead, helping to light the way for a solitary pedestrian, lantern in hand, who was making his way home along Meadfoot Road. His day's work done, this man began to smile as he realized that he would soon be sitting by a cozy fireside. There, by his side, would be his doting wife, Emma, seeing to his every need.

"Ah," he whispered aloud for his own amusement. "Soon I'll be resting in my comfortable chair. Won't that be nice? Perhaps, I'll even have some of Emma's plum pudding."

As he continued on his way, a small gust of wind, swirling up from the coast below, served to answer his quiet reflection. The mild zephyr hissed as it rattled among the bare branches, stirring up many of the leaves that had recently fallen beneath a small stand of maple trees. Nature's response seemed to please him, and he smiled once more resuming his walk up the winding slope and around a large hillock.

Over the last several weeks, this fellow had noticed that many of the sections of this roadway had fallen into terrible disrepair. He soon became acutely aware of that fact when, in the blink of an eye, his left foot caught a half-buried stump, sending him stumbling into a hedge by the side of the road. Somewhat stunned, he rested for a few moments until he had regained his composure. When he stood, with the help of a burly oak branch lying nearby, he laughed softly at his clumsiness. It was then that he noticed one of his boots was missing.

"Well, it appears that my boot has gone ahead without me. . ." he joked, jovially. "Now that's not good. . . not good at all! I'm lucky that nobody was present to witness my silly fall!"

It was now getting more difficult to see, and he surely didn't wish to go the rest of the way with only one boot. He did have his lantern though, and he gently pulled a small box from his pocket, struck a match and lit the wick. With the help of the illumination, he began his search for the missing boot, waving the lamp this way and that. Fortunately, he was soon able to locate the missing item, spying it a few yards ahead, sitting atop a small bush. After slipping it on, he secured the laces and continued his trek.

As he walked, he noticed that every step seemed to be accompanied by a dull echo. He decided to use the sound to help him maintain a consistent cadence as he moved through the brisk fall air. It reminded him of the way he used to march in his younger days when he had answered his country's call to military service. Oh, that seemed like only yesterday. . .

Looking back over his shoulder, our traveler could see the lights from the streetlamps reflecting off the cobblestone roads. He loved this peaceful little town, hard by the southern edge of the English Channel. Having lived his entire life in Torquay, he knew everything about the area. Such happy thoughts made his daily walk to and from the bank a most pleasant task, though not so enjoyable when the chilly, winter winds began to blow.

Turning his thoughts back to this night's trip, he found he was slowly being enveloped by the arrival of a foggy mist that frequented this quaint little coastal community, particularly at this time of year. The man paused to gaze at the sky, watching the twinkling stars as they slowly disappeared behind a swiftly moving band of clouds, surely a sign of worsening weather.

"Better get a move on," he coaxed, moving forward.

As he rounded another sharp bend on this isolated byway, he was pleased that he had remembered to bring along his plaid mackinaw. Residents of this region of Devon were well used to this kind of nuisance precipitation and were usually prepared for it.

The moon's light was now completely obscured by the fog, making the roadway barely navigable, though not much of a problem for one so well-acquainted with the winding trail. After all, he had his faithful walking stick and lantern to help him make his way around the many curves that lay before him.

Ordinarily, he never minded the journey, but, for some reason, there was something disquieting about this night's trip. Not withstanding the whimsical "boot" incident, something was amiss. He knew not why, but an uncomfortable feeling of dread chilled him as he plodded along. Sensing danger, the man decided to quicken his pace. A short time later, he realized that he couldn't keep going at this rate. "After all," he posited mentally, "I'm no longer a young man."

Upon reaching the top of a steep rise, he paused for a moment to catch his breath. While resting, he imagined sounds in the distance. He stood there, motionless, wondering if he had really heard anything at all. Lifting the lantern, he looked around as best he could, folding his cane under one arm and holding his hand to his ear. He tried to concentrate in an effort to discover the direction from which the noise was coming! Listen as he might, the only sounds to reach him were the mild, seasonal gusts accompanying the fog, the distant waves, and faint echoes of some late-arriving gulls as they fished the shallows along the Channel.

Somewhat relieved, he took a few more paces, then stopped once more. The peaceful, familiar sounds of the evening were once more broken!

"What's that noise?" he wondered. "Could those be footsteps I'm hearing?"

As he strained to identify the cause of the disturbance, the approaching sounds grew louder and louder. Now, he was certain that they were indeed footsteps!

"Someone else on Meadfoot Road at this time of night? Who could it be?" he pondered nervously. "Am I anxious for no reason? Torquay, after all, is a peaceful town with very little crime. Why, it's probably someone I know anyway!"

Those thoughts seemed to calm his fears for a short period of time and he continued along his route. After making his way around another sharp twist in the road, he stopped again, once more to listen. He began to twist his head this way and that, trying to better pick up the direction and distance of the approaching steps.

"Yes, those footsteps are getting nearer," he whispered, almost inaudibly.

"What should I do?" he deliberated, trying to better assess his predicament. It bothered him when he finally realized that it was highly unusual for people to be taking a walk in this remote part of the village, particularly at this time of night.

"Hmm... Let us see," he mused silently, "I've been working late, yet again. It's very dark and lonesome out here. Perhaps, just perhaps, I might be imagining things!"

Two steps later, he felt the need to state audibly his very real concern, "Still, I have rarely, if ever, found others traveling along this roadway at this hour."

"What should be done?" he continued muttering.

Once more he began to walk, still deliberating and weighing his options while trying to remain calm. "Do I simply ignore what I've heard, or should I..." He suddenly stopped dead in his tracks!

The footsteps were now getting much nearer, much louder! There was no longer any question as to the nature of the sounds. They were footsteps. There was no doubt about it.

Exercising reasonable discretion, Henry Dinsmore quickly ducked behind some tall bushes lying near a large rocky outcropping on the far side of the road. After extinguishing his lantern, he squatted down, hiding as best he could. He waited quietly, peering through the swaying branches. A short time later, there came into view three shadowy figures slowly trotting by, narrowly missing his hiding spot. They appeared to be searching for some thing or some one as they ambled by, whispering among themselves.

Dinsmore tried to hear their conversation as they passed his position, but the freshening wind gusts prevented any opportunity of that happening. Fortunately for him, he surmised, the runners seemed to be unaware that they were being observed. Henry watched and waited until they had disappeared well down the road, grateful that he had not been discovered. As he continued to wait, he realized that his body had begun to tremble. He could feel a cold sweat trickling from his forehead. Yes, he was now genuinely frightened, wondering if, indeed, he could have possibly been the object of their search!

"What about my footprints?" the thought nervously crossed his mind. "They'll realize that my prints have disappeared and they'll surely head back to see where I may have turned off the road!"

"Oh, what shall I do now?" he wondered in yet another nervous audible whisper.

He was genuinely troubled over this matter until he remembered that this part of the trail was composed of crushed rock. It would be virtually impossible for anyone to be "tracked" along this stretch of the road, especially in the darkness.

Though somewhat relieved, he remained extremely uncomfortable. A million thoughts ran through his mind. He began to consider the options available to him. Should he continue home or make a quick return to his office at the bank? Even though he was most anxious to act, he decided to wait a few minutes more before making up his mind. While he squatted behind the boulders, he felt another shiver shoot up his spine.

Again he questioned, "Is my body trying to tell me something? Could this be some kind of sign? Perhaps, it would be best for me to turn back tonight. Yes, I can spend the evening safely in my office. I'll simply 'ring-up' my wife."

His mouth continued to ramble, "Explain? Explain what? Explain that I was scared of the dark? No... that simply wouldn't do. I'm no coward. What might she think of me? No, dash it all, I'll stay where I am for a few more minutes and then proceed home."

When he was satisfied that all was in order, he stepped back onto the roadway and renewed his homeward journey.

After several more kilometers, he relaxed his pace, content in knowing that he was closing in on his destination, for his own neighborhood was just around the last hill. Soon he would be sipping that favorite glass of wine before retiring for the evening, this frightening experience merely an unpleasant memory to be laughed at and forgotten.

"Ah, that would be the thing to do," he happily concluded, and almost immediately he began to feel more at ease.

He found his earlier anxieties slowly diminishing with each new step. Now, a much calmer, more relaxed Henry Dinsmore walked on. Thinking back on the evening's events, he regretted his frightful behavior, and tried to make excuses for what he now believed to have been cowardly emotions.

"Why, anyone might have felt the same?" he posed. "I simply overreacted to an ordinary occurrence. Other people were out getting some air. That was all that it was."

Laughing quietly, he felt genuine embarrassment, happy that no one had been around to witness the way he had behaved.

At that moment, his comfortable self-reassurance was suddenly fractured by the sound of a snapping twig.

"Hallo? Who's there?" Henry Dinsmore moaned nervously, once more returning to his previous condition.

Silence. There was no response to his request. Again, Dinsmore's body tensed up and he felt the urge to run! The impulse was overwhelming, but as he prepared for the dash, a darkly-clad figure stepped out from behind a large oak tree and stood directly in front of him, blocking his way.

Dinsmore stopped dead in his tracks, and timidly muttered, "W-w-who are you? W-w-what do you want?"

There came no response from the stranger in the darkness, at least initially.

After a seemingly interminable delay, Henry's frightened inquiries were answered by a horribly sinister laugh.

The tall, dark shadow's husky voice began to taunt Dinsmore, " So, Mister Dinsmore, you wish to know who I am. And, you want to know what I want."

Henry now realized that he was in grave danger and his body began to tremble violently. He stood there, shaking, much the same as any cornered prey might react when threatened!

The terrified man tried to think of some sort of escape plan, when the muffled menacing voice started up again, whispering hideously through the chilly night air.

"I say, Mr. Henry Dinsmore," the voice continued, "do you think it wise to be out this late alone?"

Henry shakily raised his lantern, its light now showing the features of the scowling inquisitor who was staring directly into his eyes.

"Oh, it's you, is it," Dinsmore nervously replied, with some relief evident in his voice.

Now, feeling somewhat at ease, Henry offered, "You know, friend, I might ask you the same thing. What in the world are you doing out here all alone?"

After a brief pause, came the reply, "Ah," returned the other wearing a sinister smirk, "but I am not alone, councilman."

The words were hardly out of his mouth, when, without warning, Dinsmore was seized from behind and violently forced to the ground. Try as he might, he was unable to wrest himself from the clutches of his assailants. Before he could react, one of the attackers forced a dirty rag in his mouth, muffling his calls for help.

It was all over in seconds as two villainous ruffians quickly stood him upright to await his fate. They quickly turned him around to face his destiny. The man Henry had recognized began to slowly move toward him, carrying something in his right hand, swinging the object back-and-forth.

"Good bye, Mr. Dinsmore," the leader voiced in slow, measured ominous tones. "You'll trouble us no longer!"

The last thing Dinsmore would see on this earth was a strange hammer-like object being directed toward him. Unable to move, he felt a sharp, searing pain as the weapon pierced his cranial cavity and then, there was only darkness. . .

Henry Dinsmore had left his place of work only a short time before, on that fateful October night. As was his usual custom, it being Wednesday, he had been working late. His wife knew his work schedule, which seldom varied. Wednesday was the day Henry chose to catch up on his work. Everyone who knew the man, knew where to find him on Wednesday evenings. He was much admired by the town folk who had happily chosen him to be a member of the council. He was a decent man, God-fearing, sensible, hard-working and a most reliable friend to all.

Dinsmore was the kind of person often referred to as "the salt of the earth." Always eager to help his fellow man, he never could have imagined that it would be his last night alive.

Likewise, the town he loved so much could never have anticipated that this murder would be the beginning of a tragic period in the little town's history.

Chapter 2 Dark Days for Torquay

December, 1905

Christmastime is said to bring out the best in people all over the world. In the Christian religion it celebrates the birth of the Savior, Jesus, the Christ. To a lesser extent, this time of year also evokes the arrival of Father Christmas, bearer of special gifts for the children of many European countries. Of course, other groups find this time of the year meaningful, as well. For example, many follow and celebrate the seasonal equinoxes. Some of these folk conduct elaborate rituals heralding the earth's annual journey around the sun.

In this respect, the residents of Torquay were certainly no different. Preparations for this happy season would normally begin very early in December with Torquayians flitting about, decorating their homes and shops. It had always been a joyous time of the year for the inhabitants of this seaside village, one of Britain's many attractive communities along the South Devon coast.

This part of the country had long been a premier holiday vacation locale for residents of the many smoke-infested urban areas of London, Birmingham, and Manchester. Indeed, it had become a favorite respite for those wishing to escape the harsh conditions of those industrialized cities. This charming little town was also a popular spot for many on holiday from other nations as well. Travelers from other European and Scandinavian countries had been coming to Torquay for decades, seeking to enjoy the peaceful beauty and serenity of this lovely region of England.

Though primarily known as a summer resort, it could also prove most attractive during the Yuletide with its colorful displays, beautiful parades, lovely craft shops and winter festivals. Hoteliers and local merchants were the fortunate beneficiaries of this happiest time of the year. Everywhere throughout the small city could be heard the laughter and songs of children, joyfully anticipating the approach of Christmas, and more importantly, at least for most, the annual celebration of the birth of the Savior.

Sadly, this Christmas would be different, much different for residents and visitors alike. Recent events had placed a pall over the entire region. Oh, there would still be the carols, present-giving, religious ceremonies and all of the other winter holiday activities that served to brighten this time of year. Yes, there would be traditional Christmas celebrations for Torquay, but this year, other, more serious concerns were on the minds of its populace.

Much of the joy of this holiday season had been taken away from these residents. For you see, the people of Torquay were living in fear! This terrible change all stemmed from a string of unsolved murders. Yes, several of the town's more illustrious citizenry had met with tragic ends. Initially, it was believed that the first fatality, Henry Dinsmore, community bank officer and one of the town's councilmen, had tragically died from head injuries received from a fall along his daily walk home. Sad though that was, members of the town knew that such an unfortunate event could happen from time-to-time to anyone, anywhere. Their feelings on the matter, however, changed radically after detective work by the local constabulary had determined that the poor man had been murdered!

For the last several months the local newspaper had been churning out more and more details as they became available. Opinions differed as to how, why, and where the crime had been perpetrated.

According to the official police report, on Wednesday evening, October 18th, Mr. Henry Dinsmore had been clubbed to death while returning home from work. The instrument used in the crime had been some type of hammer-like device. The report continued with a description of how investigators believed the event had taken place. Officials surmised that Dinsmore's attacker(s) had come up from behind him, delivering the fatal blows, sight unseen. They further speculated that the poor man had died almost immediately, so deeply had the skull been penetrated.

They further determined that the crime had been committed in an isolated section along Meadfoot Road, an area known for its extremely dense vegetation. All who knew that particular parcel of land agreed that it would have been a perfect spot for foul play. It was further stated that police were continuing their search for the murder weapon and the perpetrators. Law officials assured residents that they would not stop until those responsible were arrested and duly brought to justice.

Many citizens, it must be stated, were quick to criticize the report. Indeed, many supplied theories of their own. Rumors abounded. Some suggested it had been the work of a pagan blood cult that had recently moved into Devonshire. The newspaper followed up those comments with an investigation of its own, sending reporters to visit other parts of England where similar cults had lived and practiced their beliefs.

Their findings indicated that a small band of Druids had recently moved into the outskirts of Torquay. Leaders of this local cult were called into a meeting with town council members. At that gathering, officials and townspeople raised concerns as to the activities and practices of the group. Many concerns were put forth by the locals, some of whom advanced the belief that this atrocity could be the result of this cult's appearance on the periphery of Torquay.

After much discussion, the chieftain of the group, a man called, Terra, was allowed to address the populace. Ignoring the derisive and threatening verbal abuse that arose from the angry audience, he offered the following remarks:

"My dear people, we only wish to live in peace and harmony with all of you. We are merely following our religious convictions, that is all. Some of our practices might seem unusual to you, but let me assure you, they are of no danger to anyone. Please know that we are willing to cooperate with community leaders in all ways possible and hope to allay your fears."

"As proof of our good intentions," Terra continued, "I invite any of Torquay's council members or groups of citizens to come to our encampment to see how we live. You will certainly find that ours is a peaceful band that only seeks to worship nature. That is what we do and what we will always seek to do."

Councilmen were quick to take the clan leader up on his offer.

Under the direction of Chief Inspector Miles Davis, council members Trent Hall and Eldridge Fenwick made plans to visit the encampment to observe how the Druids conducted their daily enterprises. They announced that they would "see for themselves and report back to the community" at the next town hall meeting. That plan seemed to settle the crowd, at least for the moment, but they would eagerly be awaiting the findings.

When next the council met, those who had visited the Druid camp provided a detailed follow-up report. The main conclusion drawn, after much discussion, was that members of the sect, while different from the local citizenry, seemed to be an honest, hard-working lot. They followed and honored the changing seasons of Mother Earth. Their religion was based on harmony and friendship. Other descriptions of the cult's daily duties and rituals that had been observed were also put forth during the meeting and further analysis of their lifestyle seemed to quell much of the early fears expressed by many of the local citizens.

Indeed, after hearing those findings, many curious Torquay inhabitants visited the cult grounds to have a look for themselves. Town records indicated that several villagers were so attracted to what they had seen and discovered that they, in fact, had actually joined the sect!

Still, once that discussion had concluded, the town folk continued to return to the Dinsmore murder. Again came more rumors as to how Dinsmore may have met his death. Some believed that he had been killed by his jealous wife, who, it had been speculated, had caught him in some illicit adulterous affair.

Another outlandish accusation had Dinsmore victimized by

hired assassins over gambling debts he had supposedly accrued. It seemed as though every member of the village had an idea as to why Dinsmore was singled-out, and each suggestion appeared zanier than the one before.

Why some of the townspeople even resurrected the legend of the "Demon from Daddyhole"! While most in the area thought that the legend of the Daddyhole Demon was just that, there were those who truly believed! In fact, in the days that followed, the town newspaper began to interview locals who had claimed to have witnessed strange happenings on, or near, the Daddyhole. Many of those who had come forward to testify seemed strangely delusional. Officials who had interviewed these people suggested that perhaps they were looking for some attention to validate their own existence. Other accounts, however, were not so easily dismissed.

It seemed that one of the town's seamstresses vowed that she had seen the Demon speeding along the edge of Daddyhole Cliff atop his black charger. She was soon joined by others who likewise imagined they had heard his fearsome cries and eerie shrieks echoing along the shoreline below!

Officials were, naturally, very concerned about these reports. They tried their best to dispel the fears that were now tearing their quiet little community apart, but it would not be an easy task. Town meetings were now being conducted each and every Monday, not once a month. Citizens were encouraged to attend these gatherings to voice their continued concerns and to help develop plans to put an end to these many spurious and often ridiculous speculations.

Citizens were growing more and more frenzied. They began to

exhibit complete frustration with those in authority. Police officials soon became the main targets of the collective town wrath. Most of those in attendance were sensible residents who understood that the law enforcement officers were doing their level best to solve the horrendous crime. But there were others in the audience with very different points of view.

At one of the gatherings, a group of residents produced a list of questions that they felt needed to be addressed. They were tired of the official responses that had been given in an effort to assuage their very real fears. One particularly interested individual, Vicar David Prentiss, headed a small, but passionate group that believed Torquay had been targeted by demonic spirits.

Prentiss offered, "My dear council and citizens, do you not see the reason for this atrocity? It is us, all of us, who are being punished by the Almighty for our wicked ways. It is that simple! All that we need do is turn from our sinful ways and repent. Don't you see, my good people?"

The vicar's words were met by a mixed chorus of "Amens" and "The Vicar's a Looney" coming from the anxious crowd. Clearly, this cleric's position was not unanimously held.

Next to express their concerns was a group represented by Molly Stone, who spoke on the matter of the demon that she and several others believed they had seen at Daddyhole.

"Before it is too late," she pleaded to the law enforcement community, "you must gather the area constables and even our army, if needed, and investigate and close up the Daddyhole!"

Her brief remarks were accompanied by some raucous behavior

by some of her followers, along with repeated chants of "Destroy Daddyhole... Destroy Daddyhole..."

The ensuing demonstration lasted several minutes before order could be restored. At that point, Mr. James Cary, council president, suggested that the entire community needed to "calm down and begin to work together."

"My fellow Torquayians," he began, "I know that we are all committed to solving this crime, for that is what it is, first and foremost. While many of you seem to think that this murder is due to some sort of demonic activity or our town's failure to observe God's laws, and let me add, that at this point there might be some justification for those feelings, I believe that this atrocity was committed by the actions of ordinary, flesh-and-blood, evil-minded humans. These individuals will be caught and they will pay for their actions. You have my word on that."

"It's easy for you to speak those words," came the reply from one of the townsfolk, "but what if there are additional killings, and still there are no arrests?"

Cary raised his hand and started to respond to the comment, when another resident loudly voiced, "Yes, Cary, words are cheap, aren't they? We demand actions..."

That last remark fomented renewed riotous chanting, pushing and shoving, and chairs heaved about, willy-nilly, necessitating the abrupt adjournment of that night's town meeting. In fact, due to that outbreak, town leaders decided to postpone the next scheduled meeting until further notice, hoping that time might allow tempers to cool.

For a while, things seemed to be getting better. Normality had returned and the day-to-day occurrences of life in a small town were once again observed, even though the community was still trying to deal with the Dinsmore murder.

Suddenly, the relative peace that had returned was fractured when constables announced that another councilman's body had been found, this time at Belgrave Road. On November 22nd, Trent Hall, another well-respected citizen, had been killed, and his death added even greater turmoil to an already terrified populace. Town leaders immediately scheduled an emergency meeting and spokesmen again demanded answers from police officials. Mothers and fathers prayed for an end to these terrible murders and demanded swift apprehension and prosecution of the guilty parties. Chief Inspector Davis could only restate that his men were doing their level best, and once more promised full prosecution once the murderers were finally apprehended.

Clearly, that was not enough for the town folk. They suggested hiring additional peace officers to patrol the town until the criminals were captured. Again it was up to Councilman James Cary to try and sooth their concerns, offering reward monies to any information that might lead to solving these heinous crimes. His offer, while well-meaning, had little effect on the frenzied residents.

Several more weeks passed and things seemed to be better with the addition of some additional police personnel, newly hired in response to the angry townspeople. Business was picking up and residents appeared to be less apprehensive, though most anxious for the killer(s) to be found. Still, stark reminders would continue to haunt the villagers until the murders were solved.

Yes, things had once again settled down for a time until December 15th. On that fateful day, a wagon pulled by two Clydesdales came rushing through the center of town, with a much-agitated driver screaming, "They've found another body on Babbacombe Road. It's Tom Dennison."

At that, an angry crowd began to form and follow the wagon to police headquarters. Members of the group appeared ready to riot against the very people whose job it was to protect them! Women were sobbing as they hugged their children, and when Chief Inspector Miles Davis walked out to speak, he was pelted with rocks, sticks, and anything the crowd could find.

Suddenly, and most fortunately, Vicar Prentiss climbed the front stairs of the headquarters and, raising his hands to quiet the demonstrators, spoke loudly, "My friends, what are we doing? I implore you, in the name of the Almighty, please stop what you are doing and think! Look at what you are becoming!"

Seconds later, an angry shout came from one of the assembled townspeople, "Vicar, get out of the way. We don't wish to hurt you. It's them.... They don't do anything to protect us. Don't you see, yet another member of our community has been murdered. . . .That's three. . . three councilmen!"

The crowd again appeared ready to riot, but Vicar Prentiss again raised his hands and offered, "My friends, I ask you to be reasonable. Do you really blame these horrendous murders on our fine constables? Do you wish to make things worse by punishing the very people who have been working day and night to try and solve these hellish events?"

"Please, turn around. Go back to your homes and workplaces.

Allow these fine men to do what they need to do. That is all that can be done, for now. And, we can pray to the Almighty for His help," the minister advised.

Slowly, the crowd broke up and departed, many still mumbling as they slipped away.

The next day's newspaper described in some detail what the investigating officials had found at the murder site. There was a brief statement which indicated that Tom Dennison had been strangled and his lifeless body left in bushes along Babbacombe Road.

With each passing day, the community continued to wallow in uncertainty and fear. Few were the smiling faces among the citizenry, for the crimes remained unsolved. Once more, area commerce and local craftsmen experienced lost revenue, for people were afraid to venture too far from their homes.

What had long been a peaceful, welcoming community had now become a suspicious, fearful one. People began to lock their doors and windows. They kept their children indoors, only allowing them to venture outside in the company of family members.

Yes, the days were dark, indeed, in the quiet little town of Torquay.

Chapter 3 A Gathering Storm

Thursday, December 14th

The blustery weather that had recently pelted the southern coast of Devon was slowly making its way out across the Channel. It would probably be nearing Cherbourg within the hour, bringing with it the same cold, damp, wintery mix that it had only recently dumped on the quaint English seaside town of Torquay.

Witnessing the storm's departure was a young local girl, who decided to take a break from her music practice. She had been compelled by the elements to remain inside her cozy home, and she was most anxious to put away her mandolin. For several hours, the girl had whiled away her time, practicing finger positions on the instrument's frets.

Aggie was very impatient waiting for the sleety mix to cease. She knew her mother would never allow her to leave the house in such poor weather conditions. The skies would have to clear for her to have any chance of visiting Margaret Cary, her closest friend.

Aggie rose from her chair and hurriedly walked to the front window hoping to find that the sky had brightened. Smiling, she was pleased to discover that her luck had changed, watching the sun's bright, warming rays racing across her lawn. It's light was up to the walkway; soon it reached the window pane and flashed into her joyous eyes. Quickly, she placed her mandolin back in its case, returned the sheet music to the corner desk, and made her way toward the delicious aromas coming from the kitchen.

Upon entering the cozy room, she found her mother humming one of her favorite songs while stirring a steaming pot of home-made soup. "Oh, that soup smells so wonderful," Aggie imagined as she listened to her mother's voice. It wasn't because her mother was such a great singer. Nor was it because the tunes were so lovely. Rather, she knew her mother's singing meant that Clara Miller was in a good mood. That was always a good thing, particularly whenever Aggie knew she might need her mother's approval.

Clara Miller was a fine woman and a loving parent. She had been forced over the last several years to raise and school her youngest child without the benefit of a husband. Sadly, Frederick had passed away four years prior, and since that time life had become so much more complicated.

"Is that you, Aggie dear?" the girl's mother spoke softly, returning the soup ladle to the steaming pot.

"Yes, mother," her daughter replied.

Turning to meet the young child's anxious glance, Clara offered, "Well, Aggie, I can see that the weather's clearing. Why don't you wrap up and take a nice walk down to Torquay Road and watch the storm heading out over the Channel?"

"Mum," she replied, fastening her bonnet, "how are you able to read my mind so easily? Why sometimes I think you're 'Clara-voyant', if

I might be so bold as to suggest."

Her mother sighed softly as she continued preparing the soup, for that witticism was now quite indicative of her clever daughter's intelligence and love for language. Gazing at the young girl, she realized how much Aggie had matured over the past several months. In truth, Clara hadn't expected much scholastically from this child.

When Aggie was much younger, Clara believed her to be a problem learner, perhaps the slowest of the Miller children. She had home-schooled all three of her brood and it was simply her honest appraisal of her last born. Clara sensed that Aggie would have much more difficulty adjusting to life than her older brother and sister. Aggie was so different from them. This worried Clara to such an extent that she made a point of keeping an extra close eye on her.

The young mother saw much of herself in Aggie, for she had experienced the same loss of her own father at an early age when he was killed in a riding accident. At the time Clara had only been nine years old. Naturally, such an event would have a traumatic effect on a youngster, and in Clara's case, it had left her very much a loner.

During those early years she formed her own theories on many subjects, some of them quite unusual. For instance, Mrs. Miller did not want her children to learn how to read until they were at least eight years old! Perhaps it was something about having them hold on to their innocence or some effort to try to keep them from growing up too fast. At any rate, this was one of her heart-felt beliefs and she demanded her students obey those dictates.

Aggie, however, despite her mother's wishes, had secretly taught herself to read, and quickly acquired a deep enjoyment and appreciation for literature. When Clara discovered that her daughter was able to read, she was initially very upset. Still, there wasn't much that she could do about it, after the fact. Instead, she chose to praise her daughter's cheekiness, hoping it might lead to continued development of Aggie's self image.

"Why Aggie, you know I've always been able to read your mind!" she voiced, responding to her daughter's clever comment. "And it's no great mystery that you enjoy watching the clouds streaming across the Channel after a storm. You've always been infatuated by the elements!"

A funny thing, Clara remembered being the very same way when she was a child, and now her youngest had inherited her own appreciation for all of the joys of nature.

"Now, Aggie, you may go, but mind, you get home before dark, young lady! That would be around 5 o'clock," she softly suggested, pointing to the grandfather clock in the corner.

"Oh, and don't forget to say 'hello' to Margaret for me," she added as Aggie finished tightening her boots.

"Thanks, mum, I will," the daughter called, as she bolted out through the back door.

As Aggie continued to fasten her outer coat, she began to laugh, realizing that she had not asked if she could visit Margaret. Yes, her mother had surmised that probability and led Aggie to mumble quietly, "That's my mum. She's always a few steps ahead of me. It's no wonder that I love her so!"

Aggie sang happily as she made her way down Barton Road through the remnants of the light slush. Suddenly, for no apparent reason she stopped, turned and looked back at her home. How pretty it appeared, sitting back on a small hill, wearing a light coat of snow! That her home, Ashfield, was a lovely residence, there most certainly could be no doubt. In truth, with its appealing location, large greenhouse and lovely acreage, it had been described by many citizens as one of the town's most beautiful homes. There, together with her mother, father, brother, and sister, they had once enjoyed such an idyllic life. Now, only Aggie, her mother and a maid remained in this stately home. Her older sister, Madge, had married and moved to nearby Cheadle Hall, while her brother, Monty, had decided to join the army.

Sadly, the passing of her father, Frederick, in 1901, had completely altered conditions and nothing would ever be the same. Aggie had truly loved her father and still missed him terribly. Frederick Miller, an American, had inherited quite a bit of money, and thanks to him, the family was able to enjoy a most comfortable lifestyle. The young girl was only eleven at the time of her father's death, and with his passing came new concerns and worries. Still, her mother was a strong figure. The family knew that their mother would be sure to provide for them, no matter what situations might arise.

A twenty minute walk was all that it took for the young girl to arrive at her favorite spot. From her very first visit to Torre Abbey, Aggie had been captivated. The expansive home sat back from a small cliff which overlooked a modest inlet on the southerly coast of Torquay. There were all kinds of trees, floral arrangements and bushes everywhere. Palm trees and other species were evident along with the branch-covered pathways that wound their way in and out of the wondrous property. Most importantly, however, Torre Abbey was the home of her best friend and confidant, Margaret Cary.

It was here, in this lovely, sylvan setting with the weather cooperating, that she loved to sit and read. It was here, overlooking the sea, where her active imagination could soar, filling her mind with so many wonderful stories and mysterious questions that needed answers!

Her friend, Margaret, was like her in so many ways, and together they would enjoy the magical beauty of the surrounding landscape. They would run, jump and play outdoor games for hours and hours at a time! It was only when the conditions were less than ideal that they would go indoors. But that was a treat, as well, for the building was much like a playground. There were so many rooms and passageways that the friends never tired of exploring the immense former abbey, once home to monks of the Premonstratensian order.

As Aggie approached the huge building, she observed several dark storm clouds moving out over the coast, blocking the warmth of the sun. Since the rain and sleet had turned to a gentle mist, she wasn't too concerned about getting soaked. Skipping along the roadway, the young girl hastily approached the large front door, eager to see her friend.

In no time at all, she climbed the old steps and anxiously grabbed the large brass doorknocker. Aggie loved to lift it up as high as she could and allow it to freely swing back into place. It always produced a very, very loud, somewhat menacing "thump!" In fact, the noise was so voluminous that she seldom had to employ this strategy more than once

In less than a minute, Aggie heard someone approaching from inside the entryway. Slowly, the huge door swung open and a kindly face offered the frequent guest a most cordial greeting.

"Why, look who's come for a visit." the Cary family butler continued with his familiar smile. "Say, aren't you the famous Miss Aggie Miller?"

Aggie would always return Malcolm's smile with a polite and sincere, "Why, Mr. Malcolm, yes. Of course, it is I."

Malcolm Randolph was a distinguished looking, gray-haired gentleman who had been in the employ of the Cary family for over 20 years. Always nattily attired in his freshly pressed butler-wear, he loved to fuss when Aggie came to visit.

Smiling broadly he offered, "Miss Aggie, am I to assume that you are looking for the lovely and talented Miss Margaret Cary?"

"Brilliant, Malcolm," Aggie teased.

"Would you please announce my presence to Her Royal Highness?" she continued.

"Aggie," Malcolm lowered his voice and returned to his more traditional role, "I'm afraid Miss Margaret is not home, and isn't expected back until later this evening. Shall I tell her that you called?"

"Thank you, Mr. Malcolm," the young girl replied, fastening her outerwear. "Please tell her that perhaps I'll come by tomorrow."

And after a polite "good-bye", she was out the door, making her way toward the nearby sea cliffs.

Looking out over the vast watery expanse, Aggie moved closer to the edge of the slight drop-off, impatient to scan the churning waters below. Finding an ideal spot, she rested, studying the rhythm of the waves as they washed ashore. While the passing storm continued to move away, the sea still remained very active, as it spatter-dashed the rocky shoreline. Positioned some ten meters above the dark foamy waters, she looked up and down the alternating small coves and stark cliffs which comprised this piece of the 35 kilometer shoreline of her hometown.

Here and there, she could spot a few brave individuals, moving from one rocky outcropping to another, challenging the breaking waves that so noisily splashed around them. Several residents were walking their dogs, enjoying their innocent canine playfulness as they waded in and out of the swirling tidal pools.

She next turned her attention toward the eastern horizon, in the direction of Cherbourg and the continent. The raging storm was still stirring up the Channel waters; an exciting sight, unless you happened to be aboard a vessel caught up in the fury.

While she sat there pondering such a situation, the young girl suddenly stood up. For out in the distance, much to her dismay, Aggie saw that there was a ship in the Channel, fighting those waves. What a sight it was! Aggie began to think about those aboard, and how horrible it must be for them in such hazardous conditions! She sent a prayer their way, just in case, for she believed that most sea captains who piloted ships from England to France knew the ways of Channel storms.

Turning away from the sight, she began to daydream. Aggie found much symbolism in storms. There were storms that mankind had to face, like it or not. Sometimes, she reckoned, the dangers must have seemed insurmountable, for indeed, many times, they were. Yet, with the passing of every storm, there came a calm time for healing, recovery, and repairs that might need to be made. Mankind, throughout its history, had to adjust to all kinds of storms that inevitably had to be faced. It was the way of the world, after all.

Suddenly, Aggie realized that she had, once more, completely lost track of time. It hadn't been the first time that it had happened, nor would it be the last. She simply enjoyed walking along the Channel, and the time seemed to slip by so quickly. It had always been that way, for as long as she could remember.

"Time to go," she whispered to no one in particular as she crossed Torbay Road, picking up her pace as she neared her home.

"It had to be near dinnertime," she reasoned while turning up Belgrave Road and away from the coast. Her mother had told her that she was to be home by 5 o'clock. She knew it was going to be close! While racing up the street, Aggie peeked over her left shoulder only to find the sun slowly disappearing over the rooftops. As she rounded the corner at South Street, the church clock tower began to ring. Five reverberating chimes. . . Hmm... the young girl would be late again.

By the time she arrived at her house, the lights were already illuminating the classic Victorian structure. With great care, she made her way toward the sweet sounds of her mother's voice and the wonderful aroma of freshly baked bread. She quietly slipped through the back door, hoping to get to the table without being noticed. Unfortunately, her plan came undone when her mother glared at her while continuing to stir the soup!

"Hmm, well if it isn't Miss Aggie Come-lately," Clara teased her nervous daughter, pointing her in the direction of the wash basin. "Don't forget to wash up, now."

When Aggie had finished drying her hands, she sheepishly made her way back to the table and took her seat.

"Dear girl, I'm wondering what kind of outlandish excuse you are going to devise this time for being late again," spoke her mother in a most deliberate manner.

Clara knew her daughter could be a dreamer, much like she had been, way back in the day. By now, the mother was well-used to the foibles of her adolescent daughter, and occasionally enjoyed making her uncomfortable.

"Mum," the young girl began, "I'm only a few minutes late after all. Why must you carry on so? You know that I can be trusted."

"Yes, I know you can be trusted, and it had better remain that way, young lady," her mother spoke freely. "After all, Aggie, you're becoming a young woman. You need to act in a more mature manner. Part of growing up is learning to act more responsibly. Can you promise that you'll try?"

"Yes, Mum," Aggie replied penitently as she unfolded her dinner napkin and placed it upon her lap.

While Clara was still stirring the soup, she casually inquired, "By the way, Aggie, how is Margaret? What's new in her life?"

"Mother," she replied, "Margaret was out for the day and apparently wouldn't be home until later this evening. Malcolm was kind enough to explain."

"Any idea where she and her family might have gone?" asked the curious cook.

Aggie looked at her mother, issued a slight scowl and voiced, "Mum, you know it's really not any of our business, if you will excuse me for remarking."

Suddenly Aggie stopped talking. Realizing that her mother wasn't trying to be nosy but simply furthering the discussion, the young girl apologized. "Sorry, Mum, please forgive my rudeness. I meant to say, Malcolm didn't offer any additional details, and I suppose I didn't think it my place to ask. Please forgive my callous remark."

"Why thank you, dear!" her mother responded, happily surprised by the sincerity of the apology. "I'm glad that you didn't read more into my innocent statement than was intended."

At that, Clara gave Aggie a warm hug and kiss, allowing, "You know how proud I always am of you, don't you?"

Aggie acknowledged her mother's kindness, "Yes, Mother, I know how you feel, and I know how fortunate I am to have a Mum like you!"

"I say, mother," Aggie continued, "will we be spending New Year's Day with Auntie in Ealing this year? You know how wonderful it is to see London at this time of the year! I miss her, as well."

As she ladled out the soup, Clara seemed to pause before answering. "We'll see, young lady. We'll see."

Noticing the joy leave her daughter's questioning eyes, she elaborated, "That is, unless we decide to take our holiday on the continent this year. How does a trip to Paris or perhaps, Rome sound to you? Might you enjoy that, Missy?"

"Mother," the startled girl blushed out, "why that would be simply marvelous! I can hardly wait!"

In short order, mother and daughter were both sitting at the table enjoying delicious bowls of homemade chicken soup. Some small talk ensued until they had cleaned their plates and finished washing the dishes.

It was only after Aggie had completed her piano practice that her mother sat her down for a good talk. Clara had received a letter earlier that day that needed some explaining. She thought that this would be a good time to bring it to her daughter's attention.

"Aggie," her mother began, "I have a letter here from Miss Guyer. In it she remarked that you are not doing the best that you can do. Furthermore, she states, you are still not making friends with the other girls. And another thing, while your grades are acceptable, they could be better."

Aggie's face suddenly reddened. She couldn't believe that Miss Guyer was so cruel! Oh, how she despised that woman. . .

"Now, I know we've had some problems with that school, Aggie," her mother continued, "but you promised that you would try harder to fit in. Remember?"

"Yes, Mum," Aggie whined, "but I . . ."

Aggie didn't get to finish her answer. When she saw the look in her mother's eye, she began to sob mildly.

"Aggie, dear," her mother reacted, "crying will not get you out of this predicament. You broke your promise to Miss Guyer, and whatever you may think about her or the school, we are going to finish the semester."

At that point, Aggie had to respond, "Yes, mother, I know what I promised. But you have to know that I tried, really tried to get along with those girls. No matter what I said to them, they were most off-putting to me."

"Worst of all," Aggie continued while wiping the tears from her eyes, "they told stories about me, and if another girl even attempted to befriend me, they would treat her most poorly. So poorly, in fact, that they would force her to turn against me!"

"My dear," Clara instructed, "assuming that is the truth, and I know that you would have no reason to lie, surely, the teachers would support you if you were to bring those events to their attention. Wouldn't they reprimand those nasty girls?"

"Mother," Aggie offered weakly, "even if they did chastise them, that wouldn't make them accept me. It would be worse than before! Also, there are those ridiculous school rules that must be followed or else!"

"Now, daughter," Clara tried to reason, "we've been through this all before. If the other young girls can abide by the rules, then so can you. I'll hear no more about it."

Clara's stern look told her daughter that the discussion was over. Aggie couldn't imagine what could be worse than that school. It seemed like prison to have to follow rules merely for the sake of obeying authority figures. But that was not for her to decide. She only wondered how much worse it was going to get.

"What is more, Aggie, you will apologize to Miss Guyer," her mother paused, then continued, stating, "after which you will get your books and respectfully submit this letter from me."

At that, her mother handed the missive to Aggie. Aggie placed in on her arithmetic book and replied sadly, "Yes, Mother, I will do as you say."

As the mournful young girl began to walk away, her mother inquired, "Aggie, don't you want to see what's in the letter?"

"Not really, Mum," she whispered, "I'll just give it to Guyer, er I mean Miss Guyer."

"Well, I want you to know just what kind of trouble you're in young lady," Clara continued. "Please read it aloud so that there can be no mistake in what it means to all parties concerned."

That was the last thing in the world that Aggie wanted to do, but she complied. Sliding open the top of the unsealed letter, she returned to the table and slowly began to read the communique.

> My Dear Miss Guyer,
>
> Please believe me when I say to you, most sincerely, that I had hoped that it would never come to this. After the many conferences that we have had both privately, and in the presence of your very competent staff, I wanted to believe in your school's reputation for molding young girls into model young women.
>
> Your school is famous throughout the entire United Kingdom, and surely, there must be good reasons for it. Well, I, for one, do not see these good reasons.
>
> In my dealings with my daughter on these matters, I have demanded that she adhere to every school rule, even though I find them, for the most part, totally lacking in merit and much too punitive. While Aggie has found them to be somewhat arbitrary and silly, she has agreed to follow them religiously.
>
> Yet, I find that although her grades are acceptable, her demeanor is noticeably not. She is a wonderful girl, and I am extremely proud of her. The fact that your school can choose to ignore her worth by allowing her to be a constant target of a group of undisciplined, unruly, uncaring girls, is beyond the pale.
>
> Please accept this letter as my formal request for our contract to be terminated. Aggie will be leaving your institution upon submission of this letter.
>
> Good Day,
> Mrs. Frederick Miller
> Barton Road, Torquay, UK

After she had finished reading, Aggie squinted her eyes, turned her head and looked at her smiling mother. Then it hit her!

"Mother, dear," she squealed in absolute delight, "could this, er, would this, er....Does this mean that I won't have to spend another day in that miserable gaol? Could it be that I'm free of those superficial, egotistical, snooty rotters?"

Clara moved slowly toward her daughter with tears in her eyes, issuing, "My fine young lady, that school will trouble you no longer. And, I was wondering how you might feel about finishing your education in Paris. I've learned of three fine boarding schools if you are interested. There is one called Mademoiselle Cabernet's, another one by the name of Les Marroniers and of course, Miss Dryden's."

This was almost too much for Aggie to take at one time. Why only a short while ago, she had been so terribly frightened by a letter her mother had received from that awful Miss Guyer. Her mother's reaction to that letter had seemed even more disappointing. When, next, she learned that she would have to apologize to Miss Guyer herself, she was on the verge of being totally disconsolate!

Oh, what an incredible turn of events had just transpired!

"Mother, dear mother," she gratefully spoke, "you cannot conceive of the relief and joy that I am now feeling! Am I interested in attending school in Paris, France? Why, who wouldn't be delighted by such a wonderful opportunity?"

Totally out of character by now, Aggie skipped over to her mother's side and dragged her from her chair. The two of them began dancing an imagined rendition of a Strauss waltz.

Kissing her mother, she sobbed, "Oh, Mum, you've always been able to make things right! Thank you so much!"

Chapter 4   Aggie Moves On

Friday, December 15th

The next day could not come quickly enough for a certain Miss Aggie Miller, Barton Road, Torquay. She smiled her way through a bowl of breakfast porridge, sipped some tea, kissed her mother good-bye and took perhaps her happiest walk down the road to Miss Guyer's School for Girls, arriving in plenty of time for morning call.

Unlike most days, Aggie found that she was actually anxious to enter the gray-walled schoolhouse. Instead of heading to her homeroom, however, she quickly ascended the main stairway leading to the second floor principal's office. Standing outside the large wooden door with its smoked glass insert, Aggie brushed back her curly locks, straightened out her school uniform, and knocked three times.

Mrs. Trelawney's voice called out, "Come in, please."

"Good morning, Mrs. Trelawney," Aggie greeted the Guyer School's long-time secretary, continuing, "I'd like to speak to Miss Guyer, please."

A scowl came to the secretary's face as she responded, "Well, I'm sure you would like to do just that, Miss Miller, but I see that you haven't scheduled an appointment. I suggest that you come back later, and we'll see if Miss Guyer can make some time for you."

Ordinarily, this response would have been enough to send the young student hastily back to her classroom, feeling embarrassed and worthless. Today, however, she would not be having any of it. Undaunted, she stood her ground, waiting for the secretary to raise her eyes from the letter she appeared to be writing.

"I'm sorry, but I have to see her now, right this minute," the young girl offered with a great sense of urgency.

"Well, now, Missy," the secretary responded, somewhat annoyed by the young girl's tone. "What is so important that you can't wait like everyone else? Who do you think you are?"

"I'm sorry, Ma'am, but it's really none of your business. I'm prepared to wait all morning if I must," Aggie sternly remarked, folding her arms across her chest.

"Is that so?" Mrs. Trelawney snootily replied. "Well, sit here, and I'll see if Miss Guyer, who is extremely busy, has any time for such a rude young woman."

Aggie quietly took a seat, feeling a bit nervous, but at the same time most anxious to see the headmistress who had made her school life one bad dream after another. While she sat there, the young girl couldn't help thinking that Mrs. Trelawney was cut of the same cloth as her employer.

As she waited patiently in the main office, Aggie could hardly contain her emotions, for the search for Guyer seemed to be taking quite a long time! Ah, but it would most assuredly be worth the wait. How she had dreamt of this moment. Aggie decided to use this time to rehearse her upcoming conversation, making certain that she knew exactly what she was going to say.

Finally, the door opened and Miss Guyer entered the office with Miss Trelawney. The administrator was a plain woman in her early forties who always displayed an air of sophistication her actions never reflected. She glared at Aggie, surprised to see the young girl sitting there, smiling broadly. Aggie knew that Guyer could never have imagined what was about to take place.

"Thank you, Gladys," Guyer suggested, motioning to her secretary. "You can get back to work."

"Well, good morning, Miss Miller," spoke the headmistress, turning her head and running her index finger through her graying hair.

"Good morning to you, Miss Guyer," Aggie returned the woman's cold greeting.

"May I ask what is so important that you are out of class?" Miss Guyer inquired in a most pejorative manner.

"To tell you the truth, Miss Guyer," Aggie continued, "my mother asked me to meet with you today to apologize for any discomfort that I might have caused while attending your school."

"Why, how wonderful!" the still dubious Guyer spoke, squinting her eyes in a troubling manner. "Come with me, please," the head mistress motioned, opening the door to her office.

As she made her way behind a large ornate desk, she inquired, "Does this mean, Aggie, that you will behave like a proper 'Guyer girl' for the rest of your days with us?"

"That would be. . . Why that would be..." she stopped, for she couldn't find the words.

Aggie interjected, "Unbelievable... Incredible... Impossible?"

"Hmmm," Miss Guyer shook her head in agreement, adding mischievously, "ah...yes, particularly impossible!"

"Well, I happen to agree with you, Miss Guyer," Aggie spoke with genuine maturity and aplomb.

The young girl began, "I wish to thank you for providing me with an excellent example of the worst that the teaching profession can offer. You, your staff, and most of your students are at best, a pretentious, self-aggrandizing lot that I no longer need stomach."

Miss Guyer sat there, staring, shocked and speechless. She looked like she was about to say something, but Aggie continued. . .

"Here is a letter from my mother allowing me to leave the premises. I shall finally be rid of this horrible, horrible place, never to return." Aggie spoke in a most diplomatic and calm manner.

Guyer still hadn't moved. She had been duly chastened and sat frozen in her chair.

Aggie, displaying great poise, placed the letter on the desk of the "warden", politely curtseyed, and left the building wearing a very broad, well-earned smile.

Marching home, Aggie felt like a new person. No longer would she have to dread walking into that cold, hostile environment. To her way of thinking, only certain kinds of individuals could handle the type of harsh discipline students of the Guyer school were expected to endure. Clearly, they would not be her types. She couldn't imagine how anyone could accept the terribly controlling environment which that school provided. Guyer was now only a dark memory, still, one that would never be forgotten.

Arriving at the front door of her house, she found her mother nervously standing in the foyer, folding her hands, this way and that. Clara couldn't wait to hear how her daughter had handled the situation.

"Quickly, Aggie," her mother begged, sitting her daughter beside her on a large couch. "Tell me, tell me. . ."

"Mum," Aggie began, "it was so wonderful. Miss Guyer never saw it coming. I did apologize for my behavior, although we both know that I did nothing out of the ordinary to ever have warranted the kind of treatment that I received at that school."

"Aggie, dear," her mother excitedly inquired, "tell me more. Was there more? Did Guyer, er I mean Miss Guyer. . . Did she yell or scream at you? Were there any theatrics?"

Clara started again before her daughter could respond, "You know, Aggie, I was truly concerned about sending you down there alone. It wasn't two minutes after you were out the door that I began to shake, worrying about you."

"Mum," Aggie responded, "that's all well and good, but it was so much better for me to have faced her on my own. It felt so very wonderful to let her know what I really thought about her."

Clara could not restrain her joy, and smiling broadly, clapped her hands and reached over to give her youngest child a warm, heart-felt hug. That moment became one of the most important in her life and she would long remember and appreciate her mother's caring decision to remove her from Guyer's school.

Next year, Aggie decided that she would redouble her efforts in a different educational setting. She would make her mother proud of her for the rest of her life!

While the school had demanded much too much from a quiet, shy person like Aggie, the young girl knew that there was some truth in Miss Guyer's references to her being a bit of a loner. Clearly, she had few close friends, excepting Margaret Cary. Prior to her captivity at the Guyer school, she spent much of her time doing things alone. Much of her loneliness had been filled by caring for her pets and her love for nature. Still, she had always been a pleasant, happy child. That is, except for the terrible recurring nightmares that she would experience from time to time.

One particularly horrid character seemed to haunt her sleep on a regular basis. Her dreams would start out pleasantly enough. She would be going for a walk or present at a house party or attending some such event, when she would spy **him**. This man would be following her or suddenly appear at her table while she was having tea. Sometimes Aggie would see him along the beach, coming her way. She had named him *the Gunman*. Whenever his pale blue eyes looked her way, she would wake up shrieking and sobbing.

Happily, Aggie had not received any such visits recently, and now, newly removed from the Guyer school, she was a changed person.

After a light meal with her mother, she hurriedly worked to complete her chores. Permission had been given to visit Margaret that same afternoon, and she couldn't wait to share the good news with her best friend. When the dishes had been washed and put away, Aggie slipped on a light winter coat and kissed her mother good bye, "I promise I'll be home today before dark, Mum. I love you very, very much!"

She seemed to fly down the road to the Cary home. As she made her way, Aggie tried to think how best to disclose the good news to her best friend. She knew how happy Margaret would be, especially since all of the details of her unhappiness at Guyer's school were known to her dear friend.

"What if Margaret was still away?" she wondered.

"Oh, well," she reasoned, "it would still be the best day of my life."

The sun was now shining brightly, and the rhythmic waves could easily be heard as they steadily crashed over the rocky shore. Aggie felt a sudden urge to share her good news with the shorebirds, but that could wait for another time!

As she approached the huge house, she noticed that there were several large carriages and drays pulled up along the main entrance. Some of the house staff were busy loading these huge conveyances with trunks and other such storage boxes that apparently had been taken from the house. Aggie hesitated, watching the events transpiring directly before her eyes. This would not do. She simply had to know what was happening.

Nearing the front door, she hoped to see a member of the Cary family, preferably Margaret, but only the servants were visible, still busy with their tasks. Could it be possible that her friend and her family were leaving the area? How awful that would be.

She was becoming very nervous, and all of this speculation on her part was not helping, not helping at all. Finally, she spied someone who could provide an explanation. She waved to Mr. Malcolm who was looking her way. He quickly made his way around the busy workers, issuing a stout warning to one of them, "Be careful now, Beatrice. That's Mrs. Cary's favorite outerwear!"

"Aggie," he called out, observing her apparent discomfort. "My dear, you look somewhat anxious! How may I be of service?"

"Mr. Malcolm," she asked in very sincere, caring manner, "is the Cary family moving away?"

"What? Why no, certainly not," spoke the family butler.

"Oh, dear," she responded, showing some relief, "I simply couldn't bear such a thing."

Malcolm had surmised what her next question would be and offered, "Don't worry, Aggie, your friend and her family are only going to visit some relatives outside of Liverpool. I believe that it will only be for a few days."

Aggie's head drooped slightly at the information and Malcolm reacted quickly, "Miss Miller, would you like to see Miss Margaret before she leaves?"

The young girl smiled broadly and nodded in the affirmative, saying, "That would be splendid, Malcolm. Thank you!"

He quickly made his way back inside the house. Seconds later, Margaret appeared at the top of the front steps, calling, "Aggie, please come in. It's much too cold for us to stand out in the air and converse. Please join me. We'll go to the kitchen and have some cocoa!"

As they made their way down the long hallway, Aggie started to speak, "Margaret, wait until you hear what happened to me today."

Margaret answered excitedly, "Oh, please tell me. I've been so nervous the last several days that I need some cheering up!"

"Well, I started down to school this morning. . ." Aggie began to relate the day's memorable events to her good friend. As each part of her story unfolded, Margaret grew more and more animated, issuing, "No....Is it so? Did you really? Oh, my goodness, gracious!"

When Aggie had triumphantly finished, Margaret stood up and applauded, as if it was the end of a good picture show.

"I'm both proud and very happy for you, Aggie," Margaret spoke with true joy upon hearing that Aggie would no longer have to deal with Miss Guyer's Girls School.

"Good for you, my friend," she continued, smiling, "I really don't know how you could have endured that woman and those snobs for so long."

Before Aggie could reply, Margaret continued, "Well, I suppose you are curious about the commotion you are now witnessing?"

Aggie, nodding in the affirmative, was about to respond, but her good friend gave her no opportunity.

"If you must know, I'm a bit miffed," she stated, adding, "we are going to visit our relatives in Liverpool, but the trip simply came out of nowhere!"

Rolling her eyes, Margaret elaborated, "Last evening, upon returning from dinner, father informed us that we would be going to see Aunt Ellen and her family for a few days. I was stunned, for we had only recently spent time with them!"

"I tried to find out why this decision had been made so quickly, but father sternly reminded me that it was not necessary for a father to ask permission from his children," Margaret explained, frowning. "After hearing that response, I knew better than to ask father any more questions."

Aggie didn't know what to say to Margaret. It wasn't her place to interfere in other people's business, but her friend looked so confused. Gazing across one of the serving tables as she nibbled on a cake, Aggie was trying to find some kind words.

Finally, she spoke, "Tell me, Margaret, do you know how long you might be gone? Did your father mention when you would be returning?"

Margaret began to nervously wrap her fingers in the pretty bow at the top of her blue dress, twisting the tie, this way and that, while her other hand reached for her cocoa, "No, Aggie," she replied, "and I sensed that there was something that he didn't want to tell us. Don't ask me why I felt that way, I simply did."

"But let's not let my feelings ruin our afternoon," Margaret insisted. "Let's enjoy our time together, for I'm sure we'll be away over Christmas, and I know that I'm going to miss you very much."

After that conversation, the two friends spent the rest of the daylight hours playing games, drawing stick-figures and making up story-lines for their creations. Time always flew when the two young girls were together.

As the afternoon wore on, Aggie realized that it was getting late. She decided to start back home and said her "good-byes" to her best friend at the door, stating, "Now make sure that you write, Margaret. Come see me at Ashfield the moment you return."

"You can be sure that I'll do just that, Aggie," Margaret replied as the door creaked shut.

Aggie quickly made her way home trying to enjoy the salty sea air, but she was still concerned about Margaret's recent disclosure. She felt it a bit strange at how quickly the Cary family had decided to leave their home to visit the same relatives they had only just recently seen.

Clearly, there was nothing Aggie could do. Instead, she decided to revisit her happy thoughts on the success of the morning. Tonight, she and her mother would once again celebrate her final hours at the famous Guyer School.

Chapter 5 Your Services Are Requested

Sunday, December 17th

"Holmes, Holmes," I queried after entering our humble residence at 221B Baker Street that wintery December evening. After whisking the snow flakes from my hat and removing my scarf, I carefully positioned my seasonal garb on the coat rack, once more trying to capture his attention, "I say old boy, where are you? Holmes, are you there? Hello. . . Hello. . ."

Still, my calls went unanswered. That seemed very strange to me, for I had only recently left our apartment for a brief walk and to enjoy the brisk, refreshing winter night air. Making my way around the corner leading into our modest living room, I wondered why he hadn't responded to my greeting. Much to my surprise and, might I say, aggravation, I found Holmes quietly reading *The Times*, his pipe smoke wafting gently to the ceiling, while comfortably resting in his favorite armchair.

Stopping abruptly, I crossed my arms upon my chest, and after issuing a loud sigh, angrily offered, "Holmes, didn't you hear me? Why haven't you bothered to acknowledge my calls?"

He never bothered to look up, but after resting his pipe on its holder, calmly responded, "Oh, there you are Watson. . . Ah, did you say something?"

Looking to the ceiling, I merely cocked my head to one side and began impatiently tapping my left foot in a most agitated manner. This had become my all-too-familiar signal of displeasure to my frequently preoccupied roommate. I continued my routine for another thirty seconds until he finally capitulated to my obvious annoyance.

"All right, old chap," Holmes offered, "I'm sorry for my poor manners. Please accept my most sincere apology for not immediately responding to your greeting!"

What, I thought? There, he's done it again! I wondered if I should once more accept his sarcastic apology with my accustomed good manners. No, not this time. I'm not going to graciously acquiesce to such a casual reply.

"Holmes, I'll not accept your token apology," I flared. "This happens all too often. What am I, merely a piece of furniture that you treat me with such disdain?"

He immediately got up from his chair, walked over to me and grabbing me by the shoulders implored, "My good man, what in the world has come over you? I certainly meant nothing other than the genuine apology that I have now extended to you! Please, tell me what is vexing you to such a serious degree?"

Pulling myself out of his grasp, I walked toward the window, and gazed out at the swirling white flakes that were fluttering beyond the gaslights along Baker Street. Perhaps I had overreacted to my friend's somewhat measured reply. He was simply being Sherlock, after all. Holmes was not doing anything new in ignoring me. I knew that it wasn't done out of malice, but due to his makeup. That's who he was. When something had captured his interest he became so immersed in the topic, he could easily block out everything else!

"Holmes, forgive my reaction," I softened my intensity while moving to the sofa. "There was no reason for me to have gotten so upset with you, especially when I know how wrapped up you can get with your investigations."

"That's my Watson," Holmes smiled, continuing, "I thought for a moment that perhaps your stuffy nose and head cold had gotten the better of you after your walk with Quincy through Helmsford Park. I, too, can sometimes fly off the handle when I'm suffering from a sinus infection. I hope you'll be feeling better soon, for we may have a new case on our hands!"

"Really, a new case?" I stammered excitedly, for we had not seen a client in well over a week.

Suddenly, I thought about what he had just remarked.

"Just a moment, Holmes," I piped up, "what do you mean fly off the handle? And how do you know that I'm suffering from a sinus infection?"

Sherlock Holmes had returned to his chair, and after sliding his pipe to the left side of his mouth, replied, "Really, Watson? You want me to explain how I knew the condition of your health?"

After a brief pause, he proceeded to explain, "Watson, you come into our living room huffing and puffing, unable to have noticed the dog excrement with which you have been staining our carpet these past several moments, and you want to know how I knew you were suffering from some form of nasal congestion?"

Hmm, I quickly glanced at my boots, finding evidence of my travels with Quincy, Mrs. Hudson's Irish Setter, still sticking to my right heel.

"Holmes, confound it," I inquired further, "yes, I see the proof of the dog, but how did you know my sinuses were acting up?"

"My dear man," Sherlock continued, holding and pinching his fingers over his long nose, "surely your olfactory senses, had they been working correctly, would have warned you of the hideously egregious odor that is now polluting our cozy quarters."

"Well, that was easy enough," I answered, "but how did you know that I had been to Helmsford Park?"

"Watson," he said shaking his head, "I noticed some of Quincy's reddish fur adhering to your trouser leg. I also know that Mrs. Hudson's canine prefers to mark his territory, if you catch my drift, at that very locale! When you add to that the fact that you left our rooms at 5:30 PM and have now just returned at 6:15 PM, you have the final piece of this rather simple explanation. Helmsford Park is a mere 20 minute walk from here, and the average time for a 3-year-old dog to 'take care of its business' is approximately 5 minutes! It most certainly was not a difficult deduction to make."

Once again, trumped by the master. I, too, would have been able to come to the same conclusion, had the situation been reversed, I reasoned. But Holmes had once more made it seem so obvious! On occasions like this I would sometimes find that I both hated and admired him at the same time. My, what a very rara avis. . .

He laughed at the expression I must have had on my face, but then added, "Well, Watson?"

"Well, what, Holmes?" I sternly responded.

"Are you interested in the contents of a letter that arrived yesterday? I opened it while you were keeping Quincy company," he offered. "By the way, would you mind cleaning that dog detritus from your boot and our carpet? There's a good lad."

While I used some old rags to clean my footwear and scrub the newly stained carpet, Holmes began to read the communique:

> December 12, 1905
> Torquay, Devon
>
> Mr. Holmes,
>   I am inquiring as to the availability of your services in the not too distant future. My family and I have recently been subjected to a rather bizarre series of events, ranging from property damage to actual threats.
>   While I have been somewhat successful in allaying many of their concerns, I fear that there are certain aspects to what our family has encountered that are well beyond my ability to remedy. I must report that I am truly at my wit's end, so to speak.
>   Having read of your many successes in resolving conundrums and various other mysterious goings-on, I am now actively seeking your assistance in this matter. Should you wish to examine my troubling situation, you may contact me at our family home on Belgrave Road, Torquay, Devonshire.
>   I realize that this request comes on short notice, and that you must travel three hundred kilometers, but I promise that you shall receive just compensation if you succeed in bringing my case to its proper disposition.
> Respectfully,
> Mr. James Cary, Esq.

After quickly folding the missive, Holmes slowly rose from the chair, rekindled his pipe, and stared solemnly in my direction. He took a few steps toward his desk, then turned back to me and issued, "Well, Watson, what are your thoughts? Do you feel that Mr. Cary's request merits our attention? Are you up for this one?"

I was still engaged in cleaning up my mess when Holmes had finished reading the letter, but I had been paying attention. Rising from the floor, I removed the waste basket and quickly disposed of the dirty rags.

Upon returning to the living quarters I ventured, "Holmes, I'm really not sure if this case merits anyone's consideration. After all, what information about his problem has this attorney, Cary, really given us?"

"You do raise an excellent point, Watson," he continued, "but the letter, if you examine it closely, has much to tell us. Come here and see what you can find."

Quickly moving under the reading lamp, I took the letter from his hand and tried to glean some of the information that Holmes had apparently been able to decipher. I read and re-read Cary's letter with very little to offer Holmes in the way of any detailed analysis.

"Hmmm," I suggested, "Holmes, this letter seems rather direct in asking for your help in solving a mysterious problem of some kind. . . I'm afraid that's all I can determine. I'm sure that you, of course, have already found much, much more. . ."

Holmes smiled at my comments as I returned the letter to his outstretched hand. His eyes began to twinkle as he reached for his magnifying lens. He slowly moved the paper up against a lamp as he began to explain his findings.

"Clearly, Watson," he continued, "Mr. Cary's practice is doing well. That much we know from both his street address and the quality of his writing paper. Belgrave Road in Torquay is among that quaint town's most affluent areas. The writing paper is of the finest Brighton weave, usually reserved for the nobility, and coming at a very dear cost, I might add."

As was his custom, Holmes, moistened his index finger and smudged the man's signature, adding, "I further believe, Watson, that the ink with which he composed this message is Charman #5, a new brand that also comes at a premium." The consulting detective continued, "Cary's bold handwriting shows that this man is very stern, yet at the same time, very compassionate. Can you see the way he curls his end letters? A most telling attribute in his penmanship."

My friend was not finished with his extrapolations. One could sense the excitement slowly building as Holmes quickened his pacing back-and-forth along the bookcase. Striking a dramatic pose, head tilted back with his left hand over his eyes, he briefly paused before disclosing his final remarks.

"Mr. Cary demonstrates his educational pedigree in the way that he communicates, Watson," he concluded, adding, "the man is also extremely frugal when financial transactions are concerned.

When he had finished making his last point, I noticed a remarkable change of expression on his face and he quickly disappeared into his room. Almost immediately, he re-entered the front room loudly exclaiming, "Oh, my, Watson, what a fool I am!"

"What, what's that?" I continued, rising from my chair. "What are you talking about, Holmes?"

He quickly sat at his desk and opened a copy of our local train schedule. His eyes followed his index finger down the departure column until he found the information he needed.

Ignoring my comment, he began, "Ah, yes, Watson, the next train to Exeter leaves in one hour and if we plan to be on it we need spare no effort! Once there, we can hire a landau to take us the rest of the way!"

"What's going on here, Holmes?" I once more inquired. "Exeter? Why? Please explain what's going on!"

"Watson, old man," he hurriedly exclaimed, "it may be a fool's errand, but if my suspicions are correct, we will need to reach Torquay in the next several hours if there is any hope of saving his life!"

"Whose life? What's going on?" I voiced with a great deal of incredulity.

He didn't reply immediately, but after bringing his packed suitcase from his bedroom, issued, "Doctor, see if this article helps you see our need for immediate departure. And it's Mr. Cary and his family that I'm concerned about!"

With that having been said, Holmes picked up the day's *Daily Telegraph*, another of London's finest newspapers, and tossed it in my direction, issuing, "Watson, page 5, third column. I refer you to the article entitled 'Another Body Discovered in Torquay'. Please be so kind as to read it carefully and you shall have your answer."

Sensing his urgent behavior, I scanned the article with some alacrity, looking for any information that could have led Holmes to his latest determination. Hmmm....the article described the town as a friendly seaside community that owed much of its survival to tourism. It further indicated that the residents were outraged and horrified over the terrible murders that had been perpetrated. The newspaper disclosed that over the last few months two of that community's most established citizenry, both members of the town council, had met with horrible deaths. According to the coroner, the first victim had been found bludgeoned; the second man died from a deep head-wound; while now, a third councilman, Tom Dennison, had been strangled.

"Oh, my word, Holmes," I spoke softly, "really, now, these people were all murdered and all of them from this one small community!"

He paid no attention to my comment, but continued nervously going about his business.

"Read on, Watson, aloud if you would," he whispered over my shoulder, his pipe now fully ablaze. "There's more."

I immediately went back to the article. It wasn't until I had reached the final paragraph that I found the reason for his concern.

I once more began to read, "The Torquay Town Council met last evening, December 16th, to discuss what might be done to better protect its citizenry. Local constables in attendance advised everyone to keep a sharp lookout for any strange goings on. The last order of business was to appoint local attorney, James Cary, another council member, and one of the town's most accomplished civic leaders, to head a commission which would be in charge of investigating these crimes."

"Holmes," I said, rising from the chair, "I now understand why you are so concerned. Cary is a member of the council and has just been appoirnted to head a commission. He's now in even greater danger! Why, certainly I wish to accompany you. It will only take me a few minutes to pack my traveling bag and we'll be ready to. . ."

I was interrupted by my roommate, "Here, Watson," he spoke. "Here's your luggage. I've taken the liberty of preparing a bag for you. Time is our enemy. Oh, by the way, I do wish to thank you for joining me on this adventure."

"What?" said I, "You mean you have the nerve to assume that I will simply drop whatever plans I may have made and head off to Torquay. . . just like that?"

"Of course, my friend," Holmes casually remarked. "I could

tell that you, too, have been somewhat lackadaisical these last few weeks. I felt that the proper prescription for you might be a change of scenery."

"Before we leave," he suggested, "you had better contact Dr. Tulley to cover your patients until this problem is resolved"

And with that remark, we were out the door, down the stairs, and on our way.

As we traveled to the train station, I simply had to ask him how he had determined that Cary was a bit of a cheapskate. I had read the same letter and could not see how my friend was able to deduce such a fact.

"Holmes, please, please explain how you have come to your theory on this matter," I implored. "I understand the paper, the ink, and the location of his home giving us a clue to his wealth, but I saw nothing in that letter that suggested his thriftiness."

"Watson," he issued, "don't you recall that he referred to receiving 'just compensation'. Surely that indicates that here is a man who would insist on getting his money's worth. To me that comment implies that Mr. Cary is tight with his shillings."

"Yes, yes, I suppose that makes sense," I agreed, and before long we found ourselves arriving at Paddington Station.

After entering the busy lobby area we quickly purchased tickets and were able to find an available compartment on the fourth car.

The 8:05 left the busy depot on time and began its long trip to Exeter. With several stops along the way, Holmes estimated that we would arrive there at 5 o'clock on the morrow. He further speculated that an uneventful carriage ride the rest of the way would have us arriving in the seaside city of Torquay by 7:30, just in time for an early breakfast.

As the train rumbled through the night, Holmes was too keyed up to sleep. The same could not be said for yours truly, for the rhythmical click-clack-click of the locomotive riding the rails had placed me safely in the arms of Morpheus in relatively short order.

The next thing I heard was the voice of Holmes calling me awake, "Up now, Watson. There's a good lad. It's time to find our carriage."

"Yes, yes, Holmes," I mumbled, still quite groggy, my body aching from sleeping on a hard coach seat. "Oh, my word," I uttered, "I say, my good fellow, where are we?"

He ignored my inquiry, and hiking me up by my left arm, laughed, "All right, old boy. Don't forget your luggage."

With that, I stretched rather impolitely, slowly rising to my feet. Then, bag in hand, I quietly followed him up the aisle and down the steps onto the Exeter train station platform.

"Egad," the expression floated before me in a misty fog emanating from my exhaled breath. "Brrr. .. it's rather cold this morning, Holmes. Wouldn't you say?"

"Yes, Watson," my comrade spoke sarcastically, "it is December, after all!"

We were soon bundled up in our carriage, trotting down the trail toward Torquay and eventually, to the Belgrave Road home of one James Cary. It was still dark here at this time of the year, but at least now, I was fully awake, as was Holmes. His mind was already working on the case. Even though nothing tangible had been posited in the letter, there had to have been something that caught his interest. We were about half way to Torquay, when he decided to strike up a conversation.

"You know, Watson," Holmes began, "this area, in addition to being extremely popular in the summer, is also famous for its place in early British history!"

"Is that so?" I casually responded to his remark.

"Yes, Watson," he continued. "If my history is correct, this part of England had been invaded by the Romans as they continued exploring and conquering the known world. There was speculation that Vespasian himself had led his legions to this part of Devon around 43-44 AD. I believe there was a great deal of evidence to that fact unearthed in this area: Roman coins, artifacts, etc., all serving to substantiate these stories."

"My word, Holmes," I offered, "you certainly are a fount of information this morning. Why might any of those facts be of interest to you in this case?"

"Watson, dear Watson," Holmes responded in a most teasing manner, "do you mean to imply that my stimulating conversation is not of interest to you? This is the history of our England I'm talking about, you know!"

He began to laugh when I shrugged my shoulders. Sensing that his audience was not appreciative of his lesson, Holmes turned toward the window of our carriage and peeked out. The dawn was breaking in the East and we would soon be arriving to our destination. Until that time, Holmes decided to slide down into his seat, close his eyes and ride the rest of the way in silence.

Imperial Hotel, Torquay

Chapter 6 Torquay and Torre Abbey

Monday, December 18th

    We arrived in Torquay shortly after seven o'clock that morning, on the eighteenth of December. There were still icy remnants underfoot when we stepped out of our landau in front of the formidable Imperial Hotel on Park Hill Road. The sky over the Channel was slowly clearing, but harsh winds from the northwest still made for a chilly morning. Our stylish hotel's close proximity to the coastal waters also made it seem even colder than the 6 degree Celsius reading listed on the chalk blackboard standing adjacent to the entryway of the historic building.

    Minutes later, we found ourselves in the lobby of one of

Torquay's most charming establishments. The dark mahogany wall panels gave testimony to the Imperial's excellent reputation as one of England's finest hotels. While registering at the front desk we were very surprised to learn that there was only one room available. I began to scratch my noggin, wondering how that could be, for it was not really the best time to be visiting the seashore.

Holmes easily read my mind and offered, "Come now, Watson, that so many hotel rooms are taken should come as no surprise, particularly at this time of the year. Now think, Watson, it's almost Christmas! Why this area, I'm very certain, enjoys a great number of shoppers as well as former residents returning to celebrate the holidays with their families!"

Of course, he was spot on. Once more I was embarrassed by another one of his simple deductions. I had long since tired of missing the obvious and being the target of some of his frequent barbs. Wait a minute, I thought. Why was I so cross ? Then it came to me. I was famished. There was nothing wrong with me that a good rasher of bacon and fried kippers wouldn't fix.

After finding our suite, sorting our luggage and freshening up, we headed down for some breakfast. I went directly to an available table near the tall windows which looked out upon the busy waterway. I could see several small vessels steaming about the quays, stopping to load and unload both passengers and packaged goods. While waiting for Holmes to return from his talk with the hotel concierge, I glanced hungrily at the morning's breakfast offerings. Hmmm, scanning the menu I quickly came across my selection, bacon and kippers with freshly-baked corn scones. Ah, yes, that would certainly do just fine!

Minutes later Holmes entered the room, glancing about the crowded tables. As he made his approach to our table, I noticed that he had secured a copy of the town paper, the *Torquay Directory*. He had a most forlorn, concerned look on his face.

"What is it Holmes?" I inquired timidly. "Is something gone amiss?"

"Yes, Watson," he replied, handing me the issue, "do have a look at the headlines!"

Fourth Body Discovered at Brandy Cove

Looking up at my good friend, I ventured, "Holmes, my word, it isn't our man, Mr. Cary, perchance?"

"Thankfully not, Watson," he remarked. "Still, it's a most unfortunate event for a poor man by the name of Mister Eldridge Fenwick. The paper stated that he, too, was a member of the town council. According to witnesses, he was last seen leaving the meeting house after the evening's committee gathering. Watson, I suggest that we pay a visit to our client as soon as we can. But first, I believe we need to come to terms with our appetites."

After ordering our morning fare, I began to carefully read the article. As of yet, no arrests had been made. Authorities indicated that they had gathered several suspects initially, but, according to detailed reports, all of them had legitimate alibis for their whereabouts at the estimated time of the recent murder. The remaining paragraphs delivered several graphic details of how the poor man had come to die. Officials speculated that Fenwick had been chained to some large boulders along the rugged cove in such a manner that he would drown with the arrival of the late evening's tide.

The remainder of the report dealt with Fenwick's family and his community involvement, noting the man's popularity and the many good works he had performed for the little town. By the time I had finished reading the article, my breakfast had arrived, and I must admit that in my famished condition, I hardly remember having had time to chew my food!

"I say, Holmes, it looks like the local constabulary must have their hands full with these foul doings." I commented, quickly realizing how obvious my remark must have seemed.

Holmes, for his part, after giving me a strange look, merely shook his head in agreement while he continued to eat his porridge, savoring every morsel.

Within the hour we had procuredthe use of one of the hotel landaus, and in less than fifteen minutes we found ourselves at the home of Mr. James Cary, Esquire. To describe the residence as anything less than palatial would have been wrong, very wrong, indeed! The large Georgian structure was set back from two main thoroughfares, Belgrave Road and Torquay Road. Large trees and gardens were meticulously maintained all throughout the sprawling estate. It was splendid to behold, even at this time of the year with few leaves on the branches.

"My word, Holmes," I spoke softly, "this property is among the most beautiful I've ever seen! The view alone is spectacular and the grounds themselves. . . so well kept!"

Holmes seemed similarly affected. In fact, I had rarely seen the man so transfixed! He took his time looking over the wondrous scenery which lay before us. He was already at work, quickly turning his attention to the exterior of the stately building as we pulled up to the main entryway.

A young stable boy quickly appeared, taking the reins, holding our team of horses while we stepped out of our landau. After watching him move the conveyance toward the stable grounds, Holmes tugged my sleeve, pointing to a path leading away from the house.

"Watson," he suggested, "what do you say to a brisk walk around the grounds, prior to our interview with Mr. Cary?"

I nodded in agreement, knowing his ways. Holmes had long ago seen the value of examining the lay of the land as it were, whenever he accepted a case. Torre Abbey's grounds were quite extensive, strewn with many pathways that crossed and criss-crossed the wide expanse. As we started down a wonderfully scenic lane toward the coastal cliffs, we could see a tall, slender woman pushing a baby carriage in our direction. Holmes took the opportunity to tip his hat as they passed us.

"Hello, Madam," he voiced in a most friendly manner. "It certainly is a lovely day for a brisk walk with your fine-looking charge."

The woman politely bowed, acknowledging his kind greeting, but seemed uninterested in continuing any type of conversation. As she pushed the carriage out of our way, I couldn't help sneaking a peek at the child within. I've always been smitten by infants.

"Awk-k-k," I stuttered thoughtlessly, for I had never seen such a child.

"Oh, forgive me, Madam," I tried to excuse my surprise, "I seem to have gotten something caught in my throat."

At that, the woman stuck up her nose and promptly continued

along her way.

"Watson," Holmes queried, smiling, "what the devil was that all about?"

Blushing in embarrassment, I whispered, "Holmes, I feel terrible about what I have to say, but I have never seen such an ugly child! My word, why it took the wind out of me!"

"Don't be absurd, Watson," Holmes issued, "all babies are beautiful. I'm very much surprised at you."

I thought I saw him smiling as he turned away, continuing our examination of the grounds. When we had reached the end of the property line, we began our trip back toward the Abbey's main house. Holmes, I sensed, was deeply engrossed, seemingly taking mental notes about the design of the large garden.

As we neared the huge edifice, I noticed that the exterior of the historical structure exhibited many signs of wear and tear. After all, I remember having heard that Torre Abbey had been constructed by a religious order several hundred years ago. That, in addition to its close proximity to the Channel, all combined to explain its somewhat worn and haggard outward appearance. I could only wonder at the interior, but we would soon find out, once inside.

Seconds later, we were at the base of the grand entryway and started to ascend the stairs toward the huge front doors.

As we prepared to engage the huge door knocker, suddenly there came a loud, grating screech as the large, ornate door slowly opened. There, standing ready to greet us, was an immaculately dressed tall, stately gentleman.

"Ah, Mr. Holmes and Doctor Watson, I presume," he offered.

"Yes," replied Holmes, continuing, "and we are pleased to make your acquaintance, Mr. Cary. I sincerely hope that you'll forgive us for dropping in on you, unannounced as it were."

"Not at all, Mr. Holmes," he stated with a refined confident smile. "I'm so very pleased to see you and the famous Doctor Watson. I pray that you may be able to help us to put an end to these dreadful goings on."

"Where are my manners?" Cary quickly apologized as he showed us into the large foyer. "Please, do come in. I believe that the library will be a most comfortable spot for us to conduct our conversation. There is much to tell you, and before beginning, let me assure you that I'll do everything I can to help with your investigation."

We turned through the first door to the left and found ourselves in a large room with two armchairs positioned near a magnificent oaken desk. The spacious room was bordered on all sides by bookcases containing writings on many, many topics. The storage units ran from the floor to the ceiling, requiring a library ladder for access to the higher shelves. A series of rails allowed the ladder to easily slide from one wall to another. The Cary book collection, I decided, could easily have served as a main library for most of the towns and hamlets in the United Kingdom.

After we had taken our seats, my friend began, "Mr. Cary, Doctor Watson and I have already begun to examine your situation. Please know that we will do all in our power to see this matter to a satisfactory conclusion. I take it that your concerns are related to the spate of curious deaths that have occurred lately in this part of Devon?"

"Well," Cary remarked, "I should have known that you've read about these deplorable events in this, our normally quiet corner of the world. You are correct, Mr. Holmes. To date, the deaths have remained unsolved, but my immediate interests have to do with some personal concerns, those that I hinted at in my letter."

"That would be most logical," Holmes replied, as he reached into his pocket and unfolded Cary's letter. Holmes quickly scanned the document and carefully replaced it in his front coat. My friend was about to say something, when Cary suddenly turned toward the open doorway.

"A moment, Mr. Holmes," Cary offered, waving to a member of his household staff.

"Malcolm," the lawyer called to the family butler, "I would like you to meet Mr. Sherlock Holmes and his good friend and associate, Doctor Watson. Gentlemen, this is Mr. Malcolm Randolph. This fine man does an outstanding job handling the many needs of the family Cary."

"Pleased to make your acquaintance, gentlemen," the stylish manservant replied, bowing cordially after he had shaken our hands.

"These men are visiting Torquay and they are to be accorded full run of our property. Is that clearly understood, Malcolm?" Cary remarked in a rather off-putting manner.

He continued, "And Mr. Randolph, would you be so kind as to bring tea?"

"Certainly, Mr. Cary," the butler replied with another courteous bow, disappearing around the corner.

"Please, gentlemen," the lawyer suggested, "I invite you to have a look around while we're waiting. I have some wonderful cigars from the colonies that you might enjoy. Please, please, be my guest."

"Thank you, Mr. Cary," Holmes responded, smiling as he reached in his coat for his favorite briar pipe. "Actually, this form of smoking is more to my liking! It's become an old friend."

At that response, Holmes slowly rose and began to make his way around the periphery of the cavernous room, stopping here and there, perhaps taking more mental notes that could be of use later in the investigation. While he moved about, I happened to notice that he seemed to pay particular attention to one corner of room, dusting off one of the shelves while we waited for our beverage.

The sprawling library was located in the front portion of the regal building, overlooking the vast gardens and walkways that led to the harbor. Holmes peered out through each window, apparently to become more familiar with the size of the huge estate. For my part, I stared around the magnificent room, intrigued by all of the legal books and maps that were present, as well as the varied selection of titles I was able to see, all neatly organized by topic.

Along one wall, Cary had a black telescope near one of the windows, positioned or aimed at a large promontory extending into the Channel. A glowing fireplace, located directly behind his large desk, served to warm the regal work space.

A short time later a bell signaled the butler's return. After adding some honey to my still-steeping cup, I took my seat on a sturdy oaken chair that faced Cary's work desk. Holmes hovered over my left shoulder, munching on one of the warm biscuits that had been brought into the room.

Cary opened the conversation, asking, "Well, Holmes, where

shall I begin?"

"Mister Cary, you may start wherever you like," Holmes replied. "And, please do not qualify your statements. Nothing is too trivial or obvious to be dismissed from consideration. In fact, in many instances, seemingly unimportant items become the most valuable clues in helping to solve a mystery."

"Very well, then," Cary remarked as he slowly paced around his massive desk.

"Gentlemen, let me properly introduce myself before we go any further. I am Atty. James Cary. I currently have an office in Torquay and have spent the last 15 years operating my law office. My wife and I are the proud parents of two fine youngsters, Thomas, who is six, and our daughter, Margaret, who has just turned fifteen.

My father, Christopher, bought this former Premonstratensian Abbey when Thomas Ridgeway put it up for sale, and it was willed to me upon his passing. Our family has been living here for more than twenty years. I spend much of my time as a member of the Torquay town council, having recently been appointed to head a commission."

Cary paused for a moment, then added, "I must state that I have a rather strong constitution that makes this nonsense hard to tolerate. I've had to perform some difficult tasks in my time. I've witnessed some horrible things, and, as you might imagine, the nature of my council work has sometimes placed me in harm's way. By that I mean that I have received threats for having chosen to defend certain unsavory individuals, as well as those who have sought my assistance in prosecuting their cases. Let me assure you both, that I have never broken the law, but rather I have spent most of my life seeing to it that all of my clients received their proper day in court."

He went on. "That having been said, I have recently come to believe that my life, indeed, even the lives of my family, are in great danger!"

"Pray continue, sir," Holmes insisted, tapping his pipe on the teacup saucer.

"As I have suggested in my letter to you, our family has been the brunt of several mischievous actions over the last month or so. Most have been relatively harmless in nature with short notes attached, all suggesting that our family leave our home. I'm sorry to say, but I simply tossed them into the fireplace, never giving them a second thought. However, seven days ago, I received this message," Cary completed his remarks, handing the missive to Holmes.

Holmes took the somewhat soiled paper, and after a cursory examination began to read aloud, "Leave this property. . . It is cursed land. . .More need not die!"

After reading those words, Holmes looked my way, passed me the note, and inquired, "What do you make of this, Watson?"

I shuddered when I saw the way the letters were formed. Each seemed to have been written in a most alarming, quaking manner. There was no signature, but as I looked more closely, a shiver went up my spine, for there was a reddish spot that looked like blood!

"Um, ah, Holmes," I blurted out, "this is outrageous. . . Why it must be taken seriously, especially with the bloody stain!"

We both looked at our host, Mr. Cary, who, by this time, had once more, taken his seat behind his desk.

"I'm not so concerned about my own person," Cary remarked

with his hands folded. "It's the welfare of my family. . . their safety!"

I returned the paper to Holmes and he quickly began a more thorough examination of the warning. Moving over toward the window, he held the paper up to the sunlight that shone into the library. Apparently satisfied with his findings, he made his way back to his chair and re-lit his pipe, caressing his wrinkled brow.

"Mr. Cary," Holmes inquired, once again holding the letter to the light, "may I ask how you came by this letter?"

Cary responded, "Sir, I found it on this very desk when I entered the room the morning of December 11th, seven days ago."

"Have you any thoughts as to 'why' it was all crumpled up in your ashtray?" the great detective offered.

"What did you say, Mister Holmes?" Cary queried. "How did you know that?"

"Forgive me, Mr. Cary," Holmes replied, "surely the many visible creases hinted at its having been crushed or folded several times. As for the ashtray, you can clearly smell the ashy odor and see the tobacco marks."

Cary smiled at those comments. I sensed that the local lawyer was feeling the same way I was often made to feel whenever Holmes had posited one of his astute observations.

"Well, Mr. Holmes," Cary went on, "my first impulse upon receiving such a note was one of great anger. I was so furious that I crumpled up the paper and threw it in the cigar ashtray. My home had been violated. Our family's well-being threatened. I angrily made up my mind to ignore this vile warning. That was my first response."

"Upon further analysis, I decided that I simply had to take the threat seriously, for the safety of my family. I knew that I needed to take certain precautions and prepare my home for the possibility that some kind of attack might be made upon me and my loved ones."

"A short time later, I decided to pick up the note and save it as possible evidence."

"Ah, that was wise indeed," my friend acknowledged. "Such warnings cannot be taken lightly!"

Holmes continued his questioning, "Mr. Cary, what did your staff have to say about the matter?"

There was a slight pause with Cary looking away.

"Sir," Holmes went on, "surely, you met with them?"

Shaking his head Cary spoke, "Actually, Mr. Holmes, I didn't. I decided to keep it my secret... that is, except for Malcolm. He has been a loyal member of our household for many years. Indeed, he is like a member of my own family. I would, and do, trust him in all things, even with my life."

"That's all well and good," Holmes remarked. "And what did he have to say about it?"

"Mr. Holmes," Cary stated with some consternation, "Malcolm was extremely upset. He naturally assumed the blame for allowing someone to have reached the inner recesses of our home. I can't tell you how cross he became. When alluding to the intrusion, he felt that he had let me down. Indeed, he even tendered his resignation, offering to leave his position!"

"And you, sir," Holmes remarked, "obviously, you refused to accept his offer."

"I would hear none of it, Mr. Holmes," Cary spoke, assuming a rather stern posture. "I looked him straight in the eye and informed him of my wish that he stay on. I expressed our family's deep affection for him. I only asked that he keep the matter to himself, suggesting that it would be better not to worry the staff. He, for his part, bowed, thanked me for the kind words, and agreed to do as I had requested."

Holmes seemed content with Cary's response, and facing the window, once more, re-lit his pipe. Already it had become a two-pipe conundrum!

"I see," remarked Holmes, scratching his left ear.

"And you're certain," he continued, "that this man, Malcolm, won't discuss this threat with any of the other servants or family members?"

"There can be no question of his discretion in this matter, Mr. Holmes," Cary remarked with much annoyance.

"That is very good," Holmes commented. "Let us turn our attention to the actual murders. Mr. Cary, did you know any of the victims?"

"Actually, Mr. Holmes," he replied, "I did know them, but mostly through our work on the town council. The most recent victim, Mr. Fenwick, however, was a dear friend of mine. I'd known Eldridge for over fifteen years. He was one of the finest men I had ever met."

"Do continue," Holmes prompted. "If you would, tell me all you can about the crimes. Spare no detail. As I've mentioned, no fact can be deemed to be insignificant when it comes to performing a thorough investigation."

With that having been put forth, Cary reached into one of his desk drawers and placed what appeared to be a journal before us.

"Mr. Holmes," he stated, "while I don't pretend to be any kind of detective, I have been blessed with an orderly disposition and a healthy, possibly perverse, curiosity for all things criminal. When the first atrocity was reported, I began to jot down what officials had discovered, placing their information in this journal, along with some of my own thoughts about the event. With each additional murder, came another set of facts for me to ponder, analyze, and add to this record. I have not yet had time to enter the horrible account of poor Eldridge's demise into this journal, but was planning on doing so."

"Perhaps you might find these writings useful," Cary suddenly offered. "If so, I would be most happy to submit them to your keeping for further examination. Along with them goes my sincere hope that these humble efforts on my part, might somehow help you in your investigation."

Holmes nearly dropped his pipe at Cary's offer. I have never seen my friend so confused. Holmes eagerly accepted the journal from Cary and quickly leafed through the neatly written details, shaking his head up and down as he scanned the informative passages. Several minutes passed before Holmes carefully closed the book, and gave Mr. Cary a most incredulous look.

"My word, Cary," a smiling Holmes offered, "I am truly delighted with your impressive reporting skills. Why, Lestrade and Gregson of Scotland Yard have never even approached this level of investigative ability. I am stunned at your attention to detail in these case descriptions. Why, I almost feel as if you were a witness to these tragedies!"

Cary smugly bowed at Holmes's remarks, but suddenly the smile quickly faded as he construed that Holmes might have just accused him of being the murderer.

"Just a minute, Mr. Holmes," a now, somewhat-agitated Cary roared. "Are you suggesting that I might be involved in any of these deplorable crimes?"

"Heavens no," smiled the consulting detective, "I would never accuse you of having done the deeds, Mr. Cary. My remarks were meant as true and genuine compliments to the thoroughness of your reporting and your written reflections of each of the crimes. I am duly impressed with your findings."

Cary's grimace had relaxed and once again, a bright-eyed, contented smile returned to his countenance as he remarked, "Really, Mr. Holmes, I'm delighted to hear that you appreciate my efforts."

"Sir, I do sincerely applaud your work," Holmes replied, extending his hand. "You know, if you should tire of the court room, you might consider opening up your own detective agency!"

All of us smiled at that comment, as it was evident that the mood had been lightened somewhat by the jovial remark.

"Mr. Cary," Holmes earnestly implored, "I hope that you understand that we may need a day or two to go through your reports to see how they may corroborate what has been officially reported. You've really saved Doctor Watson and me a great deal of time and effort. Let me assure you, once again, sir, that it is most appreciated."

"Certainly, Mr. Holmes," spoke a now-strutting, smiling Cary, "I am honored to have such approbation from a man of your reputation. Feel free to make of it what you will and return it to me whenever you are finished."

Cary suddenly moved across the room to the bookcase opposite the front windows. He lifted a pile of books on the third shelf and carried them over to his desk.

"Mr. Holmes, Doctor Watson," he advised, "these books might aid you in your investigation. Each offers information about our little village. One is a book of local maps. Another is a brief history of Torquay. The last book describes our own home. It traces its beginnings as a working Abbey and continues to the year 1900."

He continued, "Please feel free to browse through them if you feel they may be of use to you and Doctor Watson."

That having been said, Cary sat behind the stack, looked around the room, winked at Holmes, and picked up his letter opener, taking great care while placing it atop his desk.

I noticed that Holmes was staring at Cary, and Cary noticed the same thing.

"Mr. Holmes," the lawyer inquired, "will there be anything else?"

My friend quickly responded, "Not at this time, thank you."

Reaching over to shake Cary's hand, Holmes called, "Watson, old chap, let us take our leave for now. Thank you for the journal, Mr. Cary. Rest assured that I will take the utmost care in its perusal and safe return. We will contact you in the next several days to apprise you of our findings."

"Good day, Mr. Holmes. . . Doctor Watson," waved the lawyer as he walked us to the front door. "Please feel free to come and go as you please in the course of your investigation. I will be back and forth over the next few days, while I move my family to safer surroundings."

After bidding Mr. Cary adieu, we started down the steps, when Holmes, suddenly stopped and turned toward back to the servant, "Malcolm, I wonder if we can have a word with you?"

"Why, certainly, sir," he responded anxiously. "Please feel free to ask me anything at all Mr. Holmes. I am completely at your disposal."

"Ah, that is well, Malcolm," the detective whispered. "Watson and I have a few questions for you. Is it possible for us to meet with you when we visit tomorrow?"

"Sirs," he bowed, "I will be most happy to oblige. Is there anything else?"

"Not at this time, Mr. Randolph," Holmes remarked, waving to the butler. "Until tomorrow, then. . . "

"Good day, gentlemen," Cary's servant offered as the door closed behind him.

After taking the reins from the young stable boy, Holmes and I started back to our hotel. The skies were starting to clear, but a cold, damp wind had come up, inducing us to pull the plaid carriage blanket around us. It would only be a short ride back to the hotel, but the elements made our trip seem so much longer. At least the scenery along Torquay Road did help to make our return trip somewhat more palatable. I had begun to occupy my mind by observing the many quaint architectural styles of Torquay, when my friend suddenly stopped our carriage.

Holmes straightened his deerstalker, turned quickly and inquired, "Well, Watson, what do you make of Mr. Cary? Be sure to hold nothing back."

"Really, Holmes," I replied, "what do I think of the man? My word, I've only just met him!"

"Yes, yes," he impatiently offered. "Surely you've formed some opinion, Watson. Have you not?"

"Hmmm, well, Holmes, if you must know, I judged him as being extremely nervous. But, having received such a threatening note, and under the circumstances of the recent murders, anyone in his position might feel the same."

"I know, I know," Holmes continued in a somewhat agitated manner.

"What else, my good man?" Holmes questioned as our carriage started up again, approaching the last hill before arriving at our hotel.

I suddenly caught his drift, "Oh, I see what you're looking for. You want to know if I believe his story. Is that what you're looking for?"

"Watson," Holmes continued, "I hold you to be as fine a judge of human character as there has ever been. I simply want your honest opinion of the man."

"Well, then," I responded, "as I have already suggested, he seemed to be very nervous upon meeting us. Certainly, more about meeting you than me, I would suggest. I further sensed that, though most cordial, he couldn't wait for us to leave. Do you share that opinion?"

Holmes, placing his right hand over his furrowed brow, posed, "I'm not certain what to make of the man, Watson. I, too, sensed that he seemed to be acting 'on script', as it were. Perhaps, that is just his way, but I felt that he was keeping something back from us. And yet.. "

Our conversation was interrupted by the hotel stable boy, for we had pulled up to the Imperial. After helping us from the carriage, we watched the young man quickly return the horses to the hotel livery.

Continuing toward the main entrance, Holmes began again, almost as if he were thinking aloud, "Still, he was kind enough to give us his journal. That should count for something. I'll just have to give these notes the utmost scrutiny. Hopefully, we may find something there for us to go on."

As we entered the busy hotel lobby, I noticed that a young girl was standing near the main desk. She seemed inordinately interested in Holmes, who had stepped away with the hotel manager. It appeared to me that she recognized him or, perhaps had believed him to have been someone else. In any event, I kept a close watch on her out of the corner of my eye until we had rounded the corner leading to the main stairway.

Holmes and I slowly ascended the steep marble steps and turned down our hallway, when Holmes suddenly grabbed my arm and dragged me behind a doorway alcove.

Holding a finger to his lips, he smiled and whispered, "Quiet, Watson, we are being followed!"

As the young girl slipped furtively around the corner, Holmes called out in a most comforting manner, "Hello, young lady. May we be of any assistance to you?"

The poor girl stopped instantly, and as she slowly backed away, offered, "Gentlemen, please excuse me. I thought that I recognized you, but perhaps I was wrong."

At her comment, Holmes gave me a wink, as if struck by her confident manner. I must admit, we both were surprised by her pluckiness. She didn't seem ill-at-ease in the least!

As she turned to go, Holmes called out, "Come now, young lady, you've already gotten past the difficult part. Let us see if, in fact, you may have found whom you've been searching for!"

Instead of rushing away in embarrassment, our spy turned quickly and walked over to us, remarking, "Sirs, I do apologize for my brazen affront, but my curiosity simply got the better of me. Is it possible that I'm now in the presence of Mr. Sherlock Holmes and the eminent scribe, Doctor John Watson?"

We were somewhat caught off guard by her inquiry, but Holmes acknowledged her suspicions.

"Yes, my dear, I'm Holmes and this is, indeed, the 'scribe', Doctor Watson," Holmes conceded. "May I inquire as to the reason for your venturing out, alone, to a hotel and accosting two strange gentlemen?"

"Oh, this is most wonderful," the young girl happily replied, turning a bright pink. "I know this was most rude of me, but I just had to discover if I was correct!"

The child continued, "My name is Aggie Miller. I'm a resident of Torquay, but I'm certainly not here alone. My mother and I just finished our afternoon tea at the Imperial. This is where we come to celebrate special occasions."

"Well, Miss Aggie," I remarked, "it is quite good to know that you're here with your mother. Now, might I suggest that you return to her care, for she is probably searching for you as we speak!"

The girl's eyes almost popped out their sockets when she realized that her mother would indeed be quite concerned over her sudden disappearance.

She quickly said her "good-byes" and stormed around the corner and back down the hotel staircase.

Holmes and I exchanged whimsical shoulder shrugs, laughed a bit, and continued on our way.

"Most interesting young girl, Holmes, say what?" I inquired.

"Of that, there can be no doubt, Watson," he agreed, as he inserted the key into our hotel suite. "You know, my good fellow, I wouldn't be surprised if we come across this young lady again in the not too distant future!"

I smiled at his suggestion, as we entered our suite, wondering why I had felt the same way. After closing the door, I quickly made my way to my bedroom. I found I was totally exhausted. This sudden surprise trip through the middle of the night had exacted its toll upon my aging frame. Even though it was only 12:30 in the afternoon, I simply needed to rest.

After removing my outer coat, I called out to Holmes, "If it is acceptable to you, my friend, I fear I need a nap."

"Off you go, Watson," he offered, lighting his pipe. "I'll have no time for sleeping until I've studied Cary's documents."

The last thing I remembered before nodding off was Holmes studying the journal and then, peaceful dreams held sway.

Chapter 7 Cary's Journal

Evening of December 18th

"Watson, Watson," a most familiar, annoying voice suddenly rang in my ears. "Get up old boy!"

"What? Who? Where?" I sputtered, wiping the sleep from my still squinting eyes.

"Dear chap, you've been out for nearly three hours," he added, "and you've lost the best part of the day!"

"I am sorry, Holmes," I offered humbly, "I was physically and mentally spent, what with all the travel, threats, murders and all the other goings on."

Holmes went back to the corner table and once more sifted through the pages of the Cary journal. His pipe was blazing fiercely in the side of his mouth, exaggerating the size and scope of his protruding jawbone. Since I had seen him in that type of frenzy only on rare occasions, I gathered that he had found some interesting points in Cary's crime narratives.

"Have you solved the murders yet, Holmes?" I teased.

"Well, if I had had the support of one sleeping lummox, I might have!" he joked, shaking his pipe in my direction.

"Sadly, no Watson, not yet," he divulged, adding, "however, there are some bits and pieces in these reports that may merit some closer scrutiny."

"Uh... Is that so?" I queried, still a bit groggy from my afternoon refresher.

"Come, Watson, I would like your opinion on the Cary commentaries," Holmes beckoned.

While I made my way over to the small table, Holmes was already laying out the journal for my inspection.

"Watson, I believe that you will find these notes most interesting, particularly in the manner in which Cary responds to each of the articles," Holmes offered.

"Let us begin," he said. "Would you please read the first newspaper article aloud? And, after you've read it, please close the journal, placing this page marker where we've left off."

I knew better than to ask him his reasons for such a request and so I began to read the article which had been clipped from the local paper and pasted into the leather-bound case:

Torquay, Thursday, October 20, 1905

Body Discovered Along Village Road

Early Thursday morning, Officer Philip Bennett discovered the body of Torquay town banker, Mr. Henry Dinsmore, on Meadfoot Road. It is believed that Mr. Dinsmore, one of our town's leading citizens, succumbed from head injuries he had received from an apparent accidental fall on his way home from work sometime late Wednesday evening.

Officials in the department notified the family of the deceased immediately upon discovery of the body. After additional inquiries, police learned that his wife, Emma, had reported him missing very early on that same Thursday morning. When asked why she had waited until the next day to file a missing person's report, the widow offered that her husband often kept late hours due to the many responsibilities of his position. She further informed authorities that her husband was in the habit of staying up late and very often she wouldn't see him until the next morning's breakfast.

After completing the reading, I rested the journal on my lap and voiced, "Holmes, it appears to be a simple police report printed in the town paper."

"Ah, yes, Watson," my friend continued, "just a matter-of-fact police report. Now go back to the journal and tell me, dear fellow, what you think of Mr. Cary's notes. And, carefully read them aloud, as well, if you would."

I was somewhat off-put by my friend's implication, for he frequently accused me of not paying enough attention to all of the possible details. Nevertheless, I continued my perusal of Cary's notes which he had neatly written directly below the newspaper article. They consisted of the following remarks:

> **Poor old Dinsmore should never have been out that late.**
> **Beaten to death with some type of hammer-like instrument.**
> **Judging by rumors from coroner's office, it could have**
> **been a Druid ceremonial dagger of some kind. Ah, Dinsmore...**
> **All of us have enemies, and I'm sure you had your share of them.**
> **He had been warned, but he wouldn't listen to his friends.**
> **Will there be others? I wonder... I certainly hope not..**
> **Meadfoot Road served as a perfect locale for an ambush.**
> **There are many turns and hollows where evil might be done.**
> **Could Dinsmore simply have been in the wrong place at the**
> **wrong time? Perhaps, perhaps not... It is most alarming!**
> **Despite the official police report, I have my suspicions.**
> **I, for one, don't believe his death to be accidental!**

"Oh, dear me," I stopped suddenly. "Yes, Holmes, I see what

you mean. What might Cary be hiding? What do you think he means when he refers to 'others'?"

"Exactly, Watson! What is the man implying?" the great detective inquired with some consternation. "Suspicions indeed. Let's examine his other remarks. Go on, now, read the next newspaper clipping."

Torquay, Tuesday, November 22, 1905
Councilman Hall's Corpse Discovered
Town Residents Shocked by News

Our peaceful little community suffered another terrible loss when it was revealed that Mr. Trent Hall's lifeless body had been found in some dense shrubbery off Belgrade Road. Hall had gone missing for several days before family members elected to notify the local constabulary. After a preliminary examination, local officials announced that they suspected foul play.

Cause of death was believed to have been from severe loss of blood, the result of a huge gash atop his cranium. When asked to comment on what might have created such a deadly strike Chief Inspector Davis issued the following statement:
"Gentlemen, while we are hard-pressed to state with any real conviction the exact nature of the weapon that was used to murder Mr. Hall, it appears that a very sharp ax-like instrument may have done the damage."

When pressed for additional commentary, Chief Inspector Davis offered, "At this time, our criminal investigation has just begun and it would be foolhardy to speculate on mere preliminary findings."

Upon concluding this account, I immediately moved down to Cary's notes regarding this particular newspaper report.

**Now it's Hall? Good Lord, they're after the Council!
Belgrave Road. . . Too close for comfort. Is it possible?
Could this be a reaction to Article 7, I wonder?
Surely, they are capable. . . From what I've observed. . .
I do believe that these people are dangerous.
They hate all of those who refuse to follow their beliefs. . .**

> **Hall's skull was opened up like a melon! Probably done with a trench-cleave, another Druid tool!**
> **Our community will never accept their heathen ways.**
> **I'm very worried for our future. We must protect ourselves.**
> **But how? Even the local magistrates seem to be against us!**

"This is most curious, Holmes," I said. "Why would anyone choose to make such notes? To me, they seem to be merely reactive remarks to the events that have taken place! Furthermore, who are these 'dangerous' people to whom he refers?"

"Watson," Holmes stated, "I am of the same opinion. While Mr. Cary clearly needs our help, and while he was most kind to offer these journals for our examination, his remarks do seem to be simply reactionary and somewhat theatrical!"

"Thus far," he continued, "he has hinted at some possible perpetrators but has not seen fit to identify them, other than to mention the Druid cult. We must find and examine 'Article 7'. Hmm.... I can only surmise that it must refer to an edict the town council enacted with respect to this local band of Druids! And yet, as you continue reading the journal entries, you will find additional information that may shed some light on this case."

"Holmes, do you wish me to continue?" I asked, "or, have you had enough of this morbidity for one day?"

Shaking his head with a wry smile, he waved his hand casually, signaling for me to go on.

The third article was the same one that had only recently appeared in the London Daily Telegraph. This time I gave it much greater attention as I once more offered my rendition to my "audience" aloud:

Saturday, December 16, 1905

Another Body Discovered in Torquay

Residents of the peaceful town of Torquay, well-known tourist destination for summer holiday-breaks, may soon be receiving notoriety for other, more sinister reasons! Police officials have just released the name of a third apparent murder victim, Tom Dennison, yet another town council member.

Dennison's body was discovered on Friday, December 15th, along Babbacombe Road by Dan Tate, a local resident, who had been walking his dog. Over the last three months, the council has now lost three of its more illustrious members, all of them under suspicious circumstances! Residents are naturally outraged by these events and are demanding answers from the community's law enforcement authorities.

According to the local coroner, the first victim had been found bludgeoned; the second man died from a deep head-wound; while Mr. Dennison had been strangled. Constables found a wire-iron device at the site, indicating that Dennison had been garroted.

This most recent murder led the Torquay Town Council to hold an emergency session last evening to discuss what might be done to better protect its citizenry. Local constables in attendance advised everyone to keep a sharp lookout for any strange goings on that they might observe.

The last order of business was to appoint James Cary, another council member, and one of the town's most accomplished civic leaders, to head a commission which would oversee the investigation of these heinous crimes.

Cary's journal entry for this report read as follows, issuing some additional thoughts including his reference to contacting Holmes.

> Dennison? Why would they kill Tom? He was a fine young man, newly elected to replace old Dinsmore. Why as far as I know, Dennison wasn't even aware of these brigands. All of our decisions were made long before Tom was appointed. . . .
> Babbacombe Road. . . logical location for a murder! Plenty of ground-cover and densely wooded. . .
> A garroting.....common enough method of execution. . .
> I'm glad I contacted Holmes. . . I trust he can help.
> He may be our only hope!

When I had finished the last of Cary's brief notations, I turned and slowly glanced at my friend. He was now pacing back and forth, peering through the window curtains that overlooked the Channel. As he turned in my direction, I noticed that he had a most anxious look on his face. Slowly, he made his way over toward the table and retrieved the journal.

"Well, Watson," he paused, closing the work, "what do you make of the notations? Obviously, you have identified the common thread all throughout his remarks."

When he had finished his challenge to me, I felt pressured to react, and react quickly. To me, it was as if what I had read was so obvious that it needed no additional confirmation on my part. But, like it or not, I offered my opinion.

"Holmes," I spoke almost in a whisper, "of course, I observed the references to Druidism. How could one not?"

I continued, "Still, they were mostly Cary's thoughts and feelings about those horrid events. He wasn't there, so how much credence can we place on his notes? Why even I might have arrived at similar findings had I been in his position. "

Holmes made no response to my remarks. Instead, he quickly extinguished his pipe, rose, grabbed his Mackinaw and headed for the door, calling back, "Watson, I'll see you for dinner at 7:00 P.M."

"Holmes, what....where.....whoa!" I exclaimed while the hotel room door slammed shut behind him.

I must have sat motionless in my chair for at least five minutes while I pondered such an abrupt exit. Surely, something must have triggered his actions, but what could it have been? Clearly, had he wished to have told me, he would have done so. It was too late to speculate, knowing his ways. I would simply have to wait until dinner.

Rather than dwell upon the point, I decided to return to the bed and continue my physical restoration. I would catch another forty winks and let the matter rest for a short time. Conditions for my nap were ideal with the winter wind whistling through the cracks of the warped old windows of our suite. I curled up under the soft sheets and sleep came easily.

Almost immediately I found that I was in the middle of a most vivid dream. It seemed so real that it remained with me long after I had awoken. While I sat waiting to go to our evening meal, I carefully tried to recreate what I had only recently experienced. It would be something to share with Holmes!

In the dream, I was being followed by a group of shrouded figures on horseback. Black robes covered their heads, hiding their features. As their steeds came ever closer to my speedy sorrel, I knew that I would soon be overtaken. Pushing my mount ever faster, I was fortunate in spying a deep, dark cave ahead. Desperate to escape, I rode through the narrow opening, looking for some way to escape.

Inside the cave, I rounded a corner and suddenly, a bright light materialized, overtaking the darkness. Not surprisingly, my mount whinnied in terror and reared up on his hind legs. Try as I might, I couldn't stay in the saddle, and soon I was rolling on the ground. Fearing for my life, I reached for my service revolver and quickly took cover behind a large rocky outcropping illuminated by the light.

There, I was determined to defend my position or die trying! Several tense minutes had passed before I realized that there was no noise except for the sounds of my racing heart, my own hurried, elevated breathing and a weird, popping sound. Bravely maintaining my position, I waited for the riders, preparing for the worst. I sensed that they would make their appearance at any moment, but strangely, they were nowhere to be seen!

Questions peppered my active noggin. . . Where had they gone? What had happened to them? I remained anxiously on edge, knowing it would only be a matter of time.

Once again, my attention was drawn to the popping sound and reflecting light. Kneeling down, I crept further into the depths of the cave. Peering around another nook, I discovered a fire blazing away in a small pit. The intense light rushed into my eyes, causing some minor discomfort. Shading my vision with my left hand, I slowly moved behind my poor, exhausted, lathered horse.

Still trembling and confused, I decided to call out in the hope of getting someone's attention.

"Hello, hello, I say, hello. . . Is anyone there?" I bellowed.

Seconds later, I heard a vaguely familiar voice replying, "Hello, hello, I say, hello. . . Is anyone there?"

I quickly tensed up, cocking my pistol, ready for action. Again, there was only silence. After a few more seconds had passed, my terror turned to quiet laughter, as I realized that the response I had heard was nothing more than my own voice echoing off the walls of the enormous cavern!

Once more I continued moving toward the light, hoping to find someone to help me escape from the riders who had been pursuing me. I still sensed that they were nearby, waiting for me to emerge from this cave. One question continued to bother me. Why hadn't they followed me into the cavern? Surely, they had seen me ride my horse into the opening! This made no sense, no sense at all. Unless...

Unless, they were afraid of something that must be within the cave! Suddenly, my blood ran cold. What could be lurking all about me that would prevent a band of brigands from following?

At this stage, I decided that my best course of action would be to explore the rest of the cavern. I couldn't remain quaking in fear. I had to find out what might be lurking further within. Slowly, I approached the fire pit. It must have been my eyes playing tricks on me, for as I peered into the flames, I was certain that I saw an image of a beautiful young woman holding what appeared to have been Spanish doubloons!

As I continued to stare, she seemed to be raising her hands toward me, still holding the coins. It was as if she wanted me to have them. I began to feel a bit tipsy, deciding to put my pistol away. Slowly, very slowly, I reached into the flames to take the coins from her glowing hands.

Imagine my horror when I found that I was being pulled into the fiery pit, screaming uncontrollably as the flames engulfed my falling body. Then, there was nothing but darkness.

When I opened my eyes, I was in a dimly-lit, dirt-covered room. There were silvery Spanish doubloons all around me. Springing to my feet, I quickly searched for my revolver. Fortunately, it was still in the pocket of my coat.

Where was I ? What had happened to me? Where were the flames? Where was the young woman? She was gone, and yet, here were the coins! Questions, I had many, many questions.

Then, I remembered. While reaching for the coins, I must have somehow been whisked through these magical flames, unscathed. But why? Where? How?

I had no answers to these questions and I just sat there, wondering, wondering, wondering. . .

That was how my dream had ended, I believe, yet when I had finally awoken, there was a sense that I had shouted something. Something? Yes, yes, but try as I might I simply couldn't remember what it was?

Shortly afterward, I tried to calm down by splashing some water on my face. I was still trembling, but at least I had survived my nightmare!

After brushing my hair, I checked my timepiece. It was ten minutes before 7:00 P.M. I had just enough time to finish dressing and make my way down to the hotel dining room to meet Holmes, but I was still shaking from that eerie dream.

Cheery sounds of the season greeted me as I passed through the ornate hotel lobby on the way to dinner. Everywhere Christmas decorations sparkled along the brightly lit hallway. The soothing voices of a local choir couldn't help but lighten one's spirit at this most festive time of year. Strains of "Silent Night" drifted peacefully into the background as I turned into the large room.

I quickly spied Holmes, already seated and paging through the establishment's dinner menu. He had located one of the best tables available; directly looking out upon the Channel, whose whitecaps were still visible from the reflection of the hotel's outdoor gas lamps. Another winter storm was brewing.

As I neared the table, he rose anxiously, smiled and whispered, "Watson, I want you to know that we will have company joining us for dinner this evening. . ."

Before I could speak, he continued. "My good fellow, please don't ask me to explain at this time, for if I am correct, he has just entered the room. Your question will soon be addressed."

Turning toward the doorway, I found a rather stout older gentleman conversing with the maitre d', who was pointing in our direction. Quickly, the man was ushered through the busy dining room over to our table. As he handed over his gray tweed cloak to one of the waitstaff, Holmes and I stood politely, waiting to greet our guest, extending and shaking the man's hand.

"Chief Inspector Miles Davis," Holmes opened most courteously, "thank you so much for agreeing to meet with us this evening on such short notice. May I introduce my good friend and. . . ."

"Not at all, Mr. Holmes," replied the lawman, interrupting. "I'm very pleased to make your acquaintance, as well as the famous Doctor Watson."

After taking his seat, Davis continued, "Gentlemen, I'm very honored to meet you. Your sterling reputations precede you. I am agreeable to answer any questions you may have regarding this murderous rampage our fair community is experiencing."

"That is most welcomed news, Chief Inspector. Were you able to secure access to tomorrow's autopsy for us?" Holmes queried.

"Yes, gentlemen. It's scheduled to begin at 9 o'clock tomorrow," Davis informed us. He added, "You were most fortunate to have contacted me this afternoon, Mr. Holmes, before Judge Manson left town. It was necessary to obtain his permission to attend the examination, and with Mr. Fenwick's funeral scheduled in two days, it would have been too late if we had to wait until the judge returned!"

"Ah, Watson," Holmes sighed, "haven't I remarked how timing is everything? Chief Inspector Davis, we owe you a great deal for interceding on our behalf."

"It was nothing, gentlemen," Davis replied. "After all, it's the two of you who will be helping us in our work, as well!"

Holmes raised his hand to summon our waiter, who hastened to describe the day's special menu items. While we awaited the arrival of our evening repast, we enjoyed a carafe of Clermont's finest Merlot.

The night was proving to be most relaxing, and for a brief moment I found that I was totally unconcerned with the tragic events that had brought us here to Torquay.

That comfortable mood quickly changed when my dear friend turned to Davis and posed the following: "Chief Inspector," Holmes inquired, "are you aware of any active followers of Druidism in this region of England?"

"Hmm. . . that's a most interesting question, Mr. Holmes," remarked the Chief Inspector, squinting his eyes and moving closer to us. "There does exist an ever-growing colony of those who espouse the Druid religion 32 kilometers away, near Wildecombe. However, there have been occasional visits by one of their leaders, a man who goes by the name Terra."

"Terra, you say?" I volunteered. "Why that word translates to earth if my old Latin studies are correct."

"Elementary, Watson!" Holmes exclaimed, teasingly. "It's one of the first Latin words that we were taught many years ago in our early schooling, along with mater et pater, and amo, amas, amat, . . ."

Davis chuckled at that remark, while I must admit that I was not as amused by my friend's innocent, yet caustic barb.

Sensing my discomfort, Holmes soothed, "Come now, Watson, I couldn't help it. . You know that I hold you in the highest esteem!"

The best I could offer was a polite smile to that remark, but Holmes knew that I never enjoyed being the brunt of his clever comments.

"Terra, is it, hmmm," Holmes started up again, crossing his arms. "Might I assume that this fellow has recently made his presence known at the town council meetings?"

Chief Inspector Davis at first seemed stunned at that remark, but quickly replied, "Why, yes, Mr. Holmes. As a matter of fact he has been a regular attendee since the passage of Article 7, banning any religious ceremonies on public grounds."

Davis moved his chair closer to Holmes and whispered, "Tell me, Mr. Holmes, what made you ask about the Druids, if you don't mind? There has been nothing about this group in our newspapers for several weeks. Have you discovered anything that might throw some light upon our ongoing investigations?"

"In truth, Chief Inspector, I believe that I have," Holmes

replied smiling as he reached into his pocket.

"Earlier this afternoon, I visited the site of Mr. Fenwick's tragic death, examined the area and discovered this."

Reaching in his pocket, Holmes slowly unwrapped a cloth, exposing a strangely shaped, dull grayish object.

He carefully placed it before us.

"Well, now," Davis exclaimed, "that looks like some kind of coin or token. . . although I don't recognize the strange symbols etched upon it."

The Chief Iinspector held it up before his squinting eyes, and turned it over and over.

"Most interesting," he remarked.

Holmes suggested, "Watson, see what you can make of it? Perhaps you've come across something like this in your travels. . ."

Taking it in my left hand, I carefully rubbed my thumb across the surface of the object, pinching it to determine its weight and composition. Much like a half-pence, I reasoned, while continuing to examine the symbol thereon.

"Holmes," I ventured, "I believe that I've seen this symbol someplace before, but I can't exactly remember where. Perhaps, it was near the monoliths at Dartmoor when we were called to investigate the Baskerville case. . ."

"Very good, Watson," Holmes affirmed, adding, "if I'm not mistaken, the symbol on the token is of Druid origin. I believe this particular image engraved upon the object is called a sigil. Notice it appears to be a leafed, willow wreath with twin branches or staves passing through it."

"Mr. Holmes," Davis suggested, "it would appear that your visit to our little community will prove to be most helpful in our efforts to solve these murders. In fact, you are absolutely correct about Druid involvement in these heinous crimes. I have been very busy gathering information about the weapons used in the murders that have taken place. My findings have indicated that all of the weapons used, a special dagger, a trench-cleave and a laqueus, are all Druid ceremonial devices."

"Bravo, Chief Inspector," Holmes praised. "It appears that you are well on your way to solving these crimes."

"Thank you, Mr. Holmes," Davis blushed. "Coming from you, it is high praise, indeed."

"While I'm on the subject," the lawman continued, "I almost forgot to thank you for sending your advance team. They have been most helpful."

"Advance team?" I questioned, "Holmes, what advance team?"

"Watson," Holmes replied, casually dismissing my inquiry, "all in good time, my good fellow."

Davis immediately inquired, "Tell me, sir, if you would, what would you suggest we do next?"

"Chief Inspector," Holmes addressed the law official with much candor, "the autopsy tomorrow may prove to be most beneficial in helping us formulate what our next steps might be."

With that having been stated, our meals arrived, and the three of us spent the next thirty minutes enjoying our food and the festive music of the season.

After dinner and a few more glasses of wine, Davis arose from the table, thanked us for a most interesting evening and, bowing slightly, took his leave as we continued finishing our pudding.

I was still feasting on my dessert when Holmes decided to light his pipe. In several minutes, I knew that he was well-into one of his cranial comas. These events, though seldom rare, were usually reserved for much more secluded locales: living quarters, hotel rooms, libraries, cemeteries, etc. Such was the consulting detective's established methodology. Indeed, the game was once more afoot, and I believed that like a trained bloodhound, Holmes must certainly have discovered some valuable evidence.

While I was always curious when I found him so disposed, I knew better than to interrupt. He would reveal his findings in his own good time. For now, I would be content to listen to the carols that the children of the village so sweetly sang.

Chapter 8 The Plot Thickens. . .

Tuesday, December 19th

I was awakened the following morning by the familiar sounds of jingling bells which adorned all of the carriages this time of year. Outside of our windows, vehicles were everywhere busily carrying their fares to and from the magnificent grounds of the Imperial Hotel. People loved to visit the quaint little shops and their seasonal displays along the hotel promenade.

While the happy sounds echoed off the exterior walls of our historic establishment, I continued dressing, all the while imagining the morning's work. Soon, Holmes and I would be meeting Chief Inspector Davis for the Fenwick autopsy. That, however, would have to wait until we had finished our breakfast.

Although lesser mortals would argue that perhaps an empty stomach might prove the wiser choice when viewing a thorough examination by the county coroner, I had long ago become hardened to such uncomfortable procedures. The battlefield had steeled my resolve and I had some experience performing them when it was required. Still, I knew that I needed sustenance to face the day.

"What say we try the French croissants, Holmes?" I offered, happily rubbing my hands in anticipation.

"Watson," he replied as our waiter approached the table, "you continue to amaze me. After all of these years, you still try to tempt me in the direction of sweets. You know my ways. I've told you that too much sucrose in the system can stifle the brain's activity, thus dulling its creative and problem-solving potentialities!"

"Forgive me, Holmes," I cautioned. "It being the holiday season, I actually believed that you might enjoy some temporary deviation from your normal eating habits. I, for one, must have a taste!"

"Young man," I called to our server, "I would very much like to try the strawberry croissants with some Imperial Hotel Grey tea. I have no idea what my companion may decide this morning."

Looking sternly at the attentive lad who was waiting table, Holmes offered, "I believe I'll have the butterscotch croissant, thank you very much."

When the young man had scurried off with our order, Holmes turned away from me, lit his pipe, and dourly teased, "There, Watson, are you happy now?"

I immediately laughed at this smug remark. Smiling, I had to admit that I found some of his quips well-delivered, and this had been one of them. That was a side of the man rarely seen.

Soon after, we relaxed and enjoyed a most delectable breakfast. The pastries were every bit as tasty as they appeared, I hasten to add.

We were still finishing up our meal, when I suddenly recalled a mental note that I had made during last night's dinner meeting with Davis. There was a question that needed answering.

"Holmes," I spoke in a very serious tone, "I have something I need to ask."

"By all means, old man," he replied. "What is it that you simply need to know?"

"Holmes," I offered gingerly, "would I be correct in assuming that you had previously corresponded with Inspector Davis, prior to our arrival in Torquay?"

The great detective gave me a most curious look. He seemed genuinely confused by my inquiry.

"Why, Watson," he spoke with some mild agitation, setting his croissant on his plate, "are you suggesting that I've been keeping something from you?"

Pausing slightly, I remarked sternly, "Actually, yes, I believe that is exactly what you've done, especially since it's not the first time that this has happened!"

"Well, I'm quite flabbergasted by such an accusation," he answered, stirring his tea while adjusting his napkin.

Suddenly, his face brightened, "Bravo, Watson. You are correct. However, let me assure you that I had every intention of disclosing all of the facts at the proper time."

"When might that be?" I replied, scowling with no little apparent concern.

"Perhaps, now might be a good time," he chuckled, sipping his morning tea, sensing my mood.

What followed next was a detailed explanation in which Holmes described a letter he had received from Chief Inspector Davis asking for assistance in solving the murders of the first two town councilmen. Holmes continued to elaborate how Davis, his constables, and town officials had been receiving tremendous pressure from the residents. These people were terrified, and their communal fears had to be addressed. His people, the authorities, had, thus far, found very few clues.

Holmes had replied that he would be most happy to look into the case and informed Davis that he would be arriving on the 18th of December.

"What?" I interrupted, contemplating the informational timeline. "Holmes, do you mean to say that you had already decided to head here, to Torquay, even before the Cary letter had arrived?"

"And, your point is?" my friend asked calmly.

"Well, why didn't you inform me of this, this, Davis letter when you received it?" I probed, nervously. "Perhaps, you weren't going to tell me about it at all. . . "

Holmes didn't respond right away. He let me stew a little longer, finishing his butterscotch croissant.

"Watson, old boy," he dryly offered, "consider the second letter mere serendipity. Of course, I would have wished you to share in this adventure. Where would I be without my Boswell?"

"Now, think about it, Doctor," he pointed out to me, "when was the last time we were involved in solving two mysteries at one time? Or, might the two be connected? Hmm, we'll have to see."

Admittedly, he had me confused, but in the end I concluded that he most certainly would have invited me to assist in the investigation, and so, I softened my position.

After my concerns had been somewhat allayed, we discussed our plans for the day, listing some of the options that we had at our disposal. Holmes suggested that we revisit Torre Abbey and give that expansive property a much closer look. We had, thus far, only given the estate a brief, cursory examination. That would account for a portion of the day, but I wondered what other plans he had in store.

Although I now knew that Holmes had visited Brandy Cove, I was certain that he would also wish to visit the other crime scenes.

Rising from the table, Holmes restated his plans to me. "Watson," he spoke, "if it is agreeable to you, after the autopsy, we'll go directly to Torre Abbey. I believe that vital information can be gained from a quiet talk with Cary's butler."

"Holmes," I asked, "surely you are not suggesting that Malcolm is involved in any way?"

"You know, Watson," he posed, "it is always best to examine those who are closest to the situation. For, like it or not, proximity lends itself to opportunity. No one is beyond suspicion, at least not at this point in our investigation."

It was a short ride from our hotel to the local police station and along the way we observed the typical early morning goings on of a small town. Residents were actively making their way along the bustling main thoroughfare. Some smiles were evident at this time of the year, yet there was a hint of melancholy, doubtless the result of the rash of crimes that had plagued the quiet seaside village.

At 9:00 A.M. sharp, we reached our destination. Chief Inspector Davis was standing outside the station, carefully adjusting his hat when he spied us alighting from our landau.

Quickly rushing over to greet us, the law officer voiced, "Ah, gentlemen, right on time as I might have imagined. Well, shall we head downstairs and see what we can find?"

"Good day, Chief Inspector," Holmes answered simply.

"Hopefully, this procedure will give us a few more clues than we already have."

"More clues?" Davis asked, cocking his head to one side.

"Mr. Holmes," the police official continued, as the three of us rounded an open doorway, "what do you mean more clues? Why the only clue we have so far is that object that you say you discovered at Brandy Cove yesterday. Are there other bits of pertinent information that you've been able to glean that we might like to discuss?"

At that comment, I looked at Holmes. Surprisingly, he did not react to the snide insinuation made by the local policeman, at least not in any noticeable way. I did, however, recognize some minor displeasure in the manner by which he responded to the lawman.

"Ah, Chief Inspector," Holmes spoke most deliberately, "one merely has to look more closely when investigating. Quite often a vital clue can be overlooked by careless presumptions, as you are sure to discover shortly."

I smiled, being quite familiar with Holmes's well-delivered blow to the local investigator's arrogant insinuation.

Minutes later and we were within the bowels of the building, in a small, well-lit morgue, alongside the town coroner, Stanley Leonard. Mr. Leonard was a clean-shaven, stately-looking man who had held this position in Torquay for the last decade. He was most gracious in welcoming us to this somber procedure. He further advised us that while he took his important position very seriously, at times, he sometimes ascribed to what might be referred to as gallows humor. Holmes and I chose not to respond to such an unusual comment, but waited for the local coroner to begin his examination.

Leonard, after assuring us that he would do everything in his power to find all that could be found, pulled on his surgical mask, picked up a scalpel along with a notepad and started his work.

It was always a chilling experience to witness the manner in which the operation was performed, for that, in fact, is what the procedure truly was, and, I might add, it's not for the squeamish.

The first thing that Leonard did was to examine Mr. Fenwick's exterior. We watched silently as the coroner detailed some of the bruises that were present where the chains had held his wrists to the boulders. Some lesser abrasions were evident along his ankles which had been tethered to some heavy weights securing his position along the shoreline.

After duly noting these findings, the coroner put down the notepad and began the second phase of the examination, neatly slipping the scalpel down the solar plexus. Leonard calmly and expertly completed the autopsy in a timely manner with his assistant now taking notes while Leonard followed all of the established, prescribed directives for a thorough autopsy.

According to his findings, Leonard decreed the official cause of death to be drowning. Leonard painstakingly described how the poor man's lungs would have slowly burst as wave upon wave of the rising tide gradually covered his head and body. It was horrible to ponder that kind of death.

Shortly after the official results had been recorded, Davis led Holmes and me to his office and asked what we thought of Leonard's findings. A brief discussion took place as to the locale, approximate time of death, the horror of such premeditated murder, notification of the next of kin, list of suspects, etc. While the official was wrapping up his end of the proceedings, Holmes seemed to be lost in thought. I knew that look, having seen it so often before. It could mean only one thing, Sherlock Holmes had honed in on an important clue, one which, for the moment, he chose not to disclose to Davis.

Holmes quickly rose from his chair and, once more, thanked our host for allowing us to witness the official autopsy.

"Chief Inspector," Holmes calmly offered, "please know that Watson and I are completely at your disposal should you require any assistance or should any pertinent information be forthcoming. We will also keep you in mind if we discover any important developments that might aid you and your competent staff in solving these crimes."

As an afterthought, while we were leaving the room, Holmes offered, "Chief Inspector, please remember to thank Dr. Leonard for his excellent analysis."

After making our way up the stairway and out of the station, I tugged at Holmes sleeve, "I say, Holmes, I know that you've found something today. Please tell me what it was and why you chose to keep it from our friend, Davis."

"All in good time, Watson," he replied, "all in good time! For now, we need to see Mr. Malcolm Randolph."

"Hmmm," I mumbled, "I see you're doing it, again, Holmes."

The carriage ride along the coastal road to Torre Abbey was brief but most pleasant. Many of the trees along the roadway still glimmered with the sleet that had fallen, producing a silvery-shimmering effect upon the landscape. This beautiful sight wouldn't last much longer for the low winter sun had just now broken through the clouds and with it would come a rise in temperature.

While we were on our way, I invited our driver to tell us about himself, and asked him what he might know about Torre Abbey. We were happily surprised to learn that this young man was well-acquainted with the grounds, having worked there as one of the gardeners while a young man. He further spoke glowingly about the Cary family, informing us that they always treated their help most civilly and courteously.

"It was a privilege to work there, guv'nor," the driver spoke respectfully as he stopped the vehicle near the front entrance.

"Tell me, young man," offered Holmes, stepping from the carriage, "what is your opinion of their butler, Malcolm?"

"Malcolm Randolph, sir?" the carriage driver replied. "Let me say that I have only the greatest respect for the man. In all of me dealins' wif him, he was a regular gentleman to me, he was!"

"Thank you, lad," I said, slipping him a few farthings as he hopped back into his seat and proceeded to drive away.

After the carriage had departed, we made our way toward the main entrance. By the time we had arrived at the top of the steps, the butler had already made his way outside holding open the door, and beckoning us to enter the magnificent vestibule with a most formal sweeping gesture.

"Gentlemen," he voiced softly, "I welcome you back to Torre Abbey. Before I say anything else I must inform you that Mr. Cary is not on the premises today. Furthermore, I don't expect him for several more days as he is getting his family situated at their country estate."

The butler cordially guided us into the main parlor as he

continued his running commentary.

"Please have a seat, gentlemen," Randolph began. "Mr. Cary was insistent upon my availing myself to meet your needs while you are here. Let me assure you both that I am truly open to any and all requests that you may have in his absence, and so I am completely at your service."

"Why that is most considerate of you," I replied on both Holmes and my own behalf.

"I am happy to oblige," the butler responded most amiably.

"Mr. Randolph," Holmes inquired, "as you are aware, we are here to investigate the threats that were made upon Mr. Cary. That being the case, we are most anxious to begin our examination of the property. Is there any particular information that you might be able to provide that may aid us in our work?"

As Holmes was speaking, I noticed one of the housemaids slowly walking by the open doorway. She had a dust rag and was polishing one of the suits of armor that was located outside the parlor doorway.

The butler seemed momentarily distracted, and, "Beg pardon, sir, I lost my focus. Did you ask if I had anything to add that might help you and Doctor Watson?"

Strangely, the manservant appeared somewhat mystified by the detective's question.

"My good man," Holmes explained, "I only meant to give you the opportunity to give us your own account of what has been happening over the past several weeks. Spare no detail, for as Watson can attest, sometimes the smallest revelation can lead to the solution of a problem."

For several minutes, Randolph proceeded to describe his many daily responsibilities, which included collection and sorting of Mr. Cary's mail. He assured Holmes and me that he was very happy working for the Cary family, and hoped to continue in their employ. With regard to the threatening letter, he lowered his head as he recalled the day Mr. Cary shared his concerns over the event.

"Gentlemen," he slowly continued, "I am still most upset for having allowed such a message to have entered this household. I can assure you that the letter never arrived by mail, so that meant that someone had to have brought it into the house, undetected."

Shaking his head, the butler continued, "Mr. Holmes, believe me when I tell you, I am still mortified that this could have happened under my watch. Sirs, I don't know if the Master mentioned, but I offered to tender my resignation over such a terrible blunder!"

Just then, our conversation was interrupted by the same housemaid whom I had observed working a short time ago. She was a slender, middle-aged woman who, upon entering the parlor, offered, "Oh, Mr. Randolph, excuse me. I didn't know that you were busy."

Calling her over, Malcolm nervously spoke, "Mrs. Bedlam, I'd like you to meet Mr. Sherlock Holmes and his associate, Doctor John Watson. These gentlemen are here to inspect the grounds and surrounding buildings which comprise Torre Abbey. It's our annual insurance evaluation."

"Both Mr. Holmes and Doctor Watson have been given total and complete access to our estate. Perhaps, you may have seen them talking with Master Cary yesterday?" spoke Randolph.

Continuing, the butler offered, "Sirs, this is our housekeeper, Lucretia Bedlam. She has just recently begun her service to the Cary family, but she has already made her presence felt."

At that remark, I sensed a certain discomfort on the butler's face as he quickly turned away from the new housekeeper.

Mrs. Bedlam, after giving Randolph a nasty scowl, bowed courteously, "I'm very pleased to make your acquaintance, I'm sure. If you'll excuse me, gentlemen, I'll be on my way, now."

As she was leaving, she whispered to the butler, "I need to meet with you later, Mr. Randolph."

With that, the woman curled her lips and quickly scurried away toward the kitchen pantry. A few awkward moments passed while the butler turned back to Holmes and me, shaking his head.

The looks on our faces must have betrayed our curiosity, for Randolph quickly added, in hushed tones, "If you have sensed some discomfort on my part toward Mrs. Bedlam, I'm afraid that she and I have recently had some differences that need to be addressed. Hopefully, in time, she will come to terms with all of her responsibilities to this household."

"We needn't delve into internal issues at this time, Mr. Randolph," Holmes voiced, in a comforting manner.

"I'm very sorry that I'm unable to do more to help you, Mr. Holmes," the butler whispered, looking over his shoulder. "It's just that I simply can't think of anything that might be of value. **I can't**."

"Well," Holmes voiced, cocking his head to one side, "should you think of something, please feel free to bring it to our attention."

"Mr. Holmes, even though I have many things to do, I am ready to accompany you in your examination of Torre Abbey," Randolph offered, continuing, "although, I suppose that would be what the Master would want."

"No, no, my good man," spoke Holmes, reassuringly. "We don't require your company at this time. It's quite unnecessary. Doctor Watson and I should have no trouble in making our way about the property. If we have future need of your services, we shall certainly seek your kind assistance."

The genial butler seemed quite nervous at Holmes's commentary. He shook his head and offered, "That sir, will never do. I would be neglecting my duty if I were to allow strangers the run of the place, as it were. . . "

Suddenly, he realized what he had suggested. "Gentlemen, please forgive my discourteous remarks. I certainly did not mean to imply that either of you were beyond trust! I simply meant that the privacy of the estate would, of necessity, be compromised to a certain degree without some type of oversight! I hope you understand."

At that response, I must admit that my friend seemed a bit miffed. I, for one, took no umbrage at the butler's remark. Indeed, I could easily understand his position. Holmes stared at the man for several moments before issuing, "Very good, Mr. Randolph, you have passed the first test with flying colors!"

Malcolm seemed stunned at the comment. It looked like he didn't know whether to take Holmes's remark as a compliment or a pointed barb.

After briefly hesitating, he replied, "Sir, I will take your statement to me as a compliment, but I would really like to know why you felt the need to test me. That being said, might I have permission to inquire what further tests you may have for me?"

Holmes smiled and suggested, "Mr. Randolph, I do appreciate your candor. I'll be happy to disclose all in the not-too-distant future. For now, though, Doctor Watson and I will begin our evaluation of Torre Abbey. Please feel free to accompany us if you really feel it necessary."

As Holmes and I started for the hallway, the butler quickly ran to the door, but Holmes had already opened it, offering, "After you, Mr. Randolph."

The startled servant stopped suddenly, replying, "Oh, my, certainly not, Mr. Holmes. It is only right for me to open the door for you!"

"Ah, Mr. Randolph," Holmes mildly scolded, waving his finger gently back-and-forth, "you, sir, are not our servant. I mean you no disrespect, for you are well-meaning in your attentiveness. Please understand, that we are perfectly capable of handling such simple tasks without troubling you."

Malcolm began to argue the point, "Yes, yes, I appreciate what you are saying, but it would never do......Why, my Master...."

Holmes raised his hand and stopped the man from continuing. "Mr. Randolph, I must insist. Please allow us to do our own bidding in this matter!"

Stunned by my companion's remarks, the butler bowed, and started back toward the parlor, offering a parting, "Very good, sir!"

Suddenly, he stopped and called out, "Ah, Mr. Holmes, Dr. Watson, one more thing, sirs, if I may?"

Holmes and I waited for the servant as he quickly led us to the stairwell and, looking around, softly whispered, "Please remember what I said, sirs. I wish that I could provide more help, but **I can't**!"

After he had gone, I noticed a change in Holmes's attitude. We hastened up the staircase of the magnificent structure and made our way into the upper recesses of the historic building. While we were studying the windows for any signs of forced entry, I sauntered over to my companion and tapped his shoulder.

"Holmes," I began, "I noticed you perked up a bit when Mr. Randolph whispered his latest remarks to us. Tell me, if you would, what have you discovered?"

Smiling, his mysterious smile, Holmes simply offered, "Watson, now is not the time. Let us continue our work. A place this size will take a good, long time to examine in detail. Sadly, our study of Torre Abbey will, at best, be cursory, for time is the enemy!"

Our search of the main house took us several hours. My companion quickly took notes of Cary's bedroom, and his children's bedrooms, as well. From pictures and his children's writings and drawings, we discovered that the Cary family consisted of his lovely wife, Meredith, a six-year-old son, Thomas, and a fifteen-year-old daughter, Margaret. Cary had wisely chosen to remove all of them from the house, at least temporarily, while their safety was at stake and Holmes and I were searching for clues. Our presence would only have drawn questions and discomfort for all involved.

All of the hardwood floors were polished and well-maintained. The huge building, despite the years, had been meticulously kept. It was interesting to note that all of the bedrooms were adjacent to each other in the east wing on the second floor. Across the wide hallway, there was a large playroom. It contained a massive bookcase built into one wall containing many volumes of children's books. Very near to the playroom was a rear staircase that was used mainly by the hired staff.

Holmes carefully sketched the positions of each piece of furniture in a schematic he had made for each room. I must note that he paid particular attention to Cary's first floor library-office, and this time, we gave that stately room a most thorough going over, or so I thought.

We stopped to see Malcolm to inform him of our plans to examine the Spanish Barn. Holmes approached the butler and surprised him with a list of questions that he would like to have answered.

"Mr. Randolph," he politely inquired, "if possible, could you try to get those questions answered as soon as possible?"

The butler quickly scanned the list and, shaking his head to the affirmative, responded, "Certainly, Mr. Holmes. I'll get right to it!"

"Oh, Randolph," Holmes added, "there's one more thing that we need to ask."

"Certainly," the attentive butler replied. "What is it, Mr. Holmes?"

"Am I correct in assuming that Mr. Cary has sent the rest of the servants and housekeepers away until he and his family can return home?" Holmes whispered.

With some reluctance, the butler looked around to see if anyone was watching, then shook his head in the affirmative, adding, "Yes, sir, Mr. Holmes. Only Mrs. Bedlam and I have been retained to look after the property. Oh, I almost forgot, our stable boy will still report each day."

Holmes thanked Randolph and we both left the building through the back door.

As we walked along the pathway leading to the large barn, Holmes treated me to a rather detailed historical account of that intriguing building. According to several reports, the barn had been constructed to collect and store the taxes, or tithes, that resident farmers owed to Torre Abbey's religious order. Payment was usually in the form of crops and various other farm products and tools.

Holmes further informed me that in 1588, one of the ships in the Spanish Armada, the Nuestra Senora del Rosario, had been captured by Sir Francis Drake in one of the many sea skirmishes of that war. As a result, 397 members of the crew were captured and taken to Torre Abbey, where they were imprisoned by the English in this very barn. As we slowly entered the building, Holmes continued his lesson.

"Watson," he instructed, "so now you see how the building got its present name. Rumors still abound as to whether the Spanish prisoners were beaten, starved or otherwise, shabbily treated over their brief fourteen-day incarceration. The facts remain that many perished in this very edifice."

"Well, Holmes," I countered, "I wasn't expecting this kind of dissertation, but I admit that I'm impressed at your knowledge of this sad event!"

"There's more, Watson. There remains a most interesting legend attached to this edifice, dear fellow," he teased. "Shall I continue?"

"There is nothing that I would enjoy more, Holmes", I replied.

"Please continue to inform and entertain me!"

His deferential gaze at my teasing retort only momentarily delayed his tale-telling.

"Watson," he started anew, "legend has it that aboard that ill-fated vessel was a young woman, who was a fiancee to one of the ship's lieutenants. Upon realizing that the ship and its crew would soon be taken, this woman donned a disguise as one of the sailors in the hope that she would not be separated from her lover."

Holmes paused dramatically, then continued. "Soon after capture, the crew was housed in this very barn, where overcrowding in horrendous conditions led to the deaths of many of the prisoners. Sadly, this young lady was one of many who perished."

"Oh, my, Holmes," I remarked. "That is truly horrific!"

"Yes, indeed, Watson," my friend slowed, almost displaying some emotion, which was highly unusual.

"Watson," he stated, "there is even more to the story! Ever since that day, 'the ghost of the Spanish Lady' has been seen from time to time, wandering along the barn and all over the grounds of Torre Abbey, searching for her lost love."

"A ghost?" I queried, feeling a slight shiver down my spine. Surely, you don't believe in ghosts, Holmes?"

My companion smiled, but did not respond to my question, as we turned a corner and opened one of the main doors leading into the expansive open area inside the famous barn. There was very little light available to us and most of that quickly disappeared when the door swung closed behind us. Fortunately, we noticed a lantern sitting on a small stand and wasted no time in putting a match to the wick.

The dark interior gradually came to life. As our eyes became accustomed to the lamplight, it soon became clear that the barn had seen little use. My companion quickly glanced about the edges of the walls, sweeping away some of the straw that covered the dirt floor and the cobwebs which hung obtrusively from the damp mold on the walls and beams. I accompanied him, lantern in hand, busily swatting spiders that were virtually everywhere.

Next, Holmes carefully examined the massive entry doors that opened from the outside, moving from one to the other. While he continued scrutinizing their girth, I noticed that there were no actual windows, only slits along the walls allowing small shafts of daylight to enter.

"Holmes," I ventured, "perhaps, it was your story, perhaps not, but suddenly, I'm beginning to feel very ill-at-ease!"

"Watson," he firmly stated, "I'm very disappointed to hear you talk this way... Surely, the legend of *the Spanish Lady* hasn't gotten to you.... or has it?"

He followed this commentary with an all-too-familiar guffaw that always served to irritate.

"Of course not," I replied, having no option but to declare my bravado to his snide chide, although I do admit that I was extremely uneasy inside this old building.

Why was I so uncomfortable? Hmm... this room suddenly felt very familiar, but why? Then, like a lightning bolt, it hit me. I remembered the dream I had experienced earlier when taking my afternoon nap. It was so vivid! I could almost imagine the cave, the fire, the young woman, the dimly-lit room....

I was about to relate my nightmare to my companion, but as I approached him, he began to move slowly toward an inside stairway, leading to a loft. Holmes quickly stopped dead in his tracks, and placed his hand over my open mouth.

Suddenly, we heard a loud slamming sound coming from the main entryway.

"Quickly, Watson," he shouted, "get to the other doors and try to open them! I fear we have been trapped!"

Placing the lamp on the ground in the center of the building, both Holmes and I bolted to each of the barn doors. We were too late, for all of them had apparently been locked from the outside!

"What can we do, Holmes?" I whispered to my friend.

"Watson," he slowly responded, picking up the lantern. "Clearly, someone is not happy that we're here. Still, this is of no major concern, my good fellow. Let us not forget that the butler, Malcolm, knows where we are and will soon be checking up on us."

That statement calmed me to a certain degree. I was beginning to feel somewhat better about our situation until he continued to voice another possible theory aloud.

"Although," Holmes speculated, "we still don't know if we can trust either Malcolm Randolph or that maid, Lucretia Bedlam, can we?"

While offering this remark, Holmes continued his search for another means of egress. It soon became apparent, after examining the loft, that there was no other way out but through the sets of doors on the ground level. Judging from their design they were not about to be opened from the inside without a great deal of effort.

I began to feel claustrophobic and suggested, rather loudly,

"Holmes, shouldn't we holler, yell or, I don't know, bang on the doors?"

Before he could answer, we heard a soft tapping, followed by a somewhat concerned whisper, "Mr. Holmes. . . Doctor Watson. . . Please tell me. . . are you in there?"

We rapidly moved toward the voice beyond the sealed door and Holmes called out gently, "Miss Aggie, yes we are here. Are you able to lift the bar from the doorway?"

We could hear the youngster pushing and pulling at the heavy iron rod, but she was not able to move it.

"Oh, it's too heavy, Mr. Holmes!" she sadly reported while we listened to her grunts and groans.

Again she called, "Please don't worry, I'll be back momentarily with Mr. Malcolm. He'll surely help us!"

Several minutes passed with us waiting and listening intently for Aggie's return. It seemed like hours, but we soon heard the concerned voice of the butler, "Oh, Mr. Holmes and Doctor Watson. We'll get you free at once!"

After some effort, the bar was lifted and Holmes and I walked into the open air, greatly relieved.

"Mr. Randolph," I spoke for both of us, "Holmes and I are most grateful, and we thank you for extricating us from this awkward, embarrassing situation."

"You are entirely welcome, Doctor," spoke the mildly embarrassed butler, "but your thanks should be directed to Miss Aggie Miller who brought your plight to my attention."

"Of course, you are correct," Holmes piped up, turning to the young girl.

Smiling broadly, he offered, "Miss Miller, we are most fortunate that you came upon us. If it hadn't been for you, poor Watson and I might have never been seen again!"

At that remark, the butler chimed in, "Now, now Mr. Holmes, why certainly. . . "

Randolph's reply was quickly dismissed by the wink that Holmes sent his way.

"What I meant to say," continued the manservant, "is that you are certainly correct. I've been so busy lately, that I most assuredly would have forgotten that you two gentlemen were here. Thank heavens that Miss Miller found you."

The young girl began to blush, issuing, "Oh, really, it was nothing. I just happened to be on my way to the shoreline when I sauntered through the Abbey grounds. My friend, Margaret, and I always take this path to the shore."

The young girl was beaming from the attention but, when she saw Holmes staring at her, her smile vanished.

"Aggie, please take no offense by what I am about to ask," issued the detective. "Were you, perhaps, following Doctor Watson and me, again?"

At once, the butler spoke up, "Mr. Holmes, I am shocked at such a suggestion. Why Aggie Miller . . . "

Randolph was about to continue his defense of the young girl, when she spoke up, "Mr. Malcolm, there is no need to speak on my behalf, though it is most kind of you."

Brushing her hair back from her forehead, the young girl offered, "Yes, Mr. Holmes, I was following you and Doctor Watson.

Please forgive me if you can. I just can't help myself. I've a natural disposition that makes me want to find answers to questions. When I discovered that one of the world's greatest detectives and his bosom companion were visiting our little town, I couldn't suppress my curiosity. I suppose many would say that I'm a nosy young thing who needs to mind her own business!"

There was silence for several seconds while Aggie demurely rocked back and forth, her eyes looking at the ground.

Holmes turned away, momentarily stifling a laugh, and with a most winsome grin suggested, "Miss Miller, I am glad that you chose to follow the good doctor and me, at least today, for you have rescued us. There is no way of knowing what might have happened to us without your intervention."

"While we have you here, young lady," he continued, "could you describe what you may have seen before coming to our aid?"

Relieved by what my friend had said to her, Aggie began to relate her story.

"When you and Doctor Watson entered the barn, I was standing behind that oak tree by the stand of hemlock. I intended on waiting for you to emerge when I heard a loud slam. The next thing I knew, I noticed someone running from the doorway of that same Spanish Barn. At that point, I decided to have a look and found that you and Doctor Watson were trapped inside."

"Again, it was most fortunate for us that you came along when you did, young lady," Holmes spoke. "Tell me, Miss Miller, did you recognize that person?"

"I'm sorry, Mr. Holmes," the young girl responded. "The

person was wrapped in what appeared to be the trappings of a monk, I believe. . . I really didn't get a good look. . ."

Holmes walked over to the young girl to try to sooth the apparent discomfort that she was now exhibiting. As he did so, he waved off the butler, "We'll see you inside, Mr. Randolph. Thank you for your assistance."

"Watson," my friend motioned to me, "please have a look at our young lady friend and see if her condition might warrant any additional attention."

"Oh, Mr. Holmes," the young girl replied, "I'm fine, really. I'm only embarrassed at my actions. I know that I shouldn't have been following you. I'm truly sorry."

"Ah, yes," Holmes softly cajoled, "that is what you are saying my young girl, but is it the whole truth?"

Holmes did not allow the young lady to reply and continued remarking, "You see, Aggie, I am sensing that you planned to follow Doctor Watson and me from the very moment you first recognized us. And, if you will allow me to say so, you desperately felt compelled to become involved in our investigation. Is it not so?"

Aggie Miller seemed shocked at his words, but only for an instant. Bravely, she acknowledged what had been said and, looking up at the great detective, young Aggie shook her head slowly to the affirmative.

Softly, the young girl issued a most subdued, "Yes, Mr. Holmes. What you have said is true. I am guilty, as charged. There can be no excuse for what I have done, and can only beg that you will forgive me for my intrusion. I'll not bother you again. . . but I only wished to help you and. . ."

"That is well and good, Aggie," my friend stopped her mid-sentence, patting the young girl on the shoulder.

Holmes looked over at me and rolling his eyes, continued, "Miss Miller, perhaps I was too quick to dismiss your involvement."

"Beg pardon, sir," Aggie queried. "What do you mean?"

My companion cocked his head to one side, stroking his chin and offered, "Well, Doctor, if this young lady is really that interested in our investigation, her knowledge of this city might save us a great deal of time."

Holmes continued, "Aggie, mind, now, you would have to agree to follow our instructions to the very letter. Of course, you would certainly have to get permission from your mother, as well."

Aggie Miller's eyes almost popped out of their sockets when she realized that she had just been invited to participate in this investigation.

Before she could respond, Holmes suggested, "Now, run along home and seek your mother's counsel on this matter. If she agrees, Doctor Watson and I would like you both to meet us for dinner tonight at the Imperial Hotel at 6:30 P.M. Good day, young lady!"

As we watched her skipping up the road, I turned to Holmes, fuming, and stammered, "Holmes, how could you? Do you really think that this is such a good idea? This is a dangerous case in which we are involved. Is it wise to involve this young child?"

"Watson, dear fellow, think about it. This young lady is the kind of individual that would never take no for an answer. She oozes curiosity! What better way to keep her safe than to send her on missions that, while possibly proving valuable to us, most certainly will pose little risk to her person."

I must have been wearing a particularly strange expression after listening to my companion's explanation, for he continued to elaborate on his plan for Aggie.

"Watson," he spoke with some mild agitation, "you of all people should understand. Surely you must see the wisdom of my idea? This type of youngster could never be dissuaded from following us. That is where the real peril will, in truth, be felt. Surely, you must concur?"

I wanted to disagree, but I could see the wisdom of his plan. Holmes was correct, yet again. She most certainly would be much safer away from us.

"Now, good friend, let's try to pick up the trail of this monk if we can," Holmes directed, quickly heading to where Aggie had last seen the shadowy figure.

We made our way to the far side of the barn to try and locate some footprints. As we rounded the corner, Holmes quickly knelt to the ground and, pulling out his magnifying lens, began to examine what appeared to be several sets of fresh imprints alongside the exterior wall.

"Watson," he whispered, "do as I say and stoop down here. . . now. . . not a word, mind you!"

His tone was so ominous that I immediately pretended to examine his findings.

"Hmmm..." my friend spoke louder than normal, "Watson, what do you make of these prints?"

Then, in a barely audible voice he mumbled, "Watson, we're

being watched! No....don't look. When I tell you, make a run for the far wall as fast as your legs will carry you. . ."

I took notice of what he said and remained alongside him running my fingers through the sandy leaves.

"**Now, Watson, go**," he yelled, and immediately I heard the sound of a bullet rip past my ear.

I quickly ran to the barnyard wall and dove over the top, expecting to see Holmes right behind me. Strangely, he had not followed. I tried to peek around the corner of the wall when three more shots rang out, two of them ricocheting off the stonewall that protected me.

I called out, "Holmes, are you there?"

Again, I shouted, "Holmes, where are you?"

I waited, but there came no response. I readied my service revolver, peeked over the wall, and scanned the area for the shooter. I saw and heard no one.

"Holmes," I cried out again, "where are you?"

When no response was immediately forthcoming, I decided to take action, firing two rounds where I believed the shooter had been. Spying an old work wagon that was positioned between the boundary wall and the Spanish Barn, I quickly made my way across the yard, ducking behind the old wagon's sheltering sideboards. As soon as I had arrived, two more shots rang out. Carefully, I peeked over the sideboard, just in time to see a darkly-clad figure disappear behind the Spanish Barn. Somewhat relieved, I turned my attention to the back of the wagon.

Suddenly, I felt a chill ran up my spine, for there, right before my eyes, was the motionless body of my dear friend.

My thoughts were those of horror in finding Holmes in this condition. I quickly moved to his side, hoping there might be something I could do for him. Suddenly, his familiar voice shocked me back into reality and I issued a frightful gasp.

"We can relax, Watson," my resurrected friend offered, "I'm sure that our shooter is well away from here by now!"

"Holmes," I shuddered, "you scared the life out of me! Thank God you're not injured!"

Rising from the floor of the wagon, he brushed off his outer garb, and I followed his lead as we made our way back toward the Cary home. Not surprisingly, we could see Malcolm Randolph running our way, shotgun in hand.

"Mr. Holmes, Doctor Watson," he shouted anxiously, looking all around, "are you all right?"

"I heard the shots and quickly gathered my shotgun and shells, just in case," the butler offered, breathlessly.

"Now, now, my good man," Holmes soothed, "we are both quite safe, for the time being, at least. Please calm yourself."

Randolph seemed to be quite shaken by the recent events, and I couldn't help notice him looking all about the property as we made our way back to the house and the rear entrance.

As we watched the butler put the gun away and lock the cabinet, Holmes moved toward the back window, parting the lace curtains to take a peek in the direction of the Spanish Barn.

"Mr. Randolph," he questioned, "were you, by any chance, peering through this window when the shots were being fired?"

Randolph's knees seemed to buckle at the question and he slowly made his way to one of the oaken chairs around the kitchen table.

Slowly, he offered, "Mr. Holmes, please excuse me, I need to sit. This recent event has truly had an effect upon me."

Randolph continued, "But to answer your question, no sir, I was not looking through that window at that time. As a matter of fact, I don't believe that I've gone anywhere near that particular window in weeks! What, may I ask, sir, are you suggesting?"

After a somewhat awkward pause, Holmes, laughed his annoying laugh and replied, "Oh, Mr. Randolph, please don't be alarmed by my questions. I'm only trying to obtain facts wherever I may be fortunate enough to find them."

Clearly, I sensed that Holmes had, indeed, found something at that window, but, for now, he had no intention of disclosing any of that information in Randolph's presence. I noticed a considerable agitation had been manifest by the butler when my friend had posited his question, but it quickly subsided as Holmes and I headed back toward the rear door.

"Mr. Holmes," the shaken butler inquired, "shouldn't we contact the authorities about this attempt on your lives? Why, you both could have been killed!"

Holmes slowly waved his arm and shook his head, "No, Mr. Randolph. While I understand your concern I don't believe it would be in the best interests of our investigation. I think it would be best if we kept this to ourselves, at least for the time being."

"But, Mr. Holmes," the nervous manservant began again, " I still think. . ."

Holmes interrupted the man, "Please Mr. Randolph, my associate and I have been through similar situations in the past. It has been our experience that, while they mean well, the constabulary often complicate matters and that might not be in the best interests of the Cary family."

"Rest assured," Holmes continued, "Dr. Watson and I will be prepared for any further intrusions and will take every available precaution. Now, if you would be so kind, we must once more continue our work. We will be sure to stop and see you before leaving."

Immediately, Holmes and I started back to the barn area where we spent some time looking for any additional clues. Sadly, the footprints abruptly disappeared at the edge of the service road which consisted of crushed gravel. We were able to find several bullet fragments that had lodged in the side of the work wagon which Holmes carefully placed in one of his coat pockets. Prior to taking our leave we revisited the main house to report to the butler, who was still trembling from the recent events.

"Please don't bother to see us out, Mr. Randolph," Holmes issued, as we made our way past the imposing staircase in the ornate hallway. Holmes, paused briefly, at the base of the steps and peered up to the first landing. As he did so, we could easily hear footsteps rapidly scurrying across the hardwood floor above. Holmes looked at me, raising his eyebrows at the sound. I knew what he was thinking. Someone had been hiding, listening to our conversation with Mr. Randolph.

Holmes quickly turned back to the butler and clearly stated, "Randolph, when you do talk to Mr. Cary, please inform him that we are ever so close to resolving his problem. I also wish to inform you that we will be returning tomorrow to continue our investigation. Good-Day."

Together, we walked down the main hallway when the servant called out to us.

"Mr. Holmes, I just remembered. Here are my answers to the questions you had for me. If you require greater detail with any of my responses, I will do what I can to elaborate when next we meet."

The butler bowed, bid us farewell and slowly closed the main door behind us.

And with that, we were back on our way to prepare for what would prove to be a most interesting evening.

Chapter 9 Dinner For Four

Evening of December 19th

After returning to our lodgings, Holmes and I had barely enough time to prepare for the evening dinner. As I removed my winter coat, I suddenly felt weary, for we had had a very busy and demanding day. Moving toward the closet I took a brief glance across my room and I suddenly longed for a brief respite in the warm, welcoming bed which lay before me. But there really wasn't time.

Holmes, still in our suite parlor, had taken a seat in a large armchair, humming one of his favorite arias as he removed his footwear. I must admit that I was still miffed at his offer to young Aggie Miller. For me, the better course of action would simply have been to chastise the youngster and report her actions to her mother. But, again, he must have decided that the proper thing to do would be to keep her away from our investigation by enlisting her services in a much less threatening environment.

My mind seemed to be caught up in this situation but once again I realized that Holmes had charged the young lady to secure her mother's consent. I relaxed a bit, for surely, Clara Miller would refuse her daughter's request, seeing the obvious danger that any involvement in a criminal investigation might bring. That realization proved to have a most calming effect. I was relieved, believing that Aggie and her mother would not be joining us, and I posed the point to my friend.

"Holmes," I ventured, "think, man. Why, we're perfect

strangers! Can you imagine any mother worthy of being called a mother allowing her daughter to become involved in such a dangerous situation? Do you really believe that they will join us?"

Holmes ignored my question. Instead, he continued to shine his boots as dinner time came ever closer.

When I approached him, issuing, "Well? Say something!"

He slowly put down the polishing cloth, looked up and merely repeated his all-too-familiar droll remark, "We shall soon see, Watson... We shall soon see."

While I waited for him to finish his dressing ritual, for that is what it had recently become, I allowed my mind to rehash what had transpired after the shots had been fired at Torre Abbey.

To the best of my recollection, Randolph, the butler, appeared soon after the attack. He came running from the building, shotgun in hand, ready for action.

After ascertaining that Holmes and I had not been injured, he shook his head, resting the gun over his left arm, hunting style. Holmes then thanked him for his concern as we all headed back to the Cary home. Then came the uncomfortable exchange between Holmes and the butler. Next, we left the house, with Holmes intimating that we were moving closer to solving the mystery.

Holmes further informed the servant that we would most certainly be returning to complete our examination of the estate, and warmly thanked him for his concern over the gun-play.

We had left Torre Abbey discussing our plans for the morrow. One of our talking points, as we rode in our carriage back to the Imperial Hotel, had to do with Lucretia Bedlam, the Cary family's maidservant. Our conversation went along the following lines:

"Watson," Holmes began, "did you happen to notice that every time Mr. Randolph talked with us, Mrs. Bedlam was present?"

"Mrs. Bedlam?" I questioned. "Holmes, I only remember seeing her briefly inside Torre Abbey proper. Are you certain?"

"My dear Watson," he continued with a wry smile, "I am as certain of her presence at our discussions as I am that your revolver is currently missing two rounds!"

At that comment, my frown did nothing to disturb his trend of thought and he continued to disclose his findings.

"Oh, I readily admit that she was not always visible, but the curtains overlooking the Spanish Barn had been pinched as if someone had been peering from the darkness. I saw her crouching down along the outer stairs when Mr. Randolph came running with his shotgun. You do catch my meaning, Watson."

"Well, it's certainly possible, Holmes," I responded. "You have proven that you are much more observant than I, time and time again."

"That is rather obvious, Doctor," he crowed, "but I also sensed that Malcolm is most uncomfortable when the maid is in the vicinity. I'm not yet sure why that should be the case, but we shall soon reason it out."

Scratching my head I queried, "I say, Holmes, what gave you that impression?"

"Well, first off, he seemed markedly more nervous whenever he suspected that she might overhear our discussions with him," Holmes stated. "Did you not notice how his voice fell to mere whispers whenever we questioned him?"

"Now that you mention it. . ." I pondered, commenting, "perhaps it is so, but could it simply be his way or a peculiar manner of speech?"

"Possibly," he replied, "but what about the way he reacted to my question about looking out the window?"

"Hmmm," I moaned, "I see. That's why he was so tense when you inquired about the window. He might have been covering up for Mrs. Bedlam."

Our conversation quickly came to an end with a brisk knock on the door to our suite.

"Watson, would you please get the door," Holmes called, "I'm not quite ready for Mr. Wiggins."

"What? Did you say Wiggins? Not 'our' Wiggins?" I began to stammer as I headed for the entrance.

"Just get the door, Watson!" my impatient roommate scolded.

Slowly, I released the door handle, and I have to admit that I hardly recognized the distinguished young man standing before me.

"Hello, Doctor Watson," a mustachioed, well-dressed gentleman offered, as we stared at each other through the open doorway.

Pausing briefly, I cautiously studied the two visitors standing before me. In what must have seemed an eternity to them, there I was, apparently stunned and somewhat confused. The speaker was a tall, slender fellow in a stylish gray winter coat. Accompanying him was a rather short, diminutive man, peeking out from behind his Macintosh.

Suddenly, I snapped out of my stupor, recognizing the familiar smile of the tall one. I extended my hand to him, issuing, "Why it is you, Wiggins! What a wonderful surprise. It's been years since we've seen each other. How are you, young man?"

I was barely able to contain my emotions, so delighted I was to see one of our old Baker Street Irregulars!

"Step in here and tell me all about yourself," I happily offered.

As Wiggins and I began to converse, we were rather rudely interrupted by what I can only describe as a loud cough coming from the other gentleman who had stepped between us.

"Excuse me, Doctor Watson," Wiggins offered, "I wish to introduce you to my good friend and associate, Robert Roberts."

"Pleased to meet you Mr. Roberts," I replied, curiously peering down at the shortish fellow. "I hope you can forgive my lack of manners."

"Doctor," he smiled, laughing, "please think nothing of it. At my height, I'm not that easy to spot!"

"And, please, call me, Bobo. . . everyone does."

After leading the men into our suite, I spied Holmes slowly appearing around the corner, calling, "Ah, Wiggins...Bobo.....so glad you could join us. Quickly, gentlemen, please take a seat and tell us what you have discovered."

Before Wiggins had a chance to respond, Holmes, noticing the strange look on my face, explained, "Watson, I may have forgotten to mention, but Wiggins has been making quite a name for himself as a private investigator."

"What? What's that you say?" I sputtered.

"Furthermore," Holmes continued, "Wiggins and his apprentice, Bobo, have been behind the scenes helping us in this most unusual case."

Somewhat taken aback by this revelation, I recovered quickly, commenting, "Oh, I see... Of course. That is fine. Fine, indeed."

"Gentlemen, pray tell us what you have found," Holmes offered, eagerly rubbing his hands together.

Wiggins quickly undid a folder and handed the contents to Holmes while Bobo nodded approvingly in my direction.

"It's all right to stare, Doctor Watson," the little person spoke reassuringly. "I'm used to it. We tiny folk are not so common in these parts."

I was dumbstruck and confounded at the same time. It was true! I had been staring at Mr. Roberts and hadn't realized it.

"Please, forgive me again, Mr. Bob-O," I offered. "I'm truly sorry if I have offended you by my actions. I didn't mean to stare! Honestly!"

"Forgive my companion, Bobo," Holmes interceded as he issued a most threatening scowl in my direction.

"He tends to nod off now and again. It's his age you know," joked Holmes, pointing to his head. The mild laughter that followed his remark did much to soften the moment and for that I was truly grateful.

Then, turning to me, "And, Watson, it's Bo-Bo, not Bob-O," he lectured.

After briefly scanning the report, Holmes smiled, commenting, "Wiggins, Bobo, this is fine work...fine work, indeed!"

"I had a hunch about Mr. Cary and this validates my theory. I see you also had time to visit that Druid community as well. Very good. You may proceed with the next phase of your investigation. I'll be anxiously awaiting your next communique," Holmes voiced as he led our visitors to the door.

"Mr. Holmes, Doctor Watson, until we see you again," spoke Wiggins, bowing as he and Bobo left our quarters.

The door had barely closed when I angrily posed, "Holmes, what is this all about? A theory about Mr. Cary? What are Wiggins and his associate doing? Why was I not informed on these matters?"

Holmes easily understood my questioning look and tried to relieve my concerns with a casual, "Watson, my good Watson, all will be explained later this evening. For now, we have a dinner appointment with a very curious young girl and her Mum."

As we moved through the doorway into the hallway, I offered, "Do you really believe they're coming? We'll see about that."

When we arrived at our table, our precocious little lady and her mother were quietly enjoying the seasonal music provided by the Imperial house orchestra. A local choir in their Christmas robes accompanied the fine musicians, providing those in attendance with a beautiful selection of noels. The dining room was sparkling and resplendent with Christmas wreaths, candles and other beautiful decorations.

Aggie was quick to her feet in greeting us, and proudly offered, "Doctor Watson, Mr. Holmes, this is my wonderful mother, Mrs. Clara Miller!"

"Ah, very delighted that you've decided to join us for dinner, Mrs. Miller," Holmes politely bowed, continuing, "I'm very pleased that your Aggie successfully conveyed our invitation and that you were kind enough to accept!"

As she took my friend's hand, Clara Miller seemed a little uneasy, quipping, "Mr. Holmes, you will excuse me if I seem slightly ill at ease, for Agatha only told me of this dinner engagement a few hours ago. Let me further state, that if it weren't for the sterling reputations of you and Doctor Watson, I would never have consented to such a spur-of-the-moment surprise invitation!"

Holmes seemed shocked at her remarks. He raised his left hand and slowly stroked his chin, a sure sign of discomfort that I had learned to recognize in my friend's demeanor. While the pause seemed interminable, it probably lasted only a second or two. I knew that I had to say something, for the atmosphere had suddenly become very frigid, and I'm not referring to the seasonal weather.

I began, "Ah, Mrs. Miller, please be assured that there was very little planning on our part, as well. Please give us a chance to explain."

After we had all taken our seats, I poured a glass of water to slake my thirst, trying desperately to think of just the right words to sooth the situation.

"Mrs. Miller," I began, "Mr. Sherlock Holmes and I only met your dear daughter the other day. We were so taken by her engaging persona and curious nature, that we simply had to meet her lovely mother."

If I expected my charming words to have some type of calming effect on the young girl's mother, I was dreadfully wrong, for she clearly was not dropping her guard.

"Doctor Watson," she replied firmly, "while your words are no doubt honest efforts to ease my suspicions, I'll need to hear much more from you and your friend as to the true purpose of tonight's gathering."

At that remark, Holmes laughed his hearty laugh. It was rarely manifest, but always indicated some level of personal embarrassment. After another uneasy pause, Holmes smiled, bowing politely to Agatha's mother.

"You find this situation entertaining, Mr. Holmes?" Clara Miller asked, raising her voice as she rose from her chair.

"My dear lady," Holmes quickly responded, "I beg of you. Won't you please return to your seat. I'm sure that if you give us an opportunity to explain, we will all have a most enjoyable evening together. I must assure you that my laugh was in no way meant as sign of disrespect, honestly. I was merely caught off guard by both your frankness and quite understandable concern for this unsolicited dinner invitation!"

Holmes took a sip of sherry which our waiter had provided, then continued, "I fully expected that Aggie would have a most difficult time convincing you to come to dinner with two individuals who are total strangers. Still, I made the offer, sensing that your young girl, here, could be quite convincing, given the chance. Finally, having met Aggie, I knew that I simply had to meet the mother of such a talented young lady. Please accept our most humble apologies and let us enjoy our evening together. Afterward, I shall explain all of the events that have led to this meeting."

Clara Miller seemed to have softened somewhat at my friend's words and returned to her chair, replacing her dinner napkin. While this curious exchange was taking place, I turned to see how young was dealing with the recent turn of events. She sat there mouth agape as Holmes continued to try to allay her mother's concerns.

After yet another uncomfortable pause, our waiter returned and dinner orders were taken. It still took a few more minutes for Clara Miller to come to terms with Holmes's remarks. She looked over at her young daughter and smiled softly.

"Mr. Holmes," Aggie's mother spoke calmly, "I know what you and Doctor Watson do, professionally. I know why you have come to our town. You are here in Torquay, no doubt, because of the recent murders. Aggie and I have discussed these heinous crimes over the last several months, and I must admit, we are of the opinion that they may continue until the perpetrators are captured. I also believe that my dear sweet Aggie's curiosity about you and Doctor Watson has led her to spy on you. For that I am truly sorry."

"She has been particularly fond of your case accounts, Doctor Watson," Clara Miller continued, looking directly into my eyes.

Suddenly, she focused on her daughter, "Am I right, Missy?"

At her mother's remarks, Aggie dropped her head, looking away from us in youthful embarrassment.

Quickly, Holmes offered, "Well, Mrs. Miller, I can see where your daughter gets her candor."

Replacing his glass on the table, my friend continued, "Why, yes, Mrs. Miller, your daughter recognized us at this hotel and covertly tracked us to our quarters."

"I might add, it was a wonderful job of reconnaissance, by the way," the detective stated, winking at the young girl.

Aggie sat there, nervously sensing the awkwardness of the moment. I wanted to say something to lessen the tension, but the words were not forthcoming.

At that moment, the conductor of the choir of youngsters tapped his baton on his music stand and began his address to the audience seated at their tables.

"Ladies, gentlemen, girls and boys," he said, "thank you so much for your kind attention. We now invite you all to join us in a rousing rendition of Deck the Halls."

Much applause followed his directive and for at least several minutes, we all were swept up in the happier aspects of that joyous time of the year. At the completion of their performance, the carolers took their bows and quietly left the room to much fanfare from the smiling audience.

Clara Miller wasted no time in voicing her next inquiry. "Gentlemen," she posited, "would I be correct in assuming that my shy little one has offered to help you?"

Aggie turned a most elegant shade of pink and once more hid her face in the dinner napkin.

Holmes smiled and replied directly, "Clara, may I call you Clara? Ah, yes, as a matter of truth, Aggie did offer her services and for that we are most grateful. At first, I hesitated, having concerns similar to the ones you've recently postulated. Please understand that we would never think of placing anyone, let alone a wonderful young girl like Aggie, in harm's way. Why, no parent would ever allow such a dangerous request to be granted! How could we even think of involving Aggie in our investigation?"

Clara Miller began to relax after Holmes's response, but shorty, thereafter my friend continued.

"That was my initial reaction to her generous offer," Holmes confided. "Yes, I was about to politely decline when another idea popped into my mind."

Clara listened intently as my friend leaned toward her and pointed his index finger to his cranium.

"Doctor Watson and I have come to Torquay to offer our help to the local law enforcement agency. Chief Inspector Davis contacted me several months ago. Coincidentally, I received a letter from Mr. James Cary, father of your Aggie's best friend, Margaret. He was also very concerned about the recent murders and as leader of the Town Council, he believed that Dr. Watson and I might be able to hasten the resolution of these horrible murders."

"Suddenly," he continued, "I reasoned that Aggie, with her intricate knowledge of Torquay and, in particular, Torre Abbey, could prove to be a most valuable asset, simply by being Aggie! You understand, don't you? In making frequent visits to Torre Abbey, she could keep us apprised of any strange goings-on, or note any changes that she might observe in her travels here and there."

When he had explained his plans for Aggie, he looked around the table for some sense of approval. Mrs. Miller had listened with apparent interest, and was about to speak, when the table staff arrived with our dinners.

Seeing an opportunity to relieve the obvious tension that was present, I suggested, "I say, why don't we leave our conversation for a time and enjoy these wonderful meals and listen to the peaceful music of the season?"

All agreed with my suggestion and the four of us started on our meals in earnest. Table conversations turned to more innocent and less threatening topics. Whether it was the beautiful seasonal decorations in which we found ourselves, the delightful carols, or the delicious repast that had been set before us, the group mood had greatly softened. The town of Torquay, its history, beauty and many wonderful shops became the subjects of much of the evening's conversation. There were happy smiles all around.

However, the most interesting tale told that evening belonged to Mrs. Miller's young daughter. Holmes and I were delighted with Aggie's detailed account of her confrontation with her former school mistress, much to the delight of her proud mother. Things seemed to be progressing nicely. As our company finished dessert, Mrs. Miller looked at her young daughter, then turned her gaze at the detective and me.

"Gentlemen, I've been thinking about this," Clara Miller began. Several seconds passed with Mrs. Miller slowly shaking her head back and forth. Finally, smiling, she turned to her daughter, took her hands into hers and earnestly inquired, "Aggie, dear, what do you have to say to Mr. Holmes's plan? Are you interested in helping these two gentlemen? Do you think you can do what is required of you, safely?"

"Mother," Aggie offered, "I know that I would easily be able to do what Mr. Holmes has put forth. Why it's merely continuing to do what I do everyday when visiting my friend! I see no danger in simply acting the way I always act on my trips to the Cary home."

"However," the young girl concluded, "I want you to know, Mum, that if you think it's too dangerous for me, I will abide by your decision."

Holmes and I looked at each other, wondering what Aggie's mother would say next. Our telepathic query was answered almost immediately as Clara Miller rose from the table with her daughter.

"Oh, dear," Clara voiced, "why Aggie, I am completely surprised and delighted by this new-found maturity that I am seeing in you. If you think you can be helpful to Mr. Holmes and Doctor Watson, and promise to follow their directives, I have no objection."

At that point, she warmly thanked Holmes and me for the delicious meal and fine conversation. After wishing us a very "good evening," Clara and Aggie started walking toward the hotel foyer.

Suddenly, Clara returned and voiced, "Mr. Holmes, my daughter and I are at your service. Please take care of her, as you stated that you would. Remember, she is not to be placed in harm's way, but only as a fact-finder and observer. Is that clear?"

Holmes shook his head in the affirmative.

"Then," she voiced, "that being the case I hope to see you tomorrow at our home, Ashfield, for 6:00 dinner. We'll not take 'no' for an answer."

And, with that remark, our guests continued on their way.

Chapter 10 The Report

Later that same evening

After returning to our hotel room, Holmes seemed greatly amused by what had just taken place. Clearly, Clara Miller had made quite an impression on him. In fact, it would only take a few seconds before he would prove my suspicion to be spot on.

Posing briefly by the open doorway, he raised his hand, pointing at me, and questioned, "Well, Watson, what do you make of Aggie Miller's mother?"

Before I could reply, he began again, "I must admit, she had me somewhat bewildered at dinner. I truly feared that she would disappoint her inquisitive daughter after our disclosure to use the child in much the same way as our Irregulars back in the day. At least we now have her approbation."

"Really, Holmes," I cautioned, yet again, "do you still think it is wise to involve such a young girl in this case? I still believe that we may be ignoring the danger in which we may be placing her."

"Old boy," he quickly replied, squinting those deep-set eyes at me, "surely, you are not accusing me of endangering such an innocent waif as Aggie? Really! Can you not see that she will be much safer doing the kinds of things we intend to require of her? It will be much easier protecting such a brilliant and curious young lady if we make every effort to keep her away from the truly dangerous work that you and I will soon be undertaking."

As he spoke those words, he briskly made his way to the writing desk, trying to change the subject, but I wouldn't allow him to do so.

"Holmes, I noticed that you didn't discuss the ambush that we encountered at the Abbey," I voiced. "Clearly, you didn't wish Aggie's mother to know about it. Why would you choose to hold back that account?"

"Watson," he responded with obvious agitation, "of course I held back. I didn't want to tell her. Had Mrs. Miller learned of that attempt on our lives, she most certainly would have refused to allow Aggie to get involved."

I looked at him, rather harshly, once more whispering, "Well, wouldn't that be best for Aggie?"

"Watson," he issued with much agitation, "you, above all, know my ways. Certainly, the child would be much safer if we could be sure that she would stay away. By now you must understand that her tenacious, insatiable nature would demand her involvement, one way or another. Of course, I would hate to be responsible should anything happen to her. It's for that reason, and that reason alone, that I believe she will be much safer if we control her actions. Now will you, once and for all, move on? "

"I sincerely hope you are correct," I solemnly offered, for I knew I had to get the last word in this argument.

Having put that question to rest, at least for the time being,

Holmes turned to face me as I settled into a most comfortable armchair. He reached for the report Wiggins and Bobo had supplied, waving the envelope to-and-fro, as he smiled wryly.

"Watson," he offered, "I know that you were very much surprised to see Wiggins and his associate a little earlier. By now, I'm sure that you are most curious as to this report. Are you not?"

My friend truly enjoyed posing such interrogatives at my expense, and I had long since tired of playing this game. Ignoring him, I picked up the local paper, feigning little interest in his question. I slowly leafed through the rotogravure section, examining seasonal photographs of downtown Torquay. Believing my apparent disinterest would annoy him, I smiled behind that section, awaiting his reaction.

"Very well, old boy, I'll provide you with the details anyway," Holmes began.

"When I first became aware that Mr. Wiggins had embarked on a career in private investigation, I contacted him, first, to congratulate, but also to remind him, that there would be many, many more disappointments than successes in his newly chosen profession. I further informed him that to perform a first-rate job would require an inordinate amount of time, patience and attention to detail. Anything less than his best efforts would invariably end in failure," Holmes stated with some sobriety.

I sat perfectly still, pretending not to listen, allowing my ploy to continue. Glancing over in his direction, I could see him raising one eyebrow, for he knew that I had heard every word.

"Hmm…very well, Watson," my friend whispered. "Two can play at this game."

Suddenly, he turned away and quickly opened Wiggins's report. While he perused the information once more, I noticed some rather peculiar eye movements, a sure sign that some valuable points had been introduced into the investigation. He also mumbled a few words, his voice emoting some unusual timbres, indicating his pleasure with an occasional "a-ha" sprinkled here and there, as he continued to pore over the account.

I tried to content myself with the knowledge that he was bursting to tell me what had been found. This time, I would force him to come round to my terms. After all, I had tired of being a mere tag-a-long on these cases. It was high time for my services to be properly respected. Eventually, he would have to understand that I, too, needed to be given my due credit.

Several minutes had passed since Holmes had put down the report. He sat by the bay window, smoking his pipe, humming one of his favorite Wagnerian arias, his mind totally involved. This was his standard modus operandi. I had witnessed him time-after-time, day-after-day, sometimes week-after-week, employing the very same technique in formulating his plans. As was my wont, I would invariably acquiesce to my own curious nature and almost beg him to bring me in on his findings.

Tonight it would be different. I was convinced that if the report was valuable at all, he would surely divulge the facts, without my asking to hear them. It wouldn't be much longer. I would wait him out this time.

Time seemed to pass very slowly that evening. Try as I might, my self-inflicted patience had me most uncomfortable as I sat there adjusting and readjusting my position in a suddenly, most uncomfortable chair. Peering over the top of the headlines, I observed him resting his eyes. He began to tap his fingers on the envelope, rhythmically performing what seemed like a military cadence.

"Damn it, Holmes," I charged loudly, tossing the newspaper aside, "when are you going to tell me what you've found in that bloody report?"

Appearing somewhat startled by my sudden outburst, he slowly moved toward me, and wearing a devilish smile whispered, "Good fellow, why are you so vexed? I was going to tell you everything. . . everything, that is, when you were good and ready."

Placing the report on my lap, he suggested, rather nastily, "Here, old chap, perhaps you will acquire a better appreciation for the work if you read it yourself."

My reading glasses needed to be adjusted before starting on the information, but once positioned, I anxiously began reading.

Cary Investigation Report:

Wiggins and Roberts Private Investigations

At the request of Mr. Sherlock Holmes, London, our agency was hired to travel to Torquay, Devonshire, UK, to investigate the circumstances surrounding two suspicious deaths/murders that had taken place over the months of October and November. What follows is a brief summary of our findings:

Thursday, December 14th, 1905

8:15 AM - Mr. Roberts and I arrive. (Torquay, UK).

9:00 AM - Register at Biddle's Rooming House.

10:00 AM - Mr. Roberts and I meet with Chief Inspector Davis

In response to a request Davis had made to Mr. Sherlock Holmes for help in his investigation of two murders that had occurred in the village of Torquay, Mr. Roberts and I formally introduced ourselves. The law official was kind enough to supply us with the particulars of the crime scenes along with some cursory background information on the two unfortunate victims. After discussing his findings in great detail, we thanked the lawman for the information and set about our plans to visit the sites of the murders. As we were in the process of hiring a carriage, we were suddenly distracted by the sounds of an angry crowd which had gathered near the very police headquarters we had visited earlier that same day. There, we witnessed a near riot when it was learned that yet another council member had been murdered. When the disturbance had been quelled, we met with one of the town's religious leaders to glean additional information about the residents of Torquay. A Vicar, one David Prentiss, new to the area, did his best to provide our team with his perspective of the local populace.

Friday, December 15th, 1905

Preliminary investigation of Dennison murder. . . details to follow. (information gleaned from local paper)

Saturday, December 16th, 1905

Additional assignment to investigate local Druid sect near the vicinity of Ipplepen. We took a slow ride out to locate the community and noticed that the encampment had the look of a military fortress. The entire area was being patrolled by several individuals who were keeping a sharp look-out around the perimeter. Mr. Roberts and I decided to continue driving past the camp, satisfied that we would make plans to return at a later date.

Sunday, December 17th, 1905

We began a surveillance operation on the movements of a certain James Cary, Torquay. As per request we were to report on any/all of Mr. Cary's daily habits, chores, work, travels, social interactions, etc. Mr. Roberts and I spent most of the afternoon keeping watch over the Torre Abbey grounds and found nothing unusual to report.

Monday, December 18th, 1905

9:45 AM - Enter Torre Abbey grounds wearing disguises.

Mr. Roberts and I wore costumes which would allow us to blend in with the inhabitants of the area. I chose a rather matronly black shawl and grayish wig underneath a fine tweed bonnet. Mr. Roberts, much to his very great annoyance, was persuaded to ride in a child's carriage, covered by a plaid blanket. (While somewhat agitated by the arrangement, he had to agree that in those clothes, we would never have been seen as any sort of egregious threat to those who may have been watching over the property.)

10:15 AM - We continued our exploration of Torre Abbey

10:30 AM - Mr. Holmes and Dr. Watson arrive and are escorted by Mr. Cary into the main house.

11:00 AM - Mr. Holmes and Dr. Watson exited the building.

We observed them proceed to their carriage and leave the premises. At this point, our investigative team continued to examine the Abbey grounds, paying particular attention to the edifice known as the Spanish Barn.

11:15 AM - Mr. Cary and another individual leave his home.

Both of them are wearing dark winter woolen coats. They proceeded to the stable area where a landau and a fine Clydesdale team was waiting. At that point, Mr. Cary and his companion climbed into the carriage and were quickly whisked away, heading out toward King's Road. Bobo and I quickly removed our disguises and, after securing our baby tram in some dense bushes, dashed to our own carriage and began to follow Cary and the other person.

11:40 AM - After a short ride, Cary and companion exit carriage. The carriage then continued on its way.

The Cary party entered a small tavern called the Witch and Cauldron. Bobo remained outside while I carefully made my way into the dark establishment, ending up at an old mahogany bar. I quickly determined that Cary was nowhere to be seen. I asked the barman if he had seen two gentlemen come into his tavern. The barman grunted, shook his head and pointed to another door at the far end of the room. I placed a sovereign on the bar, thanked him, and exited through the doorway into an alley. At that time, everything went black...

12:00 Noon - Awakened by my friend, Bobo in the alley.

I was still a bit woozy, the result of some kind of blunt instrument having left a small bruise on the back of my skull, but a deeper wound in my self-pride. (We both knew that we had been fooled, and Cary and his companion had gotten away.) I placed a kerchief over my aching noggin, and Bobo and I stepped back into the tavern. The bartender seemed quite concerned when I described what had transpired in the alleyway. I tried to get some additional information out of him, but he calmly replied, "Sir, what I told you a few moments ago, was the truth. Those gents entered my building, looked around and left through the same door that you did. I had never seen either one of them before, and they had scarves wrapped up around their faces as well!" He seemed to be telling the truth, so we took our leave, handing him a copy of our business card with our room number at Biddle's, in case he needed to contact us or had any additional information.

12:15 PM - We return to Biddle's Rooming House.

We paused briefly for lunch after treating the wound. We reviewed what had transpired and began to plan our next course of action.

2:00 PM - Bobo and I return to Torre Abbey.

We retrieved our hidden baby tram, and after stowing it in our carriage, drove to the main entrance of the estate where we were greeted by the family butler, a Mister Malcolm Randolph. Pretending to be chimney sweeps, we asked to see the owner of the building to offer our services. Before the manservant could reply, we politely described the importance of keeping chimneys clear of any debris, adding that we were willing to do the job at half the cost. The butler offered his regrets, but informed us that Mr. Cary was not at home. He further informed us that we need not bother coming back as the Abbey chimneys had only recently been serviced. We thanked him for his time and, dragging our sweep equipment, took our leave.

2:10 PM - Mr. Roberts and I leave the Cary premises.

We drove toward the cliffs along Torbay Road. After securing our team on a rail outside of the Beresford Inn, Bobo and I entered the establishment and ordered some refreshments. Some of the locals were engaged in a game of darts, discussing the terrible murders that had plagued the community over the past several months. Polite introductions were issued and, quite to our astonishment, one gentleman actually tried to hire us to clean his chimney! Smiling, we informed him that we would get back to him when next we became available.

4:30 PM - Torre Abbey, again for more reconnaissance

After a most tedious, yet somewhat enjoyable afternoon, Bobo and I decided to return to the Torre Abbey grounds. With dusk now aiding our efforts, we had hoped to catch Mr. Cary when, and if, he returned to his home. Good fortune was with us, for shortly after our arrival, having found an excellent vantage point, we observed a carriage enter the grounds. It was Mr. Cary. He quickly looked around the property then climbed the stairs and entered the house. Mr. Roberts and I decided to spend some time in our hiding place, in the event Cary might receive some additional company, but by 9:00, we were spent. The house lights were dimmed and we decided to head back to our lodgings.

Tuesday, December 19th, 1905

7:30 AM – Breakfast at Biddle's (Scones with fresh orange marmalade)

8:00 AM – Decided to take horses back to Torre Abbey.

Back to our secure hillock on the southwestern side of the grounds, well-protected by some dense gorse. Yesterday, we found that this location allowed us to view the entire open landscape and pathways, as well as providing us excellent views of the Spanish Barn and the Abbey homestead proper.

8:15 AM – Luck was with us, for no sooner had we prepared for our reconnaissance, a familiar carriage drove up to the main entrance of the estate. It looked to be the same one that had taken Cary to the Witch and Cauldron. The carriage door opened, and a tall figure stepped out and headed immediately into the Cary home. A short time later, Cary and this individual left the house, boarded the vehicle and, once again, turned up King's Road. Bobo and I scarcely had time to get to our horses, but we soon found that carriage on the same route as the previous day. Not surprisingly, the carriage stopped at the same tavern, and the two gentlemen entered the building, just as they had the day before. We marked the time at 8:40 AM.

Once the carriage had departed, Bobo and I decided to try a different approach. He followed the two men through the main tavern door while I headed for the back alley. We were both armed and ready for what might manifest itself. A short time later, Bobo exited through the alley door. I anxiously inquired as to his findings. Bobo informed me that he found the two men sitting at a table. He ordered a cup of tea and sat nearby, trying to hear them talking. When he sneaked a gaze in their direction, he was very surprised to see two elderly gentlemen approach the table and join the other two men. Bobo next informed me, that the four men ordered a bottle of rum and began playing a game of whist!

It became clear to Bobo and me that when the carriage had stopped, two men had indeed entered the tavern, but they were not our men. The gentlemen we were tracking must have remained inside the coach. We had assumed that there had been only two people aboard, but it became painfully obvious that we had been fooled, yet again!

We decided to approach the two men Bobo had followed and asked if they would be agreeable to answer a few questions for us.

Surprisingly, they agreed, and all four of us moved to another table. After more rum was poured, they were pleased to inform us that they were frequent visitors to the Witch and Cauldron, and had been paid to ride the carriage to this establishment, no questions asked. Both smiled when we inquired if they recognized either of the two gentlemen that had joined them at Torre Abbey.

One of the men, a tall dark-eyed fellow, responded, "What makes you think we're going to tell you two strangers anything about those gents? Don't you remember that we told you we were paid, no questions asked?"

His partner broke in, laughing, "Yes, my friend and I have nothing more to say about our traveling companions. You see, we had never seen them before, and I doubt if we'll ever see them again."

Bobo and I quickly took our leave, knowing full well that we had been duped.

9:00 AM – We rode our steeds back to the livery stable and returned to our lodgings to prepare for our next course of action. After re-assessing our surveillance skills, Bobo and I once again traveled out to the Druid encampment.

10:00 AM - Bobo and I proceeded through Dartmoor in the hope of acquiring some information about the group led by the man known as Terra. The encampment was located near Ipplepen, a small village approximately fourteen kilometers from Torquay. Upon arriving, we were greeted by two men wearing animal skins and carrying long, wooden branches. Apparently, they were the men we had spotted the other day. They had been assigned as watchmen to prevent the secretive clan from being freely observed by the curious or others who might be less understanding of their ways.

When we informed these sentries of our interest in their religion we were straightaway taken to their leader. At first glance, he seemed a most imposing figure: tall, solidly built, and well-spoken. He was happy to talk with us, sharing that he had been properly schooled outside of London. He talked of studies at Oxford for several sessions, but quickly tired of the mundane, day-to-day existence that he saw all about him. When he first heard of the Druid cult, he admitted to have been somewhat amused by their simple way of life. He also offered that, while skeptical at first, he decided to pursue it more deeply.

"A short time later," he divulged, "I was completely captivated by their view of life and the importance of taking care of our earth mother."

We spoke of our interest in possibly committing ourselves to this life. He smiled, and politely told us, that his encampment welcomed all who were truly called to the faith. However, he warned that the Druids, while certainly different from most English inhabitants, would never allow those who were only curious to be accepted by their community. Bobo and I could sense real menace in that remark, but tried to reassure him that we only wanted to see for ourselves if the Druid way could be our way. That seemed to ease the tension of the moment.

Terra invited us to spend the day with his followers. We did just that. Bobo and I explored the village for the next several hours. We made note of the friendliness of the clan members as they performed their community tasks, for that is what they did. Some tended the fields. Some took care of the sheep. Others took care of the stables and horses and other livestock. All seemed to be most content as they toiled. We tried not to seem too conspicuous as we continued our research, but it was very difficult to move freely among them and pretend that we didn't know we were being watched. For that, in fact, was the truth. Eyes were on our every move.

When we had seen enough, we revisited Terra and thanked him for allowing us to experience what Druidism was all about. He assured us that we had witnessed most of what constituted the group lifestyle. He ended our meeting with what seemed to have been a most heart-felt invitation to return tomorrow to witness or even help them to prepare for the celebration of the Solstice Ritual, scheduled for 12:03 PM on Friday, December 22nd.

4:00 PM – Returned to Torquay and prepared our findings for Mr. Holmes and Doctor Watson. . . Duly reported and recorded by Wiggins-Roberts Agency.

After reading the report, I removed my glasses and peered up at Holmes, who was now standing directly above me.

"Well?" he questioned, blowing pipe smoke my way.

"Would you excuse me?" I implored, rising from my comfortable chair, "Holmes, you're fairly smothering me. Give me some room, please!"

His mood quickly moderated, and he moved aside, issuing, "Dear fellow, I didn't mean to crowd you, I'm just curious as to what you make of this report."

As I quickly made my way to a window overlooking the windblown coast, he repeated his request, "Watson, I am truly interested in your opinion. What do you make of it all?"

I was going to issue my opinion, but I held back, still annoyed that he hadn't informed me that Wiggins had become a private investigator. I was furious that he had hired the Wiggins-Roberts firm without confiding in me. It just didn't sit well and I simply had to disclose my disappointment.

"Holmes," I opened, "before I give you my thoughts on the Wiggins-Roberts report, I would like you to know that I am still fuming that you hadn't take me into your confidence when you hired them."

"Watson, Watson," he remarked, restating his excuse, "haven't I only recently admitted that it was mere oversight?"

"That was what you offered, yes," I angrily responded.

"Well, then, shouldn't that be enough for you?" my friend suggested earnestly. "What do I need to say to you to get you back on task?"

I took a deep breath, pondering what I might say next.

Looking at the volume of smoke that was now fairly exploding from his pipe, I stated simply, "Holmes, perhaps it is my ego or something symptomatic of my aging mental acuity, but I need to feel that I'm a valuable part of our enterprise. I deserve more respect and consideration from you. If you wish me to be at my best, and truly want me to help, I should expect no surprises coming from you."

Holmes stood stock-still as he stared at me. Apparently, my comments had struck him to the core, for he appeared dumfounded. Initially, he said nothing. Instead, he walked over to a waste basket and gingerly tapped out the ash residue from his pipe.

Slowly, he turned back to me and, remarked, "Watson, you are correct. It shall not happen again."

"Now, if you're finally satisfied, would you be so kind as to give me your appraisal of the report, please?" he dramatically offered.

"First of all," I began, "I now understand why that baby seemed so ugly to me. Bob-O makes a most homely child."

Smiling, Holmes returned, "Yes, Watson. It's Bobo."

"Bobo, Bob-O, what the devil do I care," I blared out, expressing some annoyance at being corrected.

Holmes suddenly burst out laughing, waving me onward, "Please continue. . ."

For the next several minutes, I offered my heart-felt appraisal of the Wiggins-Roberts report, paying particular attention to the simple means by which they had been fooled by Cary and his accomplice. I continued by questioning their visit to the Druid site, believing that we had planned to give that encampment a visit. I finished my brief analysis with several questions.

"Tell me, Holmes," I ventured, "what is the significance of the Winter Solstice ritual? Why did you have Cary followed? Don't you trust his story?"

"Excellent questions, my dear fellow," he offered. "I, too, can't believe how easily Wiggins and Bobo were fooled as they tried to follow Cary."

"As to why I had him followed," Holmes responded, "my dear fellow, just because a man claims to have been threatened, does not mean that he is necessarily telling the truth. There is more, much more, to discover about Mr. James Cary, but we will leave that for tomorrow's visit."

I was somewhat comforted by the manner in which Holmes had responded to my distress. It seemed to me that I had made my point, at last. He had confided in me, which was only right, for if I do say so myself, he could never find another companion who would understand and appreciate his sometimes bizarre ways.

Suddenly, I remembered that Holmes and I had not yet discussed the butler's answers.

"Holmes," I suggested, "you've not spoken about Randolph's answers to your questions. Would you care to share them with me?"

The look on my friend's face was comical. Clearly, he did not want to discuss the butler's responses, but I had made my point earlier that evening. I would longer tolerate being left in the dark.

Reluctantly, he took the note from his pocket.

"Watson," he politely said, handing it to me, "you may read them yourself. Perhaps you will find more in his answers than I could."

I eagerly unfolded the paper and carefully began to read them aloud, hoping this could pique my friend's curiosity.
I began:

"Question #1: When and Where did you first meet Mr. Cary?

I first met Mr. Cary while I was working at another household. My former employer was moving to London and was kind enough to recommend me to Mr. Cary, who, as it happened, was in need of household staff.

Question #2: How long have you been employed by Mr. James Cary.

I have been privileged to work for the Cary family since 1882.

Question #3: Has Mr. Cary received any visitors or strangers to the house in the last several months?

Certainly. He is no hermit! Many of his fellow councilmen have come to Torre Abbey to meet with Mr. Cary. Of course, family relatives frequently come to visit. As to strangers, I confess that there have been some new faces who have met with Mr. Cary. On these occasions, I was asked to remain in my own quarters. As you can imagine, this did seem strange, but I never questioned Mr. Cary on this point. I'm sure he had his reasons.

Question #4: Are you aware of any hidden rooms, passages, etc? Are any areas restricted from your perusal?

Mr. Holmes, in truth, I know of no hidden rooms in the house proper. There are porticoes and cells once utilized by the religious brothers who once resided here. We have a storage cellar as well, but I have rarely had need or opportunity to investigate to any great extent. And I have never been denied access anywhere.

Question #5: How often do you get to leave the estate, and if you do, where have you gone in the last four months?

I have no restrictions in regard to remaining on property. As to when and where I may have traveled, I feel no need to reply. I mean you no disrespect, sir, but it's really no concern of yours.

Question #6: Do you have any close friends with whom you visit on occasion who might be of a suspicious nature?

I do have a small circle of local residents that I have the great pleasure of calling my friends. I can assure you, however, that they are among God's finest examples of humanity.

When I had finished reading the responses, Holmes asked, "Tell me, Watson, what do you make of the butler's answers?"

"Truthfully, Holmes," I replied, "I can find no fault in most of his responses. They appear to be straight, honest efforts to answer your questions. However, I am concerned about the matter of Mr. Randolph being confined to his quarters when certain visitors came to call. I believe that situation might bear further study."

My friend shook his head in the affirmative, offering, "I, too, feel that way, Watson. Malcolm Randolph seems to be a truly honest man, but he may be hiding something from us."

"Now, good fellow, it is time to get some rest. I will see you in the morning," he whispered, closing the door to his bedroom.

Chapter 11 Return to Torre Abbey

Wednesday, December 20th

"Cra-a-a-ck, a flap-a-dap-a-dap. . ."

At that noise, I jumped from my bed, only to find Holmes standing by my bedroom window, angrily adjusting the window shade that had slipped from its bindings.

"Blast it all," Holmes blustered, still struggling with the flapping blind. "Please excuse my clumsiness, but this window shade has certainly seen better days."

"Egad, Holmes," I entreated with some mild agitation, "what is the matter with you? Can't a person enjoy a good night's rest without being shocked into consciousness?"

"Yes, yes, Watson," he replied. "Rise and shine, old boy. We have a busy day ahead of us."

Ten minutes later found us downstairs, breakfasting on some of the most delicious scones I had ever tasted. Looking out the panoramic windows to our left, we could see small vessels making their way across the Channel, slowly disappearing into a receding fog bank. A bright winter sun was slowly breaking through, signaling the arrival of a most charming winter's day.

I watched my companion dip his bread into a poached egg, much too occupied with the morning paper to notice the yolk dripping onto his sleeve.

"Holmes," I snickered, "look out, friend! You'll soon be wearing your breakfast!"

It was too late and seconds later, the sticky yellow substance had taken up residence on his right arm and also decorating his tweed vest. The look on his face was priceless as he quickly diluted the stains, dabbing them with some drinking water.

Upon seeing his actions, I couldn't resist jesting, "Hmm....it seems the yolk is on you, Holmes."

Of course, his sense of humor wouldn't allow him to credit my snide remark, but he did offer, "Yes, Watson, very clever of you," while still trying to remove the stubborn stains.

His annoyance was soon interrupted by the appearance of one of the hotel bellboys.

"Excuse me, gentlemen," he stammered, "but there is a young lady who wishes to know if she can join you."

Holmes and I quickly turned toward the entryway and spied young Aggie Miller, smiling as she waved in our direction.

"Please see to it, young man," Holmes suggested, rising from his place while still laboring over his vest.

I took another piece of my scone and sipped some tea as the young lady arrived at our table. She was smiling broadly, obviously excited about what this day might have in store for her.

"Ah, Miss Miller," Holmes welcomed her. "How are you this lovely morning? Please have a seat. Are you hungry, young lady?"

"Thank you, Mr. Holmes," she replied, adding, "I've already had my breakfast. . . my mother's excellent oatmeal."

Aggie took her seat next to me, and sheepishly offered, "Mr. Holmes and Doctor Watson. Thank you for allowing me to join you. I trust that you both are well-rested. I can assure you that I am most eager to get to work on our investigation and trust you feel the same."

Holmes winked at me as he turned to the young girl, replying, "Miss Miller, we are both of us well-rested and ready for whatever the day may bring. And you, how did you sleep last evening?"

Pausing ever so slightly, the young girl softly responded, "Actually, if you must know, I had very little sleep. It must have been because I was so excited thinking about today, that my mind wouldn't let me relax to the necessary state where sleep might occur."

Before either of us could respond, she continued, "Gentlemen, what is our next step? I simply can't wait to get started!"

Anticipating a response to her terse statement, Aggie's eyes moved back and forth from Holmes to me and back and forth again.

I gazed once more at my companion, curious as to how he might respond to our young detective's unbridled enthusiasm. Holmes slowly folded the newspaper, took a sip from his teacup, and, gingerly leaned toward our young, inquisitive ingenue.

"Miss Miller," he offered, almost whispering, "Dr. Watson and I are still formulating our plans for the day, but please be assured that we have included you. However, I must remind you, you must promise to follow our directions exactly."

Aggie beamed at his comment.

He continued, "It is now 9:00. I would like you to make your way over to the Cary residence in one of the hotel carriages, making sure to exit on Church Street. From there, you should walk to the

Abbey and meet with your friend, Margaret. If she is at home, we would like you to spend the day with her, keeping your eyes open for anything that may seem the least bit out of the ordinary. Please pay particular attention to the new housemaid, Mrs. Bedlam. Of course, you must be careful not to raise any suspicions in her. Do you understand?"

Aggie interrupted. "But Mr. Holmes, what shall I do if Margaret is not at home?"

My friend quickly added, "Miss Miller, if that is the case, have a polite visit with Mr. Randolph. I believe you told us last evening that he was most friendly to you. If we haven't arrived after a brief conversation with the butler, please say your 'good-bye' and have a nice walk around the property."

Once more the child chimed in, "but Mr. Holmes, I want to do more. How can I help if I merely wander aimlessly about?"

My friend, smiled and replied, "Miss Miller, Watson and I will find you outside and we'll simply put Plan B into effect."

"Plan B," she stated, "fine, plan B. Pardon, sir, what in the world do you mean by Plan B?"

"You needn't worry about that for the moment," Holmes assured her. "Now, if you are certain that you know what you are to do, please get along. The driver will be waiting for you. Simply go to the stable and ask for young Toby. Off you go!"

"Thank you, gentlemen," she responded confidently. "I understand, and I am most anxious to see you both at the Abbey."

After that remark, Aggie Miller skipped away from the table and waved as she disappeared into the hotel hallway.

Aggie Miller was most content as her carriage headed through the crisp morning air toward Torre Abbey. The thrill of her assignment was almost too much for the young girl. No one could be that happy, or could they? Aggie Miller was no ordinary child. There was a certain something about her that everyone who had met her came to discover. Even the carriage driver noticed something very special about the young girl.

"I say, Missy," the young hotel driver, Toby, commented, "might I ask why you seem so joyous this morning? Could it be that Father Christmas will soon be here?"

Aggie's appearance suddenly changed at his remark. She was ready to angrily deny the existence of Father Christmas, and provide a stern rebuke to the pleasant driver when her maturity held sway.

Forcing a smile across her face, the young girl issued, "Oh, sir, is it that obvious?"

"Well, it's true," she continued, "I just can't wait till he visits!"

The young driver just smiled and said, "Well, you must have been a good little girl, judging by the happy look on your face. Good for you, Miss."

After that comment, Toby yelled to his team, "Whoa, whoa there!"

"Miss," he continued, "here we are at the corner of Church Street and Belgrade Road. Now, you have a nice day and a Happy Christmas!"

"The same to you, Mr. Toby," the young girl politely replied, stepping down from the carriage. Aggie waited for the carriage to disappear before continuing on her way. One couldn't be too careful these days.

After Aggie had departed, Holmes and I had been in no great hurry to finish our meal, giving our young detective a bit of time to arrive at the grounds of the abbey before us. Five minutes later, we were back in our rooms, preparing for the day's adventures. Shortly thereafter, we headed downstairs and out through the front door, only to find that our driver was still hooking up his team. It didn't take long to complete his chores and we were quickly on the road leading back to Torre Abbey. As we traveled the wintery roadway, Holmes informed me of his plans to take a closer look at Cary's library, that is, if Cary was not at home.

"Holmes," I inquired, "what if we find that Cary is home? Won't that spoil your plans?"

"Watson," he scolded, "it matters not a whit whether he is there or not. I will still be able to examine the room. The only difference will be that he will unknowingly be helping me!"

That made no sense to me, and I was about to tell him so, when he whispered, "Watson, don't worry, you'll soon see what I mean. . ."

For the rest of our ride, we rested, quietly enjoying the slowly melting icicles as they trickled from the branches of the glorious oak trees that lined our way.

"Well, look who's here? If it isn't the legendary Miss Aggie Miller, soon to be a student in Paris, France," teased the Cary butler. "And she's come to visit her friends here in Torre Abbey. To what do we owe the very great honor of your visit?"

The friendly butler bowed as he welcomed his young friend

through the main entrance.

"Oh, Mr. Malcolm," spoke the smiling youngster, "you're so silly. You know that I've come to see Margaret. I hope that she's here today!"

The smile disappeared from the manservant's face as he informed Aggie, "Young Miss Margaret, I'm very sorry to report, is still away at the country estate. And I really don't expect to see her today, Miss Aggie."

While the butler was responding, a slender figure was furtively descending from the main staircase landing.

Frowning mildly, Aggie voiced, "That's fine, Mr. Randolph. I expect she's having a grand time there, just the same."

"I say, Miss Miller," Randolph suggested, beckoning to the maidservant, "even though Margaret's not here, would you like to join Mrs. Bedlam and me for a nice hot cocoa? It's awfully cold outside and it will give you a chance to warm up before you start back home."

Before Aggie had a chance to respond, Mrs. Bedlam spoke up, "Miss Miller, Malcolm is right. Why don't the three of us have a nice hot drink and chat awhile before you must leave?"

Aggie looked at the two servants and, shrugging her shoulders, offered, "Why thank you. I'd like that very much."

The Cary kitchen was one of Aggie's favorite rooms. A large window overlooked a tall stand of hemlocks, draped with ivy. Often, she and Margaret would sit at the large oaken preparation table, doing their drawings and creating wonderful adventure stories. They would then entertain each other, playing the parts of some of the fictional characters they had newly created.

While Mrs. Bedlam readied the cocoa, Malcolm and Aggie sat and talked. The kind butler wanted to hear more about Aggie's plans to study in France, while Aggie, for her part, was thinking about other things. She listened patiently while Randolph described his trip to Paris, many years ago. He talked of visiting some of the finer restaurants and, of course, the Eiffel Tower. The young girl sat there, feigning interest, but he kept going on and on...

Quite, out of the blue, she suddenly turned to the maid, and inquired, "Mrs. Bedlam, I hope you don't mind my asking, but where did you work before you came to Torre Abbey?"

As soon as it was out her mouth, Aggie realized what she had done, but it was too late.

Mr. Randolph appeared stunned by the question and offered, "Miss Aggie, that's really none of your concern. Young lady, I'm very disappointed and surprised at you."

Aggie lowered her head, and turned away from her friend, knowing that she had indeed, crossed the line.

"That's quite alright, Mr. Randolph," the tall housemaid softened. "I have noticed that young Miss Miller is a most inquisitive child and I certainly don't mind answering her question."

At that, Malcolm excused himself, "Very well, I'll be right back. I believe someone's at the door."

"Young lady," Mrs. Bedlam began, "I came highly recommended from a London friend of Mr. Cary's. I have references from some of the finest families in England. When I was invited to apply for this position, I was very honored to have been considered by the Cary family. Although I've only been here for two weeks, I have been made to feel very much at home by Mr. Randolph and the rest of the staff. Of course, I am still getting to know everyone, and they are likewise getting to know me, as well."

Following a short pause, the maid again spoke, "Is there anything else you care to know, Miss Miller?"

A stunned Aggie Miller quietly, mumbled, "No, Ma'am, I didn't mean to pry into your affairs. Please forgive my impertinence. I was merely looking for a polite way to instigate a conversation to try to get to know you better."

The maid smiled, placing three steaming cups of hot cocoa on the table, just in time for the butler's return.

"It was only the wind," Randolph offered. "My, that cocoa smells wonderful. Thank you, Mrs. Bedlam. Please join us."

Once the maid was seated, the butler turned to Aggie once more, "So, young girl, when are you leaving for the continent?"

For the next several minutes, all three enjoyed the sweet taste of chocolate cocoa, sharing some pleasant conversation. Aggie happily discussed the plans for her upcoming studies abroad. She thanked Mr. Randolph for the information he had imparted earlier and complimented Mrs. Bedlam on the excellent cocoa and cookies she had baked.

Earlier tensions were just beginning to ease when Aggie again struck a nerve, asking, "Mr. Randolph, I was wondering if you had ever been to the Cary country estate? I'd be ever so pleased to hear about it."

Quickly, Mrs. Bedlam rose from her chair to clean the table, stating, "Mr. Randolph, I don't think you've ever been there, have you? At least, I've never heard you talk about the family estate."

Randolph looked at the housemaid and then turned to Aggie, issuing, "As a matter of fact, Aggie, Mrs. Bedlam is correct. I have never been invited for a visit, but that is acceptable. My work is here, and I have no need to take on any more responsibilities."

"Oh, my," Aggie, responded, adding, "so you've no idea where, in fact, it's located?"

"Miss Miller," a suddenly nervous butler voiced, "I'm afraid that I've fallen behind in performance of some of my chores. I do wish Miss Margaret was here for you, but, for now, I must bid you, farewell."

Smiling, he continued, "I suppose I might have used the expression, 'bid you fond adieu' as they say in France", as he escorted Aggie to the front door.

"Good bye, child," Mrs. Bedlam spoke as the door closed behind Aggie.

As she started down the front steps, Aggie scratched her head, wondering why she was so unceremoniously shown the door. Mr. Randolph had never acted that way before, and she was left to ruminate. The new maid, Mrs. Bedlam, seemed a decent sort, she reckoned, though she did notice that Randolph seemed very nervous in the housekeeper's presence.

The winter sky was still a bright blue, and the sun's rays made the temperature somewhat bearable as the young girl scanned the horizon for Mr. Holmes and Doctor Watson. She surmised that they should certainly have arrived to the Cary home by now. Somewhat concerned, she decided to follow Holmes's directives and began to make her way down one of the pleasant pathways toward the shoreline. Aggie found that the crisp, clean salty air always lifted her spirits and she quickened her pace, moving ever farther away from the Abbey and closer to the noisy, breaking waves.

When she had reached the boulders that outlined the rugged coastal inlet, she pulled out a small notepad and began to jot down the little she had discovered at the kitchen table. Mr. Randolph had never visited the Cary country estate. Why not? She jotted that down with an emphatically large question mark. Also, Mr. Malcolm was clearly intimidated by Mrs. Bedlam. Why should that be the case? She seemed to be a respectable, though somewhat secretive woman, a bit eccentric as well, Aggie added.

Then, suddenly it came to her. Perhaps, the housemaid was lying about her previous employment! Could it be that she had some information about Mr. Malcolm that she was using against him? That might explain his strange behavior of late. Smiling at her conjecture, she quickly finished her notes and put the tablet away.

"Now, where in the world are Doctor Watson and Mr. Holmes?" she whispered aloud as the sea terns flew overhead.

Holmes and I had only just arrived at the Cary estate when we spotted Aggie Miller down by the coast.

"Come, Watson," he suggested, "I see that Miss Margaret Cary is not at home. Let us take a nice brisk walk to the beach and see what our young private investigator has discovered."

As we walked toward the young girl, I was very much surprised that she never turned our way. For being such an inquisitive child, one would expect her to be much more alert. I could never have imagined that anyone would ever be able to sneak up on her. My only guess was that she was fully engaged in her work. At any rate, we would soon find out as we came up behind her.

She was facing the sea, swaying back-and-forth, apparently very much unaware of our presence. Holmes and I stood quietly behind her, just waiting for her to see us. Nothing was happening. Clearly, the young girl was lost in her thoughts, our first indication that she was, after all, only a youngster!

A slight tap on the shoulder startled her from her reverie. Aggie quickly jumped around, fists clenched and ready to defend herself. This reaction quickly dissipated as she recognized the familiar faces of Sherlock Holmes and me, standing before her.

"Well," Holmes offered, teasingly, "have you solved the case, Miss Miller?"

Slightly embarrassed by the remark, the young girl blushed and replied, "Not yet, gentlemen, but I'm confident that we'll soon have this mystery solved."

"Bravo," I spoke, smiling at the young lady. "That's our girl, Holmes. That's what we like to hear. Now, then, what has happened and is there anything new you can tell us?"

Holmes gave me a strange look. Then, looking around, he stooped down, took the girl by the shoulders and whispered, "Aggie, is anything bothering you?"

He continued, "Obviously, Margaret Cary was not at home. Can you tell us how you've been spending your time?"

Aggie, after assuring Holmes that all was well, took out her notes and put forth all that had occurred when she met with Mr. Malcolm and Mrs. Bedlam. Aggie informed us that Mr. Cary and family were still at the country estate. Additionally, she was happy to impart her own theories about Randolph's strange behavior in the presence of Mrs. Bedlam. When Aggie had completed her report, Holmes was fairly beaming at her.

"Watson, old chap," the detective praised, "what do you think of our newest irregular?"

"I told you, Holmes," I replied, gazing at Aggie Miller, "I knew she would be a great help to us!"

"It was nothing, gentlemen," the young girl replied modestly. "I'm proud to be considered one of your famous irregulars. What's next, Mr. Holmes? I'm anxious to hear about that alternate business you mentioned, that Plan B of yours."

My companion squinted his eyes at the remark, then quickly responded, "Why, Aggie, it is quite simple. Watson and I will proceed to the Abbey, as planned. You, my dear young girl, will go to visit Mr. Francis Powe, owner of some land that is most interesting to me."

"Tell me, Miss Miller," he continued, "have you ever been to his caves before?"

"As a matter of fact, Mr. Holmes," she replied excitedly, "my mother and I are very familiar with those caves. Did you know that several years ago, Mr. Powe purchased that land from Lord Haldon's estate?"

Holmes smiled, issuing, "Please, tell us more."

Without skipping a beat, Aggie informed us that the caves, now referred to as Kents Cavern, had been used by Mr. Powe, a carpenter by trade, as a storage area for his work. Powe made beach furniture, huts and even small boats for the local inhabitants.

After her brief informative interlude, Aggie tilted her head, scowled somewhat, and asked, "Mr. Holmes, what do you expect me to discover, besides some beach furniture?"

My friend, started her along the road, insisting, "Miss Miller, I expect you to be able to describe anything and everything that you find there. Examine the entire area carefully, no matter how insignificant you believe an item might appear to be. We'll discuss it over dinner tonight at your home."

While Aggie skipped down Torbay Road, Holmes and I began our walk to the Cary household. It was nearing the lunch hour, but we were in no need of nourishment after the fine morning fare we had enjoyed at the Imperial Hotel.

"Ah, Holmes," I ventured, "this Plan B. . . What is our part in Plan B?"

"Watson, that ruse was only for Miss Miller," my friend replied. "However, I haven't been totally forthcoming with all of my plans for us today, old friend."

"Whatever are you talking about, Holmes?" I responded with some mild discomfort.

"Watson," he continued, "I will need for you to offer an excuse for me when I disappear from Cary's library."

"Disappear?" I queried, "what do you mean disappear?"

Holmes hastened to add, "You may have noticed how much time I spent examining that room when first we visited him. Well, I found evidence of a passage located behind the far bookcase, and I fully plan to explore it!"

"I see," I remarked, softening, reconciling my position. "Well, how can we accomplish this task? Won't Randolph or Mrs. Bedlam be there? Why, how might I explain your sudden absence?"

"That will not be too much of a problem, old friend," Holmes smiled. "I have planned a disturbance that should keep them busy. When they find you alone in the library, you merely state that I had forgotten some important papers and needed to return to our lodgings."

"Hmmm," I voiced, shaking my head in some discomfort, "I'll do the best I can, but how long must I remain at the Abbey?"

"My good man, simply continue to survey the property," Holmes voiced with measured impatience. "See what else you may find by revisiting all of the rooms. Take some notes, but, by all means, do be careful!"

Holmes wound up his remarks with a final, "Watson, once our plans have been put into action, you and I will meet back at the hotel at 5:00, and I'll reveal all that I may have discovered."

"Very well," I replied, as we continued our walk. "I'm looking forward to hearing all about your findings."

A strong breeze was now blowing off the Channel, and upon approaching the Cary home, I was only too happy when the main door slowly opened before us.

"Gentlemen, welcome back," the butler politely offered, continuing, "I hope you are no worse for wear after yesterday's frightful experience."

"Thank you, Mr. Randolph," I responded for the both of us. "We're fine, though I certainly don't wish to experience any more attempts on our lives, my good man."

"Oh, heavens," our greeter replied, "let's not consider even the slightest possibility that such a horrible event could ever repeat itself."

He continued, "Mr. Holmes, I reflected on what you said to me in private, yesterday, and I must say that I'm having a most difficult time with your directive. In truth, I tossed and turned all night!"

Holmes replied, "We know how you wanted to call the local constabulary to report yesterday's events, but you must not continue to worry about that. You have to trust us!"

Randolph just shook his head, and remarked, "I hope you are correct, sir."

The awkward silence was shortly broken by the sound of the housemaid coming down the main staircase.

"Good day, Mrs. Bedlam," he offered in a kindly manner. "How are you this crisp winter's day?"

"A fine morning to you and Doctor Watson," she spoke somewhat reluctantly, adding, "well, it is another cold day, but, after all, it is December."

While she was speaking, I turned my attention to Randolph, for I was hoping to observe any signs of discomfort when Mrs. Bedlam made her entrance. Was it something that Holmes and I had imagined, or were we spot on in our conjecture?

Sure enough, as the maid stormed past, I noticed Randolph rolling his eyes and twiddling his fingers. We were correct. Something was amiss. Anyone could see how nervous and withdrawn Malcolm Randolph became whenever Bedlam was in his presence. I could only continue to ponder what was causing such tension in the man.

After Holmes removed his coat, he carried it over his left arm as we slowly moved across the shiny hardwood floor toward the Cary library.

"By the way, Randolph," he inquired, "have you lately heard anything from Mr. Cary?"

"No, sir," he replied, opening the door for Holmes and me. He added, "As you recall, Mr. Holmes, Mr. Cary did explain that he had other responsibilities requiring his attention. Should he return during your visit I will certainly tell him that you wish to see him."

"Are there any other matters that I may help you with?" the butler voiced.

"Not at this time, Mr. Randolph. We will be using this room as our headquarters," Holmes informed the curious butler.

"Furthermore, he continued, "when you do talk to Mr. Cary, please tell him how much we've been able to glean from his writings. In fact, Watson and I will continue to peruse his notes for most of our morning."

"As you wish, Mr. Holmes. Once again, please notify Mrs. Bedlam or me should you or Doctor Watson have any need of our service," Randolph bowed, exiting the room.

The moment the door closed, Holmes walked briskly to the far bookcase.

"Watson," he whispered, "take a peek into the hallway to see if Bedlam and Randolph have gone."

Quietly, I opened the door and peered down the carpeted hallway in time to see the maid lead the butler into the kitchen area. She slammed the door and immediately began to admonish her companion. I was tempted to move closer to hear their conversation, but quickly returned to Cary's library.

Backing into the room, I closed the door softly, whispering, "Holmes, all is well. The two of them have gone into the cookery."

There was no response to my remark, for Holmes was nowhere to be found. It was no use saying anymore, for he had found and entered the passageway and, assuredly had begun to see where it would lead. Left alone in the room, I thought it best to get busy reviewing the notes Cary had left, and so I started for the desk. After two steps, I decided to try to locate the secret passage. Nervously, I made my way to the far corner bookcase.

"Now," I reasoned, "Holmes said the bookcase was the entryway, so he probably went behind this section."

I carefully moved a few books at a time to try to find some sort of latch or switch that would open the way, but I had no luck. Of course, I couldn't move too many volumes, for I wouldn't be able to replace them properly if Bedlam or Randolph should suddenly return to the room.

"Yes," I whispered, "that most certainly would ruin everything."

Suddenly, I heard some loud screaming, followed by a knock on the front door. Unable to contain my curiosity, I walked into the hallway only to find the stable-boy informing Randolph that three of the horses had made their way from their stalls and were now freely roaming the estate grounds.

"Easy, easy, my boy," the butler calmed the young lad, continuing, "Tom, they'll not wander too far. Don't be in such a panic. It's happened before and it may happen again. You'll see, they'll be wandering back to the barn in no time at all."

"Hmmm. . ." I thought, laughing softly, "so that was Holmes's disturbance. Jolly good!"

Returning to the library, I once more got to work perusing Cary's notes, and it was just in time. Not five minutes had passed when, suddenly, Mrs. Bedlam barged into the room. She seemed bothered to a degree and was about to leave whence she had come, when she quickly turned, looked all about the room and stared into my eyes.

"Doctor Watson," she inquired, "I don't see Mr. Holmes. Might I ask where he has gone?"

"Mrs. Bedlam," I quickly responded, "my friend had to go back to our lodgings. He should be returning in a very short time. Thank you for your concern."

"I know it's none of my business," she continued, " I just thought that I might be of some use to him in the investigation."

"I say, Mrs. Bedlam, that is very considerate of you," I politely responded, "but we have our own ways of doing things. Thank you just the same. If we need your help in any way, we'll be sure to seek you out."

Bowing, she left the room in a huff, if I can judge by her actions.

"Hmm," I pondered, "I wonder if she guessed where Holmes had really gone. . ."

Meanwhile, at the entrance to Kents Cavern. . .

Young Aggie Miller had just arrived at Powe's shop at the entrance to the cavern. The wind was up a bit and, while sunny, it was still winter, and she was feeling the cold. At that moment, she realized that Mr. Powe might not even be at his workshop.

"Oh, please, please be here, Mr. Powe," she began to pray, "it is getting so cold!"

Slowly, she walked up the path that led to the cavern, wishing and hoping that the carpenter would be at work in his cabin, for she truly needed some warming up. Rounding the last corner, her spirits lightened for she caught sight of Powe rubbing down some wooden slats. When she saw him a broad smile of relief came to her face.

"Why, Miss Aggie Miller," the kindly carpenter called out, putting his work aside. "To what do I owe the pleasure of this visit?"

"Good morning, Mr. Powe," the girl responded, smiling, "I was just enjoying a walk on a winter's day, when I realized how cold it had become. I wondered where I might seek some refuge to warm up. Then, I realized that your shop was just around the corner. I hope you don't mind me coming inside to warm up a bit?"

"Young lady," he replied, guiding her into the first chamber of the cave, "you are welcome to come and visit me at any time. Please sit and I'll make us some tea."

As he moved to the wrought-iron stove, he continued, "Aggie, might I ask you if your mother knows where you are?"

Wasting no time replying, Aggie offered, "Mr. Powe, I'm almost a grown-up, you know. My mum trusts me to go wherever I please. Besides, she holds you in the highest esteem, so there is no need for you to worry about me."

"Well, that's all well and good, Aggie," Powe commented, "but we both know that Torquay is no longer the quiet little village it once was... if you understand my concern."

"Yes, I suppose you are correct," the young girl replied, spying a small model of sailboat sitting on display atop a rock ledge. "I'll only stay a few minutes to warm my bones, and then I'll be on my way."

The two of them sat and talked for a few minutes, sipping their tea, when Aggie spoke up, "Mr. Powe, as long as I'm here, if you're not too busy, would you consider giving me another brief tour of Kents Cavern? I haven't been here in years, and I am curious to see if you have made any major renovations."

The carpenter smiled broadly as he rested his cup on the table, "Aggie, my dear young girl, I would be delighted to do so. I have to warn you though, you might become frightened by some of our recent findings!"

"Me, frightened?" she chided, "Mr. Powe, I'm surprised at you. Why I'm not afraid of anything."

Laughing again, he scolded, "Well, Missy, maybe you should be a little cautious. . . for your own good, I mean..."

He quickly lit two small lanterns and they slowly made their way behind some shelving down and through the next chamber of the cave. At once, Aggie experienced a cool, damp breeze coming from the darkness that lay ahead. The flickering lanterns provided quite a bit of light, lessening the tension that such an excursion might have on anyone. For several minutes, the only sounds she heard were their feet shuffling along the damp pathway. Powe led the way, describing some of the stalagmites and stalactites that were present everywhere in the dark surrounds.

They continued making their way further into the cave, down through low, narrow passages that wound ever deeper into the darkness.

Aggie had read that this cave had been used by smugglers in bygone days. She imagined she was one of the pirates who had sought a place to bury some of the swag they had acquired in sea battles! Oh, this was so exciting...

With every step, the air became more musty, and Aggie could clearly hear the sound of water trickling from overhead as they passed along the limestone walls.

"Mr. Powe," she said, "please tell me if you see what I see over there. Is is possible that there is some writing on the far wall?"

He laughed at her suggestion and they moved closer to take a look. Sure enough, there were inscriptions dating centuries back. Aggie raised her lantern over her head and began to read, "Robert Hedges of Ireland, February 20, 1688."

"Look, Mr. Powe," the girl offered excitedly, "there's another one... William Petre, 1571... Oh, my..."

"Yes, Miss Miller," Powe responded, "notice how these writings are covered by a thin layer of liquid calcium coming from the stalactites above. It was Mother Nature's way of preserving the script."

Powe suddenly stopped and turned the lantern on his face, smiling. "Now, Aggie," he said, "when we turn this next corner, you are in for a big surprise. This section has only been visited by archeologists who are still in the process of discovery. So, young lady, get ready to look back into the history of mankind!"

Aggie's eyes just about popped out of her head with what she had just been told. She sensed that she had issued a kind of nervous giggle at her good fortune as Powe lowered his lantern, disclosing a locked wooden door which served to secure the site.

As the key began to turn, Powe offered, "Aggie, before we enter, promise me that you will merely observe what is contained within this chamber. Please touch nothing. If you have any questions, I will try to answer them for you, but, in truth, much of what has been unearthed is far beyond my comprehension."

"Oh, my," Aggie mouthed, "Mr. Powe, thank you so very much for trusting me to experience your secret collection."

"Now, now, young lady," the carpenter voiced, "it doesn't belong to me, although it lies on my property. It belongs to all of us!"

Slowly, the door swung open and they moved into one of the largest rooms in the cave. While Aggie watched him, Powe moved around the perimeter of the huge expanse, lighting all of the torches that had been placed around the exterior recesses of the immense space.

As each torch was lit, more and more details began to emerge from the darkness. Aggie Miller was speechless, speechless for one of the few times in her young life. It mattered not where she chose to look, for everywhere she gazed there were wonders to behold. It was now Powe's chance to shine as he showed Aggie to a workbench.

"Sit down here, young Miss Miller, while I relate the little I know about the work you see spread before you," offered the proud caretaker of Kents Cavern.

"What you see is the continuation of Professor Pengelly's excavations, Aggie," Powe spoke with a peculiar reverence, pointing to a large roped-off area.

Walking to one side of the dig he continued, "Right where I'm standing, was where his crew unearthed pieces of Samian ware, produced in Gaul. They also discovered, bronze rings, a fibula and other bone articles along with chisels and combs. There were even some Roman coins buried in this dig!"

Pointing to another area of the large room he said, "Aggie, the archeologists dug down through at least two additional layers, going further back in the history of man. There they discovered bones of the cave bear, the wooly rhinoceros, bones of the mammoth and even two human skulls!"

Aggie Miller just sat there in rapt attention. She could have stayed in that cave for hours, listening to Powe continue to describe all of the archeological findings, but she remembered that she had been given a job to do.

"Mr. Powe," she suggested, "this was, indeed, a wonderful surprise and I wish to thank you most sincerely. I can't wait to go home and tell my mother where I've been and what you've been so kind to divulge. I think, though, that I'm ready for some fresh air."

Powe smiled at her remarks, voicing, "Aggie, my dear young girl, I agree wholeheartedly. Let's go back to my workshop. I think I have some cookies that I might share with you before you start back on your way home."

Twenty minutes later found Aggie Miller waving to Mr. Francis Powe as he stood at the cave entrance.

"I can't ever thank you enough, Mr. Powe," she shouted as she skipped up the street and around the corner on her way back to Ashfield.

It was a most tiring walk back to her home, but Aggie was so excited, that she easily handled the weather and the distance. Upon reaching her back door, she found her mother busily preparing for the night's meal.

"So, Miss Aggie," Clara Miller hugged her daughter, "I'm glad to see you home safely. Pray tell me where you've been all afternoon and what you've found for Mr. Holmes and Doctor Watson."

"Mother," the young daughter spoke with unbridled excitement, "you'll never believe what an extraordinary afternoon I've had. I can't wait to tell you and Mr. Holmes and Doctor Watson all about it. But, if it's acceptable to you, I would really like to write down my findings and present them to all of you after dinner."

"That's my girl," spoke Clara, smiling broadly. "Go ahead, my dear, I know that you're most anxious to impress all of us. I can wait for your grand disclosure."

"Oh, thank you, mother," Aggie sighed, "I knew you would understand."

And, after a warm hug, the young girl disappeared into her room to complete her report.

Torre Abbey

Chapter 12 What Holmes Discovered...

Meanwhile Holmes is at Torre Abbey

As soon as Holmes had entered the passageway behind Cary's bookcase, he took out a match and lit the candle he had brought along, having sensed the presence of this passage during his initial visit to the Cary library. Slowly and carefully, he made his way down a dark, narrow stairway leading to a small storage area.

At first glance, all that the consulting detective was able to see was a lantern sitting atop an old wooden table that had been pushed flush against one of the surrounding earthen walls.

"Hmmm," he pondered, "surely, there's got to be more here than a table and a lantern."

He began to walk along the periphery of the small enclosure, studying the walls and the ground over which he shuffled. Nothing... There was nothing! When he turned his attention back to the wooden table, he reached for the lantern only to find it securely fastened to a rear corner of that piece of furniture.

"Well, now, here is something of interest," Holmes whispered softly, as he turned the top handle of the lantern.

Immediately, the wall behind the table began to open, disclosing another passageway and yet another stairwell.

The detective quietly slipped through the narrow opening, and after sending the wall back to its original position, began to descend another narrow stairway that had been carved out of the limestone. Down he went, several stories, in fact. When he had reached the lowest level, Holmes noticed that there were two tunnels, both going in opposite directions. He quickly decided to take the pathway to the left, marking that side of the wall in an obscure location with a piece of white chalk he had taken from the hotel menu board.

When he rounded the first corner, he noticed that this tunnel was remarkably straight. He quickly made his way through the darkness to where it abruptly ended. At first, it appeared to be a dead end, but when he glanced about, he spied a wooden latch, tucked along the left side of the tunnel wall. Wasting no time, he slid the latch down and, at once, a large section of that wall began to slowly slide open. At that, Holmes, quickly dimmed his candle, and cautiously peeked around the opening. A sliver of light shone through the half-opened space and he carefully ducked under an exposed beam to enter the large open space.

"Just what I expected," he voiced softly.

Holmes was once more in the Spanish Barn. Though there was sparse light, he could still see well-enough to explore the interior without needing the candle. He checked all of the doors and found them locked from the outside. It was good to know that he was alone. The last time he and Watson had examined the tithe barn, they hadn't had enough time. For when the doors were slammed shut, imprisoning both men, their main concern was to escape that situation. This was different. He had discovered a secret passage from the Cary home to the Spanish barn. Questions flooded his eager mind. Who had done this? When had the tunnel been constructed? And why? At this point, he could only wonder.

Holmes began taking measurements of the interior walls. He examined the loft and tried to discover if there were any other additional means of egress from the edifice. After jotting down a few notes, he headed back to the hidden passageway, securing the sliding wall behind him. He had found a lantern inside the barn and he decided that it would provide much more light than his candle. In no time at all, Holmes was back to the main stairwell.

Once more he decided to use the piece of chalk to mark his trail along the second underground tunnel. Every two-hundred meters he would hide a mark to show the way back to the Cary home. Later, he would be grateful for having used the chalk for this path went on for several kilometers!

Holmes continued to follow the winding tunnel, trying to map his way as he went. With each step he took, he believed he was getting closer to solving a part of the puzzle that Cary had posed. This was only one component of the mystery, but he believed it an essential one. He would find out soon enough!

Along this subterranean pathway, there were many other side paths, leading to dead ends. Of course, Holmes had to check them out, for he knew not where each might lead. These areas likewise needed to be mapped so that any future spelunking would be more expedient.

One path led to a large expanse, where a small pond had formed from ground water dripping from the cave walls. Holmes noted that this pond appeared to empty out under one side of the cave wall, possibly leading to the beginning of an underground stream. Another dead-end pathway took Holmes to some type of storage area, filled with large empty wooden kegs. From the smell, Holmes determined that they had, at one time, been filled with gunpowder.

Continuing along, Holmes suddenly realized that he had lost track of time. It was almost 3:30 PM when he came to the end of what he believed was the main passageway. Holding up his lantern, he saw that he was now in a vast cavern. The ceiling was at least 8 meters above the cave floor. It seemed very strange to him that such a long, serpentine underground passage had been constructed only to end in this enormous space that seemed to be completely empty.

While he was still sketching his map of the huge space, he thought he heard voices. They seemed to be coming from the far side of the cave wall, and as he moved ever closer, the voices became louder. Yes, he could hear people conversing, but he was unable to hear what was being said. Holmes was certain that there had to be some way to get to the other side. He searched and searched, sometimes stopping to try to hear the voices on the other side. He was too late. The voices had stopped. There was nothing but silence. . . silence in a vast, empty space.

After charting this last room, Holmes knew it was time to return to the Cary library and get back to the hotel, so he began to retrace his steps. He hadn't realized just how deeply into the cave he had traveled and he was surprised that it took him close to forty-seven minutes to get back to the secret library stairways.

He was almost ready to ascend the narrow steps when he heard the bookcase swing open. Quickly, he hid behind a large boulder, barely avoiding discovery by Lucretia Bedlam. The housemaid slowly made her way along the tunnel that led to the Spanish Barn. Holmes waited until she was out of sight then quickly made his move. In a flash he was up the stairs and carefully peeking through the library bookcase opening to see if anyone was in the room. Fortunately, there was no one in the room and he quickly moved toward the center of the office-library.

As he neared the large desk, Holmes noticed that Watson had left Cary's journal opened to the last entry. Checking his time piece, he slowly opened the library door, and seeing no one about, promptly stepped into the hall, closing the door behind him. He was able to make his way to the front door unseen, and after stepping outside, turned and looked around. He saw no one. Taking advantage of the situation, he knocked at the very same entry door through which he had most recently passed. In very short order, Mr. Randolph arrived and welcomed him back to the Abbey.

"Ah, Mr. Holmes," Randolph spoke, "we wondered if you would be back again today. Dr. Watson notified Mrs. Bedlam that you had forgotten something at your hotel and went back to get it. Might I ask if you were successful in finding that which you sought?"

"Randolph, my good fellow," Holmes replied, "I am happy to report that I have indeed been successful in my search. Thank you very much for your concern."

Before the curious butler could react to the comment, Holmes continued, "Randolph, is my companion still here? Before I left the library, I told him that I would be returning for him to continue our work here. Unfortunately, I became involved with other matters and am late in my return."

"No, Mr. Holmes," the butler commented, "I'm sorry to inform you that Doctor Watson has only recently left our company. Tom, our stable-boy was good enough to take him back to the Imperial Hotel."

"Well, that is all that I need to know," spoke Holmes.

"Ah, Randolph," continued the detective, "by any chance have you heard from Mr. Cary?"

"He has not been in contact, Mr. Holmes," the butler offered, "but I haven't forgotten your message and when I hear from him I'll be sure to pass along your concerns."

"Oh, well," Holmes smiled, as he and the butler made their way to the front door, "I guess I should be getting back to the hotel. I'm afraid I'll have a great deal of explaining to do. You see, my friend, Watson, will surely chide me on my tardiness."

When the outside door had closed, Holmes started down the path to the sea cliffs and Torbay Road. He decided to walk back to the Imperial Hotel. After all, it was only a mere 2.2 kilometers to reach his destination. He imagined the trip would require a thirty- minute walk, and the weather appeared to be easing somewhat.

As he walked, he tried to focus on the relevance of such a tunnel system. He could readily understand a passage to the Spanish Barn, for it would have required less than one hundred meters of digging. Additionally, it could have served as an escape route for the

Torre Abbey residents or the reverend fathers who built the structure, should the home be attacked. The other one, the longer tunnel ending in a dead end, however, puzzled him greatly. That would require some additional thought. It would have taken a great deal of time to fashion such an elaborate tunnel system. And, for what purpose? He couldn't imagine!

His thoughts on those matters would have to wait, for Holmes had nearly reached the grounds of the Imperial Hotel. He wondered if Watson had arrived safely back to their suite. He had much to tell him and hoped that Watson would likewise have information for him.

Watson's Day -(The story continues from Watson's point of view)

After returning to our hotel, my first order of business was to find a comfortable chair. I had planned to peruse the daily paper, but had trouble keeping my eyes open. There was something about the coastal sea air that made me sleepier than I had ever been in my life. Apparently, the long day and the tension had also had their effect upon me, for I was soon fast asleep. So soundly was I dozing, that I never heard Holmes enter our suite.

"Hello, Watson, Watson, old chap," Holmes whispered, gently shaking me awake. "My dear fellow, I hate to interrupt your sleep, but we have a very important dinner engagement. Have you forgotten?"

"Ah, Holmes, it's you, is it?" I sleepily acknowledged my companion's return. As I stretched, an embarrassing snort signaled my return to consciousness.

"Come, Watson," Holmes restated his earlier remark, "you

surely haven't forgotten our planned visit to Ashfield, have you? Good fellow, I have never seen you so sleepy. What is going on?"

"Holmes, I have noticed the same thing. I don't know, perhaps it's a part of growing older," I replied with some mild agitation. "And no, I haven't forgotten our dinner engagement. I'm really looking forward to it, actually. Aren't you?"

"Well, it has been rather a long day, and a home-cooked meal and pleasant conversation are always welcome diversions," Holmes suggested. "Tell me about your day, Watson, while we are refreshing ourselves. Did you notice anything of interest in my absence?"

"As a matter-of-fact, Holmes, I believe that I did," I stated proudly, continuing, "I am now more certain than ever, that Mrs. Bedlam has some kind of control over the butler, Randolph."

"Go on, Watson," Holmes coaxed. "Please tell me your reasons for such a profound conjecture."

"Certainly," I replied, beginning my explanation.

"Holmes, the moment you had vanished from the Cary library, the escaped horses produced the desired effect. The distraction, as you had hoped, provided ample time for you to find the passageway behind the bookcase and disappear. It worked like a charm!

I, for my part, responded to the commotion and entered the hallway only to find the stable boy being comforted by Randolph. He turned to me and explained what had happened and I immediately returned to the library. In no time at all, without any notice, that Bedlam woman stormed through the door. She quickly looked around, and finding you gone, immediately inquired as to your whereabouts. Just as you had directed, I informed her that you had need to return to our lodgings, having forgotten some important papers. I further offered that you would be returning to Torre Abbey in no time at all.

She seemed to accept my story, then quickly marched right up to my face, stating that she would be completely at our disposal, should we need her. I was certainly surprised by this turn of events and thanked her for the kind offer.'"

Holmes stood stock-still at my words, shifting his eyes to the ceiling, a sure sign of cranial activity.

Sensing I had captured his undivided attention, I couldn't resist withholding more of my report, so I paused to clear my throat and straighten my tie. Deciding to continue my delaying tactics, I then rose and made my way over to one of the shelves and opened a bottle of spirits.

"Oh, Holmes," I questioned, "would you care for a glass of sherry? Suddenly, I feel an urgent thirst!"

"No, thank you very much," an agitated Sherlock Holmes responded curtly.

"Surely, there's more," Holmes suggested, slipping silver cufflinks onto his dress shirt sleeves.

"Of course, there's more," I continued, and went back to my findings.

"'Bedlam quickly left the room, closing the door behind her. I sensed she was in a foul mood, so I tiptoed to the door and placed my ear against it, trying to hear what seemed to have been a rather nasty exchange between the butler and the housemaid. The gist of the argument had to do with her disapproval of strangers having the run of the place. She scolded Randolph for being so kind and so accommodating to us. He, for his part, defended his actions, alluding to Mr. Cary's dictates that we should be treated properly and given every consideration in our investigation.'"

"Hmmm. . ." my friend sighed, "is that so? Pray continue. . ."

Bedlam then said, "'Mr. Randolph, have you forgotten who's in charge here?'"

"What?" Holmes questioned, dropping one of the cufflinks. "She actually made that remark to Randolph?"

"That's exactly what was said, Holmes," I confirmed.

"The poor man," I continued, shaking my head, "I truly felt sorry for him!"

"Go on, go on. . .What happened next?" my friend inquired, anxiously strolling around the room.

"Holmes, Randolph said nothing. . .nothing at all! He simply turned his back and walked away toward the back of the house," I whispered. "Now, sir, what do you make of that?"

My friend had ceased his pacing, and sat down in one of the quaint hotel wing chairs. He had now assumed his familiar steepled hands together in front of his eyes pose. Whenever he was so positioned, I knew that his mind had seized upon something. I said nothing more for several minutes; instead I continued getting ready for our upcoming visit to the Miller home. Knowing Holmes, he would comment only when he was good and ready.

"Watson," he suddenly remarked, "this is most fascinating. Is there more to report?"

I had eagerly waited for such a request, responding to the affirmative, "Holmes, there is much, much more."

I described my lunch with Bedlam and Randolph.

"'There was not a word spoken between them. In that awkward silence, I decided to compliment each for their kind attention to our needs. I suggested that we would soon be finished with our investigation, implying that we were very near to wrapping up the mystery. At that remark, Mrs. Bedlam abruptly stood up and moved toward the butler, whispering something to him. Randolph, for his part, waved her away and she quickly slipped on her winter coat and left through the rear door.

While I finished my muffin, I sensed that Randolph wanted to tell me something. I tried to get him to comment on Bedlam, but he would say nothing. Still, I persisted.

"Mr. Randolph," I began, "I may be imagining things, but is there something the matter with Mrs. Bedlam?"

"Why, no, Doctor Watson," he replied. "That's her way. She's always been most direct in her conversations. With her it's all about keeping the household in order. Now, if you'll excuse me, I must get on with my own responsibilities."

After the butler had left the room, I decided to return to the library to see if I could find any additional information for us. Moving slowly to the window, I saw that Bedlam was walking along the path toward the Channel. Knowing she would be out of the house for a brief time, I ran back to Cary's desk and tried several other drawers.

Most of them contained what you might find in any lawyer's desk drawers: billing accounts, requests from prospective clients, etc. However, when I tried to open the bottom drawer on the left side of the spacious oaken piece of furniture, I found that it was locked! Hmm... I noticed that the drawer had a lock made by a company called Bridgelock. Oh, well, I couldn't very well break into that drawer without leaving tell-tale signs of forced entry! That being the case, I quickly rose from the chair and headed to the window again, just to check on the whereabouts of Bedlam and Randolph.

I was surprised to see the two of them sitting on a bench near the Spanish Barn. They were too far for me to hear their conversation, but that gave me a chance to do more snooping. I looked at Cary's desk once again. I kept thinking of the locked drawer. Now why that bothered me so much, I couldn't tell you. For some reason, I simply had to see what was in that drawer.

Suddenly, an idea came to me. I had my own set of house keys in my pocket and also a key to my own desk drawers. I realized that my desk had been constructed by the same company, Bridgelock. Now, what were the odds that my key would open that drawer? However remote the possibility, I simply had to try. Quickly, I knelt down behind the huge desk and slowly slipped my own key into the lock. Voila!

Fortuitously, my key opened the drawer and I was able to peruse the contents, finding another journal, this one dealing with the minutes of the last several town meetings. I quickly jotted down the main points raised regarding the murders and a strange request from Terra, the cult leader.'"

At that, Holmes bolted straight up from his chair, almost foaming at the mouth, "Brilliant, Watson, I knew there was larceny somewhere inside your person! Please let me see your notes."

Enjoying the fact that I had captured his full attention, I continued, "You'll have to wait, Holmes, I've not finished my report."

"'After putting the journal back and locking the drawer, I left the house and began to re-trace our steps outdoors. I spent much of the afternoon interviewing some of the other service personnel that worked at Torre Abbey. Tom, the young stable-boy, had decided to quit school early. He said that school held no interest for him. He had to get a job and informed me that he had heard that the Cary family needed someone to care for the Abbey barn, carriage and horses. He applied for the position and was hired on the spot. The young lad had nothing but praise for Mr. Cary, who treated him very well. I concluded that Tom was most content working for the Cary family.

I returned to the home and decided to try to glean some background information from Mrs. Bedlam, but she refused my request. I sensed the woman was, suddenly, most uncomfortable. She stated emphatically that she was far too busy at this moment to be subjected to any questions that I might wish to ask, suggesting another time might be better.

Now, Holmes, I was truly confused by her reply. It bordered on impertinence, especially when she had offered to help us earlier. Well, I highlighted her behavior in these notes, knowing you would be most interested in her reaction.

Next, it was Mr. Randolph's turn. Would he be willing to talk to me I wondered? Or, would he, like Mrs. Bedlam, refuse to hear me out. I'm happy to report that he was only too happy to oblige, as long as the questions pertained to his daily household duties and responsibilities.

Naturally, I was delighted by his willingness and we quickly began our intercourse. You'll be interested to hear that our butler is an avid reader. He is most familiar with many of our adventures that I've penned over the years. He also confided that he has great admiration for you, my good fellow! As we talked, he spoke of his total dedication to the Cary family, for whom he has worked since he came to Torquay. He had little to add, though, about the threatening letter Mr. Cary had received. When I asked about Cary's recent frequent absences from the house, he simply remarked, looking around, almost in a whisper, 'I would like to be able to tell you and Mr. Holmes more, but I **can't**. . . I simply **can't**. . .'

Later in the day, it must have been near 2:30 PM, I heard the door close and caught sight of Mrs. Bedlam heading up the stairway. She was quickly followed by Randolph and, once more, I heard them bickering. Again, they were too far away for me to hear their words, but it was clear to me that there is no love between them. I decided that it was time for me to get back to the hotel and informed both the butler and the housemaid that I would be leaving.

While walking toward the front door, Bedlam inquired as to the possibility of seeing us again. I politely replied that I didn't know, and bid them adieu. As I was leaving, Randolph called the young stable-boy and had him take me back to our hotel. And here I've been, anxiously awaiting your return.'"

After a slight pause, I turned to Holmes and asked, "Well, that was my day. What about you? How did your explorations go?"

My friend shook his head and weakly offered, "Later, Watson. Now let me see those notes, if you would be so kind."

He snatched them from my hands and quickly scanned the findings that I had so quickly scribbled. Occasionally, my colleague would offer a smile of approval in my direction, finalizing his brief study of the information with a closing, "Well done, Watson."

I returned his smile, offering, "Well, what do you think our next move might be?"

"We'll get into that after our dinner," he stated, sliding my notes into his dress coat. But now, it's time we were on our way to visit Ashfield."

We started down the stairs to the hotel lobby when we spied Wiggins and his diminutive partner heading our way. Wiggins winked at our approach and pretended to stumble into us, falling to the floor.

Holmes, playing along, raised his voice, "Young man, watch where you are going. You could have easily been injured. Worse than that, you might have injured others!"

After those remarks, I watched Holmes help Wiggins to his feet and in the process, drop a small envelope into the young detective's coat pocket.

Wiggins began straightening his jacket issuing, "I'm fine. I'm fine. Now please get out of our way. You and your friend might watch where you're going as well!"

The hotel manager had been observing this brief disturbance

and quickly approached trying to quell what seemed to be the beginning of a nasty altercation.

"Gentlemen, please calm down," he spoke in a most comforting manner.

The proprietor continued, "Surely, there was no malicious intent by either party. If no one has been injured, I would suggest that you just move along and go about your business."

"Well," Wiggins spoke, "I suppose you are correct. Please accept my apology for the way I have behaved, sir. We'll be on our way."

The manager smiled as Holmes briskly replied, "Thank you sir," then he turned to me and offered, "Come, Watson, no harm has been done."

Seconds later, we were out of the hotel and into a carriage, heading toward Ashfield, the home of Clara Miller and her delightful daughter. As we rode along in silence, I wondered if Holmes was going to tell me what that collision with Wiggins was all about. Oh, I knew he had taken advantage of that coincidental meeting to pass along some information to Wiggins and his partner, but I couldn't imagine why he hadn't shared it with me. I waited for several minutes, hoping he would explain what had transpired. He remained silent.

I could take it no longer. I simple had to ask, "Holmes, why won't you tell me about the note you gave Wiggins? Surely, you know that I saw you slip it into his pocket. Why all the secrecy? I'm your partner, after all. After our last discussion, you assured me that this would not happen again!"

I continued, angrily, " I can't imagine why you are keeping things from me."

After an awkward silence, my friend responded calmly, "Watson, the note was only a directive for Wiggins and Bobo. Believe me, I have no intention of keeping anything from you. And yes, I know a man of your detective skills would easily see my drop. I would never try to fool you, dear fellow."

"Holmes," I replied with some mild agitation, "that simply won't do. Damn it, man, tell me what's going on. What are your suspicions at this point? What do you want Wiggins and Bob-o to do?"

Holmes could certainly tell by my response that I was greatly bothered. My patience at an end, I needed to know if I was essential to the success of this investigation or merely a pawn of sorts, merely playing a part in the goings on.

"Watson," he suggested, "I see that you are at the brink, so I will explain all of our plans later this evening. I promise you that. As far as the note to Wiggins and Bobo is concerned, it was only a summary of my findings in the caves beneath the Cary household. I thanked them for setting the horses loose at the Abbey, telling them it had done the trick. Finally, I further requested that they examine the sea cliffs by Daddyhole. Now, we are almost at the Miller house, so can we please save this conversation until after our dinner?"

Before I could respond, our carriage came to a stop in front of a stately home, situated on a small slope. We had arrived at Ashfield.

Chapter 13 Ashfield

The evening of December 20th

    The Miller home was most impressive. Positioned on a slight rise, it was tucked away behind a lovely stand of oaks. The light from within the stately residence seemed to warm the spirit on this cold winter's night. As we carefully proceeded along the snowy walkway, we could see the young girl peeking through some curtains adorning one of the building's front windows. Suddenly, Holmes, quite uncharacteristically, gathered up some snow and tossed it, gently striking the frosty pane. A startled Aggie Miller jumped back at the snowy, noisy surprise. After quickly recovering from the disturbance, we observed her laughing and grinning as she moved toward the front door to receive us.
    "Mr. Holmes... Doctor Watson..." she politely offered, wearing her best smile, "we are truly honored by your presence. Do come in. Welcome to our humble abode. Welcome to Ashfield!"
    Holmes bowed politely, then turning to me, offered, "Why

Doctor Watson, who is this fine young lady welcoming us into her domicile? Could it be that famous detective, Aggie Miller?"

Nodding at my friend's jest I said, "Miss Miller, thank you for that warm greeting. We are most happy to be here."

No sooner had we entered the residence, when Aggie's lovely mother, Clara, appeared, joining us in the spacious foyer.

"Gentlemen, we are so pleased that you have chosen to visit us this evening," Mrs. Miller spoke, leading us into the living room. "I trust that you've had a most profitable day with your investigations."

"As a matter of fact, we have," replied Holmes, "and thank you for your interest, Mrs. Miller."

Upon entering the parlor, I looked around and found it to be a most comfortable room. There were wonderfully scenic paintings of Torquay, the English Channel and other local points of interest artfully displayed on classic oaken paneled walls. Window treatments were stylish if not opulent, and everywhere could be seen tasteful, interesting miniature statuary.

We both soon found ourselves relaxing in a pair of armchairs that seemed to have been made for us, so comfortable were they. I, for one, was most happy to rest my weary bones. While enjoying the warmth from the main fireplace, I allowed my olfactory senses to enjoy the delightful aromas that were emanating from the cookery.

"Wine, gentlemen?" Aggie's mother offered. "Or, perhaps something with a little more character?"

Holmes and I both chose a mild claret to quench our thirst and warm our souls. Almost immediately after these refreshments had been provided, we were treated to a brief, but detailed account of the young girl's day.

"Mr. Holmes, Doctor Watson," Aggie excitedly began her concise report, "I hardly know where to begin. . ."

"Now, Aggie," her mother interrupted, "please calm down. We have the whole evening to hear what you have to report."

The young girl, bowed to mother, "Yes, Mother, I shall try to do as you've suggested. Mr. Holmes, Doctor Watson, I hope my findings prove themselves valuable to you. But, before elaborating, I want you to know how much I've enjoyed my day. Thank you so very much for allowing me to join in your investigation!"

For the next twenty minutes, Aggie carefully described her day's findings, reading carefully from the notes she had compiled. The young girl excitedly informed us of all she had experienced. She shared, in great detail, all that she had gleaned: from the cocoa and conversation with Randolph and the Bedlam woman, to her exciting adventure exploring Kents caves with Mr. Powe. As Aggie was describing her visit to the cavern, I noticed a marked change in Holmes's level of interest.

"You see, Mr. Holmes and Doctor Watson," the young girl continued, "Mr. Powe took me deeper into the cavern than I had ever been before, leading me to the furthest recesses of the caves! When we arrived there, Mr. Powe had to unlock a huge wooden door that had been installed to protect the integrity of the most recent archeological digs. While we viewed those explorations, Mr. Powe provided me with a description as to how certain levels of strata had been carefully removed, section-by-section, numbered and marked for posterity."

The girl continued, "As you and Doctor Watson might imagine, I was truly gratified to have had this opportunity to see portions of the past, now displayed right before my very own eyes. Mr. Powe seemed to be as excited as I was, especially when he proudly told me how the Ministry had entrusted care of this historical site to his keeping.

We lost track of time, but I sensed that it was getting late, and though I would have loved to have spent more time there, I knew I should return home. Mr. Powe understood, and we turned around, preparing to start back toward the cave entrance when I thought I heard voices coming from the other side of one of the cave walls! Mr. Powe listened as well, but suggested that running water, shifting limestone deposits or even cave bats were probably the cause of those sounds."

"And so, Mr. Holmes and Doctor Watson," the young girl concluded, "I hope that some of my investigative findings will prove to be useful to you."

When she had finished her report, we could see that Miss Aggie Miller was all aglow with excitement, waiting to hear our reaction to her findings. I had to admit that she had a wonderful talent for description. Apparently, Holmes felt the same, for soon after, he was beaming broadly. Why I actually thought that I had perceived a tiny smile upon his countenance!

"Mrs. Miller," my friend commented, turning to the young girl's mother, "you must certainly be proud of your daughter. She has just given us an excellent account of her day's work."

Then, turning to young Aggie, he continued, "Miss Miller, I must commend you on the thoroughness of your report. Bravo!"

The young girl smiled contentedly, bowed, and offered, "Why thank you, Mr. Holmes, but I should be thanking you and Doctor Watson for your faith in me."

Clara Miller smiled proudly, but quietly brought her beaming youngster back down to earth, issuing, "Aggie, dear, would you please escort our guests to the dining room? I'm sure they must be famished."

A delightful repast added to the enjoyment of a busy, yet productive day. While we enjoyed a modest dessert offering, Holmes put forth his day's findings, detailing his examination of the Cary journal and its grounds.

I was not surprised that he chose not to disclose his actual activities at Torre Abbey. We were still in the early stages of our investigation and, clearly, there was no need to provide all of what we had uncovered to Aggie and her mother.

When it was time for us to leave, Mrs. Miller thanked us once again for allowing her daughter to help with our work. Aggie, for her part, was still bursting with excitement. In fact, as we were starting for the door, Aggie slipped ahead of us, with her back to the door.

"Mr. Holmes. . . Doctor Watson," she spoke slowly, "if you wouldn't think it too presumptuous, might I inquire what else you might have in store for me? I'm ready to do even more!"

Clara Miller quickly spoke up before we could reply, "Now just a moment, young lady. These gentlemen were kind enough to allow you to become involved in their very important investigation. I'm sure that you are no longer needed, at least for now. Am I correct, gentlemen?"

I noticed her winking behind her daughter's back and Holmes quickly picked up on her intentions, offering, "Aggie, what you've been able to do for us will help enormously. Your mother is correct. If we have need of your services, we will most assuredly be in touch. Thank you, again."

We were barely out of the house when Holmes looked at me and said, "I know what you're thinking, Watson. I know that I chose not to tell the Millers all that I had discovered, but I hope you will agree that it would only have served to complicate matters."

"Certainly, my dear fellow," I concurred. "I knew what you were doing and I am in complete agreement."

On the trip back to our lodgings, Holmes suddenly posed, "Watson, what would you say to a slight detour to Torre Abbey at this very moment?"

"Holmes," I quickly responded, "what do you have in mind? What do you hope to find at this time of night?"

"Watson, if you have no objections, I thought we might make our way back to the Abbey to see if Mr. Cary has returned home," my friend suggested.

He further remarked, "Watson, I am beginning to think that Mr. James Cary has been deliberately avoiding us for some reason. Perhaps, we can find out why that seems to be the case."

We directed our carriage toward Barton Road and headed once more for Torre Abbey. The evening's weather, remarkably, remained most cooperative, indeed, almost mild. It is well-known that winters along English coastal areas are normally damp and bone-chilling. That evening, there was little wind, if any, on our drive to the grand estate and we soon found ourselves along the sea cliffs that border the property.

We thought we might have some trouble finding a suitable place to hide our horse and carriage, but fortune was with us. Quickly spying an excellent location behind some scrub brush, we drove our conveyance to that locale. From there, it was only a short walk to the Spanish Barn and Torre Abbey.

As we neared the buildings, there rose above the breaking of the nearby waves what sounded like high-pitched shouting.

"Watson," Holmes warned, "it would appear that someone is being read the riot act within. Quickly now, let's move to the front window."

I followed my friend as he hopped over some low-lying hedges, and we both crouched low under the window sill outside of Cary's library.

"I'm warning you, Cary, you'll do what we say or your family will suffer," an ominous voice threatened.

"Did you hear that, Holmes?" I whispered.

"Yes, Watson," my friend went on, "it is as I suspected. It appears that poor Cary may indeed be at the mercy of some very dangerous characters."

"And," Holmes continued, "while he was wise to seek our aid and support, I'm fearful that these criminals must have learned of our involvement. I believe that Cary and his family are now in even greater danger."

I was about to answer when another voice rang out through the night. I recognized it to be the voice of the housemaid, Lucretia Bedlam.

"Cary, we don't want to see anymore of those meddlers, Holmes and Watson," she commanded. "Do you hear me? You will tell them that all is well and that you no longer require their services. Do you understand?"

Cary responded, "Listen, Miss Bedlam, these men aren't fools. They'll know I'm trying to hide something if I suggest they return to London. As far as they know, I'm back and forth working out of town, visiting my family in our country estate. Let's keep it that way until you've finished this unholy business of yours."

"Did you hear that, Holmes?" I offered again.

"Watson," Holmes softly spoke, "Cary is a very brave man. His only hope for the safety of his family depends upon his total compliance with this evil band's wishes."

With that, my friend and I quietly moved away from the house and headed back to our carriage. In no time at all, we were on the way to the hotel. While we whisked through the narrow streets, Holmes observed, "Watson, we are at a most critical moment in our investigation. All of our moves, from this point on, must be done with the utmost care. I fear that we will be followed wherever we go. Eyes will be upon us reporting everything we do."

He said no more until we had reached the Imperial and had entered our rooms. After putting away our outerwear, Holmes pulled the drapes across both windows and sat down by the fireplace. Pulling out his pipe, he struck a match sending sparks and tobacco all about him.

"Watson," he began, "before we plan our next moves, I need to relate my afternoon's work for your wise analysis. I had a most interesting time earlier today below ground, and I don't mean the cellar of Torre Abbey."

"Yes, Watson, when I passed through the secret bookcase, I

followed a dark stairway below. There were two pathways leading away from a small storage area. The first one was easily spotted and it led to the Spanish Barn. I remembered that other day, when we first explored that edifice, I felt certain that there must have been a passageway to the main house, but hadn't enough time to complete that part of our investigation. The locked doors, the bullets flying, Miss Miller's appearance, Randolph with the shotgun. . . all distractions from what I had planned to do."

"At any rate," he continued, "after following that underground tunnel, there was a hidden opening that I was able to uncover which connected the tunnel to the barn. There, I spent a short time checking all of the walls and floor areas, searching for additional hidden passages. Finding none, I returned to the tunnel area which lead back to Cary's library. The second tunnel, was not immediately discernible, but after discovering it, I decided to see where it might lead."

While Holmes continued his tale, I decided to stretch my legs, still listening, and headed to the window. Peering out, I thought I saw a figure staring up at our window. I was about to relate that fact when Holmes called me back to my seat.

"Watson," he cajoled, "my good fellow, are you bored with my afternoon's work?"

"Sorry, Holmes, "I muttered, "please continue. . ."

"Well," he began again, "I moved through the gap, and continued along the dark passageway, using a piece of chalk to mark my trail. And it proved to have been the proper thing to do, as I would soon find that I had wandered many, many kilometers from Torre Abbey.

Moving ever deeper along the way, I noticed that there were several smaller tunnels that branched off the main passage, but I continued along the main underground trail. I passed many areas where running water could be heard, indicating that perhaps there was some kind of underground river nearby. Farther along, a strong odor of gunpowder led me to investigate one of these smaller rooms, an offshoot from the main tunnel."

"What?" I voiced, "gunpowder, you say?"

"Yes," my friend replied, with some mild annoyance present in his tone. "May I continue now?"

"Watson, there I found several large empty kegs, which, at one time had held the gunpowder my olfactory senses had recognized. I left that room, returning to the main tunnel, again marking my way. Several minutes later, I had reached the end of that main branch. When I raised my torch, I found that I was in a large domed room, stalactites and stalagmites all about me. The only sound I could immediately hear was the noise made by running water, echoing off the far wall of the huge room.

The area appeared empty, at first. It was then that I noticed a small chair and table set behind a rocky outcropping that protruded from the left. It was protected from view by the cave shadows created by the torch. I moved closer and was about to examine that area when I heard voices on the other side of the cave wall.

Moving my ear directly against the rocky facade, I endeavored to hear what was being said. At that moment, I realized that there had to be a way to get to the other side. I fully intended to try to find some kind of opening to the other side, but it was getting late. I knew that it would take me at least forty to fifty minutes to get back to Cary's library, so I started back on my return trip."

"Oh, and Watson," Holmes blurted out, "I almost forgot to tell you. I narrowly missed running into Lucretia Bedlam as I neared the stairway leading back to Cary's office. She was on her way along the tunnel to the Spanish Barn and fortunately, she missed seeing me."

"Egad," I said, "I can't imagine what kind of repercussions such a meeting might have brought upon our investigation!"

"I agree," spoke Holmes, and he completed his tale, "Watson, I carefully emerged into the Cary library, luckily finding no one there. Quickly, I slipped out of the house, apparently unseen. After a few minutes, I knocked on the door from the outside."

"What," I inquired incredulously, "why would you do such a thing?"

"Elementary, my dear fellow," he boasted. "Did you forget that we had to follow the story line we prevaricated earlier in the day? Certainly, Randolph and Bedlam needed to believe that I had left the house earlier and was, only now, returning to the Cary home."

"Of course," I concurred. "Cleverly done, Holmes!"

"Watson," he returned to his previous revelations, "getting back to the voices in the tunnel, as I mentioned, I couldn't make them out, and the words spoken seemed mere gibberish. Now, after hearing Aggie's story, I believe that it could have been her voice speaking with Mr. Powe. Do you understand what I'm saying, Watson?"

Stunned by his commentary, I offered, "Holmes, if you are correct, then there may indeed be a tunnel connecting the Spanish Barn to Torre Abbey and Kents Cavern!"

"Precisely, Watson," my friend remarked, drawing deeply from his pipe.

"What to do, now," he continued, as he thought aloud. He circled the hotel room around and around, again and again, puffing away much like a locomotive climbing a steep grade.

"Whoa, there," he suddenly remarked. "I almost forgot about those notes you made from Cary's council journal. What's the matter with me? I must be losing my touch, Watson."

Before I could issue my response to his rhetorical comment, he opened my notes and began to read aloud.

"According to these journal entries, my friend," Holmes stated, "It seems that at each of the Torquay council meetings, this Druid leader, this Terra person, made an appearance and indicated a strong desire to obtain permission to use or perhaps purchase the clifftop land known as Daddyhole from the community land trust."

"That is correct, Holmes," I replied, "that is, if Cary's notes are to be believed. But they can easily be checked. . ."

"And," Holmes continued in the manner of a lawyer leading the jury to follow his reasoning, "each time Terra indicated his interest in purchasing this property, it was unanimously refused. Furthermore, every time he heard his request being denied, Terra issued the same somber remarks, 'Gentlemen, these continued refusals may not be what is best for this community as you are bound to discover.'"

Holmes bristled at that last remark, issuing, "Watson, that sounds very much like a threat to the town council. What say you?"

"I thought the very same thing, Holmes," I responded. "And, especially when you consider that soon after each town council meeting, a member of that very same council was murdered! Coincidence, I think not!"

Holmes quickly placed my notes on the desk corner, atop the other papers he had amassed for this investigation.

"Well, Watson," he smiled, "this case is becoming more and more interesting. I only hope we can stop these villains before another innocent life is lost. Now, if we are to be any good, we need to get our rest, for tomorrow will be a most demanding day. We are going to pay a visit to Mr. Powe's caves and see if we can get him to show us what he shared with young Aggie."

Cliffs of Daddyhole Plain

Chapter 14 Daddyhole

December 21st

    Early the next morning, long before the onset of daybreak, the detective team of Wiggins and Roberts decided to charter a small Channel boat for a trip on the famous waterway. Captain Kirk, skipper of the *Toast of Torquay*, was quite surprised by the offer. It was not the kind of day most tourists would have chosen for a scenic cruise. But he hadn't seen much business for quite a time, and it was to be a short trip along the coastline and back.

    That anyone would wish to go out on the water in December, especially in such windy conditions, was a mystery to him. Nevertheless, these two men were interested, and seemed agreeable to pay extra for the privilege. Additionally, the old sailor could always use the money.

    So it was that Mr. Wiggins and Mr. Roberts boarded the vessel, wearing several layers to keep them warm, at least as warm as anyone could be on the deck with whitecaps breaking and splashing across the ship's prow. The men kept their eyes peeled on the steep stone cliffs that served to support a well-known plateau known as Daddyhole Plain. The shorter man used a pair of binoculars to scan the impressive formation.

While they were being tossed about and bounced by the Channel waves, they spied what appeared to be a small opening halfway down the side of the Daddyhole cliff. Having validated the existence of the aperture, they signaled Kirk and they soon found themselves back on the city dock, happy to be once more on dry land.

Minutes later, they were atop that same cliff side, preparing for their mission and enjoying the striking view out over the Channel. With the waves breaking so powerfully, they believed that their best hope of reaching what appeared to be an entrance to a cave would come by being lowered from the top of the ledge.

"Wiggins, might I have a word with you?" queried Bobo Roberts as he continued to harness his torso to a thick piece of hempen rope.

"Why, certainly, Bobo," came the response from his partner as he continued fastening the other end of the rope to the wheel of their carriage.

"Can you tell me why I am always the one to be lowered down sheer cliff walls, sides of buildings? Why is it always me that gets pushed through small, dark, holes across deep crevasses?" the diminutive Bobo inquired. "Answer that for me, if you would."

After a brief pause, Wiggins turned his head slowly, stared directly into the eyes of his partner and whispered, "Bobo, would you rather lower me down? Really?"

"Think about it," Wiggins continued. "Bobo, you weigh less. Furthermore, you're agile and supple. Your size allows you to go where others may not. Need I continue?"

"Enough, enough... You may stop, now!" Bobo Roberts interrupted Wiggins, preventing him from any further commentary. He groaned "You have made your point. Let's get on with it."

The words were no sooner out of his mouth when Bobo began to move to the edge of the rocky ledge atop Daddyhole Plain and slip over the side. Slowly, slowly, the shortish Mr. Roberts felt himself being gently lowered down the ragged side of the sheer cliff wall. Closer, ever closer, he moved toward the Channel waters below him.

"Easy there, Wiggins," he called up to his partner, "there are several sharp outcroppings over which the rope must pass. We certainly don't want to cut the cord!"

Wiggins continued to let out the rope, slowly, every so slowly, waiting for word from his partner.

"Hold it there, Wiggins," Bobo called softly, as he lit his lantern. "Tie us up right here. I'm directly across from the opening!"

"Can you see anything?" Wiggins inquired.

"Not yet, but I'll soon have a report. I'm going in," Roberts announced.

The aperture was just far enough away from the dangling investigator that he had to swing back-and-forth on his harness to reach the edge of the tiny opening. After several efforts, Bobo was able to grab hold of one side of the cave wall and maneuver into the darkness.

"I'm in, Wiggins," he called out. "Give me some slack, while I venture further into the cavern."

Wiggins followed Bobo's request and slowly loosened the rope. He watched each section of the line gradually move to the edge of the cliff and disappear.

A short time later he called down to his partner, "That's all of it, Bobo. There's no more rope for you."

He repeated his message, "Bobo, I said there's no more rope for you. Are you there? Can you hear me?"

Seconds passed that must have seemed like minutes to Wiggins as he waited to hear from his companion. He pondered what could be taking him so long to respond. Had he been injured somehow while entering the cave? Had the rope been cut? He could only wait.

Suddenly, he heard a small branch snap behind him accompanied by a familiar voice, "I can hear you clearly, Wiggins. You needn't bother to raise your voice!"

Turning quickly, Wiggins found his partner standing directly behind him.

"What? Where? How in the world?" Wiggins began his inquisition.

"Wiggins, Wiggins, Wiggins," Roberts spoke, shaking his head. "Think, man. . . how do you think I got here?"

Wiggins slapped himself aside the head, smiling, "So, Bobo, there's another way into the cave."

"Such brilliance. Is it any wonder that I chose you as a business partner?" he joked. "Come, Wiggy. It's right along this huge outcropping. Here's the passageway behind this dense patch of gorse."

They quickly removed the rope, rolling it up and returning it to the carriage they had acquired. Wasting no time, the duo entered the hidden passage, swinging a lantern to and fro. They continued downward, passing the opening through which Bobo had entered the cave. As they moved further along, they were startled by a bright light. Ducking down quickly, they soon realized that it was only light from their own lantern reflecting brightly off a huge stalactite. They once more began to move forward, deeper into the cave. The path continued, spiraling downward along the sides of the sprawling cavern, until they arrived at what appeared to be the cave bottom.

Moving further along, they could hear the waves pounding outside the cave walls, but as they wound deeper and deeper into the cave, those sounds diminished. Still, both men continued to hear the sound of running water. Their imaginings were quickly answered around the next bend, where they encountered an underground spring.

At first, the two detectives appeared somewhat stymied by the small body of water, for there seemed no way to cross without wading through the dark liquid. Upon raising their lanterns, as they glanced across the small pond, they could see where the pathway continued on the other side.

They tested the depth of the wee pond before them, and soon determined that it was much too deep and much too cold for them to wade across to the opposite side.

"Well, Bobo, it looks like we're going to have to get wet if we intend to get to the other side," offered Wiggins.

"What do you mean, we?" Roberts replied. "It's too bloody cold to go for a swim now, isn't it. . ."

Before Wiggins could respond, Bobo turned and was off to a

far corner of the cave, both he and his lantern disappearing behind a cut in the cave wall.

"Where do you think you're going?" questioned Wiggins. "Come back here. We've work to do!"

No sooner had he uttered those words, when Bobo reappeared with his lantern, dragging what looked like a long, wooden beam.

"Here's how you get across," called Roberts, smiling broadly. "You just have to learn to use your noggin, Wiggins."

The two partners carefully stretched the beam across the water and quickly made their way to the other side. Following the winding underground path was treacherous in spots, so they had to be alert. Occasionally, they would stop, look around and listen for any noises. Still, they only heard the sounds of water dropping from the stark cave walls and observed glistening stalactites that seemed to be everywhere.

They continued to follow the pathway along the winding tunnel, sometimes finding openings into larger chambers. Those areas were quickly examined by the detectives before they continued their spelunking.

On and on they walked, wondering where this damp, dark footpath might lead. According to the note Holmes had passed to them earlier, they were to search the Daddyhole cave for any signs of Druid activity. The winter solstice would soon be upon them and that, of necessity, would require a full-blown Druid ceremony. From their recent visit with Terra, the cult leader, they had learned of the event, and had actually agreed to attend the ancient rite. Terra had informed them that Daddyhole Plain was the chosen venue for welcoming the arrival of the winter season.

While they continued their examination of one of the smaller chambers, Wiggins suddenly stopped, doused his lantern, and signaled for Bobo to do the same. Both men quickly jumped behind a large stalagmite, for loud voices could be heard coming through the tunnel. Soon, dancing lights began to bounce along the moist walls as a small group of men made their way past the two investigators who remained perfectly still, safely hidden.

As the troop made their way along the passage, Bobo and Wiggins recognized two of the individuals as members of Terra's cult. In his excitement, Bobo accidentally bumped his lantern which had been sitting nearby. As it tipped, it made a very strange noise; not too loud, but noticeable.

"Did you hear something, Weasel?" one of the clan members voiced.

"What are ye' talking about?" the shorter of the two spoke. "The only thing I've heard for the last several miles, has been the dripping of water and your poor excuse for jokes."

Now, two others joined in, as the shadows from their lanterns danced about on the cave walls.

"Noise, Roachman! You think you heard noise?" they continued. "Why, judging by the terrible odor comin' from your direction, I'd say it was some Roachman bottom gas, if you know what I'm implyin'. . ."

That last remark was too good to ignore, and the small company began to carry on, their echoing laughter bouncing off the walls of the cavern.

"P-e-e-e- yuuuuu," they started, one after another. "Roachman, how were those beans you had earlier. . . har. . .har. . .har..."

Waving his fist at his tormentors, the man identified as Roachman replied with some feigned agitation, "Argh, you're all daft. That was none o' me gas, ya bunch of children. C'mon, then, let's get to the main cavern and make all of the necessary preparations for Terra."

Once more, the procession continued along the winding tunnel, still laughing at the comments that had been made.

Wiggins and Bobo decided to remain where they were until they felt it was safe to renew their exploration. Things were now different, much different.

"So, perhaps the rituals will be conducted in this cave, not on the plain above," Wiggins suggested, continuing, "or the cave might serve as an area for storing the booty they may have uncovered. We'll just have to see what happens."

Bobo shook his head in agreement, adding, "It'll be interesting to hear what Mr. Holmes has to say about these findings."

Starting out again, they found no need of their lantern. For it seemed the passing brigade had lit torches that were placed throughout the tunnel. Bobo and Wiggins wasted no time in heading in the other direction, for now they knew that there had to be another way out of the huge cave, and they were most anxious to find it.

A short time later, they saw a large unlocked door. Evidently, they had entered into what appeared to be some kind of historical archeological dig.

"Well, now," spoke Bobo, "we must have entered Kents Cavern. Just look around, Wiggins. Can you imagine what we're seeing?"

Wiggins just shook his head to the affirmative, then urged his companion to be more quiet, for his comments were still reflecting off the hard walls of the cave.

"Bobo, you're much too loud," Wiggins suggested. "We certainly don't want to be discovered down here!"

"Sorry, Wiggy," Roberts responded, "I'll have no more to say."

The two men proceeded along the dank pathway. According to Bobo's compass, the two were now heading southwest, in the direction of Torre Abbey. For the next twelve minutes the detectives were able to move quickly along the lighted way, accompanied by the damp, musty cave air and the constant noise of dripping stalactites. They soon found themselves behind a large storage shelf, wondering where they were and pondering what their next move might be.

All of a sudden, they heard a creaking noise coming from the top of a stairway that was tucked around an outcropping to their left. Quietly, they backed up against one side of the cave, hoping to avoid notice.

"How soon until the master arrives?" came a shrill, piercing voice from above.

"It won't be long now," a much deeper voice replied, adding, "He's always on time when these services are concerned."

Bobo and Wiggins were able to find a nook behind the storage shelving and dove for cover as the two voices descended the stairs.

"When do ye think the boys will be back, Mrs. Bedlam?" the deeper voice inquired.

"They'll be back when they're finished, Michaels," the Cary housekeeper answered with obvious agitation. "It's not for the likes of you to need to know. Now go on, get on with your work. It's getting late."

After her remarks, Bedlam watched the man disappear around the corner, leading back into the interior of the cave. She shook her head and then headed back up and into the residence, slamming the door behind her.

Wiggins and Bobo could see the man clearly in the light of the gas lights and held their breath hoping to remain undiscovered. After he had passed them, they simultaneously issued sighs of relief, lucky to have escaped detection.

"I say, Wiggins," Bobo whispered, " I believe that that bloke was one of the watchmen at the Druid encampment."

"I thought the same," Wiggins softly responded, raising his finger to his lips."

"Bobo," Wiggins continued, pointing to another passageway that suddenly appeared across the way. "Look, I'll wager that path leads to the Spanish Barn."

Bobo smiled and replied, "Well, what are we waiting for?"

Wiggins shook his head in agreement as both men started for the new tunnel. After a short walk, they soon found themselves at a dead end. According to their estimates, they had to be very close to the Spanish Barn. There had to be some way into the building, but all they could see was an old lamp sconce.

"Wiggins," Bobo inquired with a smile, "Do you think that it's possible that this old candle-holder might be used for another purpose?"

"Let's find out," returned Wiggins, twisting the sconce.

Almost immediately, an opening appeared to their left, and soon they found themselves at the bottom of a roughly-carved set of stairs that led them up and into a huge open area. They had entered the Spanish Barn.

Quickly, they extinguished their lanterns and moved along the dank walls in darkness until they came to one of the exterior doors.

Luckily, they were able to exit, since that door had not been locked. As soon as they were outside, they carefully moved toward the bushes along the side of the old building and ducked behind a small stone wall as a carriage entered the main yard of Torre Abbey.

"I hope they didn't see us," offered Bobo. "I, for one, need to rest a bit after the last several minutes."

"You're so right, Bobo," spoke Wiggins. "I, too, am quite exhausted, but we've much to tell Mr. Holmes. Let's get on our way back to our rooms and record what we've discovered."

Suddenly, Bobo stopped and suggested, "Wiggins, my good man, one of us has got to return the carriage. . . That would be you, Wiggy!"

"What do you mean me?" asked Wiggins. "After all, we both rode to Daddyhole."

"Wiggy, I was the one who was suspended over the crashing waves, my life in peril. I think it only fair that you do your part," Bobo offered as he scampered down Belgrave Road.

Entry to Kents Cavern

Chapter 15 Return to the Cavern

December 22nd

The next day dawned clear and bright, and I was most eager to learn what new adventures lay in store for Holmes and me. Sadly, my thoughts were unceremoniously awakened by my esteemed colleague's original rendition of one of his favorite arias echoing from the front room of our lavish hotel suite.

I had to admit to being somewhat confused, for it was not like Holmes to show any frivolity in the midst of an investigation. It could mean only one thing, a new clue had been found. My curiosity, I must say, got the better of me and I simply had to confront him, "Good morning, Holmes. Pray tell, what startling new piece of information have you uncovered?"

At first he ignored me, continuing to revel in his melodic refrain. Not that that could ever surprise me, having known the man all these many years. In the middle of a key change, he suddenly turned and tossed the morning's paper in my direction.

"Watson," he laughingly remarked, "take a look at the morning headlines in *The Observer*. Can you imagine?"

Retrieving the paper from the floor, I focused on the banner atop the first page. It read, "Ghost of Spanish Lady Returns".

"Go ahead," my partner issued, "read it aloud, slowly. For, as you know, quite often the spoken word can stir additional cranial activity in my noggin."

Looking carefully at the first page banner, I reached for my glasses and began to read the article.

Ghost of Spanish Lady Returns

Residents living near Torre Abbey have once again claimed to have seen the infamous ghost known as "The Spanish Lady". Local seamstress, Lucinda Spenser, described the sighting as "most alarming." The woman was passing near the grounds of the former tithing barn at approximately 9:30 last evening, when she was witness to a bright yellow beam of light flashing through some trees and hemlock bushes.

At first she thought nothing of it, ascribing it to one of the members of the Cary household on the way to the stable area.'The light was a swingin' back and forth,' she said. 'It wasn't the proper way to be carryin' a lantern, so I moved a little closer, out of curiosity, don't you know.'

What greeted her eyes sent the woman screaming away from the parkland setting, finally finding refuge at a local pub, "Davey Jones Inn", on Torbay Road. 'The tavern owner tried to calm me down, but it took a few good swigs afore I could describe what I saw,' the frightened woman stated.

According to Trevor Norgood, proprietor of the pub, 'She was near out of her head with fear! After Mrs. Spenser regained her composure, she gave me a chilling description of what she had witnessed. And I'd have to say that she seemed to be tellin' the truth. She said it was the ghost of the Spanish Lady!'

He elaborated on the woman's account, saying, 'The ghost appeared to be clothed in a long, blackish gown. Wearing a fiendish smile, is how she described the apparition. That gives me the shivers just thinkin' about it. And the moanin'. . . The lady ghost was screechin' and moanin' somethin' awful, Mrs. Spenser confided.'

Other witnesses were also contacted by our senior investigative writer. All of those who had claimed to have seen the spirit were in agreement. Their descriptions of the night's spectral appearance varied not an iota!

While this paper's editorial staff remains unconvinced that we have some kind of unholy visitor from the grave haunting our community, we do recommend continued vigilance, just in case.

When I had finished reading the account, I removed my glasses, holding them to the side of my face and turned to see my companion smiling.

"My word, Holmes," I sputtered, "surely, you don't subscribe to such nonsense. . . do you?"

"Well," he posed, gazing out at the Channel, "what if it were truly some form of ectoplasm reawakening? How exciting it would be for us to happen upon a real ghost!"

"What? What are you saying, Holmes?" I cried aloud. "You, you who have rebuked all forms of spiritualistic reports as utter nonsense... What, have you recanted your previous position?"

"A moment, Watson, old boy," he softened. "I was merely teasing. You know how I feel about such claims. Of course, it's some form of chicanery. That being said, we do need to find out what these witnesses think they may have seen. According to other reports, these sightings are not that uncommon."

"Along with the Demon of Daddyhole... " I chuckled, as I finished lacing my brogans.

"Yes, the town demon also requires our consideration," my friend assented, cradling his chin in his left hand. "We might as well check on that legend, as well. But first thing today, we'll be visiting Kents Cavern and a Mr. Francis Powe."

After another delightful breakfast in the old hotel's main dining room, Holmes and I headed to Kents Cavern to meet with Francis Powe. Powe had been renting the well-known caves from Lord Haldon's estate, using them as a workshop for his business. We had learned that he spent most of his time there constructing small boats, beach huts, and the like for area residents.

At last evening's dinner, Clara Miller had informed us that Mr. Powe had purchased the property only recently, in April of 1903.

When Holmes indicated that he was planning to follow up on Aggie's visit, Clara offered to contact him on our behalf. She was sure that he would be most willing to give Holmes and me a detailed tour of the underground site. As a result of her intercession, this very morning we had received word by courier that the proprietor would be waiting to hear from us.

Upon arriving at the entrance to the caves, we found Powe struggling mightily with a sailboat mast. When he spied our landau coming up the road, he paused, waved, and then gave the long wooden beam one last push, jamming it securely into the housing.

As we stepped down from our carriage, Powe straightened his hat, grabbed a wet towel, and wiped the dirt from his calloused hands.

"Gentlemen, I've been expecting you," he voiced, smiling broadly. "You come highly recommended by Miss Aggie Miller, so you must be fine, trustworthy gents."

"That's high praise, indeed," Holmes replied, tipping his hat to the property owner. "Thank you, Mr. Powe, for agreeing to lead us on a tour through Kents Cavern, especially on such short notice."

"It will be my pleasure, Mr. Holmes," spoke Powe, adding, "and, you sir, must be Dr. John Watson. Welcome, gentlemen. I'm completely at your disposal."

We soon found ourselves inside the subterranean passages, following the same path that early cave-dwellers must have traveled thousands of years ago. My mind wandered as we turned this way and that, using our lanterns to aid our tour. I began to ponder early man's existence, dealing with the day to day challenges of living life in such surroundings. Tribes seeking refuge from the elements or safety from intruders might have used these caves as havens, places of warmth where they might find protection. One could only imagine the type of lives these ancient peoples must have led!

My brief revery was suddenly interrupted by Holmes. "Watson, old man," he inquired, "are you able to keep up with us, or should we rest a bit?"

"What? What are you talking about, Holmes?" I responded.

"Well," he continued, "Mr. Powe and I have been standing here for the past several minutes, waiting for you to come out of whatever trance you seem to have encountered."

Embarrassed by their laughter, I explained my fascination with the historical significance of the location. Holmes shook his head disparagingly, and urged me to catch up with the two of them.

"Around this corner, gents," Powe said, "you'll find the actual archeological digs of Professor William Pengelly."

Upon making the turn we found a locked door, marked with the initials W.P. Excavation site 1865-1884.

"Well, now," Holmes spoke, moving the lantern nearer the carved markings. "It seems as though we have reached a dead end."

"Not at all. Not at all, Mr. Holmes!" our delighted host assured us. "I have the key to the lock. It remains sealed to keep the excavation site secure from any animals or other visitors that might wish to tamper with this treasured piece of our nation's history. Naturally, I am keen to guard the site, especially since I'm the current caretaker."

With that, Powe placed a key into the sturdy lock, and immediately the door to the large chamber opened before us.

As light from our lanterns illuminated the workspace, what first struck our eyes were the precise demarcations of the digs. It looked to have been left much the same as when Pengelly had filed his last report. Anxious to examine the well-defined sectors, we placed our lanterns on three tables, strategically placed in order to provide the necessary light to work in the huge domed area.

"Gentlemen, may I present the most valuable piece of historical property in the United Kingdom," Powe stated with solemn pride.

He continued, "This bit of property had been cordoned off by the official scientists of our government. Only recently have they accorded me the honor and responsibility of guarding this part of the cavern."

Holmes began to examine the perimeter of the large space, careful not to disturb any of the artifacts. He stooped down, moving ever closer to the bones and ancient pieces of pottery that lay scattered all about the well-defined regions. Moving quickly, from one corner of the room to the other, magnifying glass in hand, Holmes was, once again, demonstrating his unique investigative skills. No one could match the man in such endeavors. He next pulled out his notepad and began to quickly scribble a few sentences and some sketches of what appeared to be stalagmite formations.

Powe watched his every move, clearly intrigued by the energy of the world's greatest consulting detective. I, too, always marveled at the way Holmes threw himself into his work.

At this point I had to voice, "Holmes, may I ask what you expect to find that others have not?"

"Ah, Watson," he replied, "that is the point. Is it not? Friend, you know from our many investigations how nothing must be left to chance. Think about what we learned from Aggie last evening."

Powe suddenly interrupted, "Mr. Holmes, may I ask what Miss Aggie had to say about her visit with me? I can assure you that I may be able to shed some additional light on whatever it was she told you and Doctor Watson."

"Please pardon my rudeness, Mr. Powe," the detective continued, "I certainly meant no discourtesy toward you, and if you are willing, I will be happy to impart Miss Miller's report for your consideration."

Powe listened to every word of Aggie's story, as told by my partner. When Holmes had finished, Powe looked pleased.

"She's quite the sleuth, ain't she, Mr. Holmes?" Powe voiced, smiling contentedly.

"And she really said those nice things about me?" the cavern caretaker inquired.

"Yes, she spoke very highly of you, Mr. Powe," I offered as Holmes turned back to his work.

He had now moved to the far end of the room and began tapping gently along the cave wall. Here and there, he placed his ear up against the surface, listening for sounds that might be emanating from deeper inside the cavern. After several minutes, he returned to one of the tables where he had placed his lantern, picked it up and headed back to the entry way.

"Mr. Powe," he spoke deliberately, "Watson and I wish to thank you most sincerely for allowing us to visit this wondrous piece of human history. Sometime in the not-too-distant future I would very much like to return here to make a more detailed examination of these most fascinating historical finds. Of course, it would require your approval."

"Mr. Holmes, Doctor Watson," Powe replied cordially, "it has been my very great pleasure to have met you both, and you are certainly welcome to come and visit the cavern at any time."

After we had reached the cave's main entrance, we bid our friendly host a fond adieu, and, once again, profusely thanked him for his help.

It was a short carriage ride to Babbacombe cliff, alleged scene of most of the Demon of Daddyhole sightings. It was another fine, crisp winter's day, affording the two of us a wonderful view of the waters of the Channel, now teeming with activity. Ships and small skiffs were busily riding the waves, all going on about their own particular missions. A brisk wind, though, chilled one's bones as Holmes and I tied our team to a hitching post near an observation point, a short distance away from the edge of the cliff.

"Well, Holmes," I commented, as we walked along, "that was a most interesting visit with Mr. Powe in his cavern. Tell me, were you able to glean any additional information while you were studying the digs?"

"Watson, dear fellow," Holmes cajoled, "now is not the time to comment on any of today's findings."

"We still have much to do before the entirety of these mysterious doings can be understood," he continued as he turned a corner behind a large outcropping.

I paused to admire the beauty of the overlook wondering why he chose not to disclose any of his recent discoveries. Clearly, he had found something inside Kents Cavern, but, as was his habit, he was still not ready to share his theories with me. That would only occur when they became factually verifiable.

"Watson," he suddenly called. "Come and tell me what you make of this."

I carefully made my way along the well-worn pathway, moving slowly, for one slip would have me on the rugged, rocky shoreline below. As I turned the last corner, Holmes was nowhere to be found!

I quickly knelt down on all fours, hoping that my friend hadn't fallen over the edge of the precipice, and crawled out to the very end of the overlook. Peering down, I scanned the shoreline as the waves crashed menacingly over the rocks below.

"Holmes," I cried aloud, "Holmes, where are you?"

There was no response. All that I heard were the squeaking sounds of the terns and gulls accompanying the tidal surges along the coastline below.

"Watson," a familiar voice comforted my fears, "get up off the ground and get over here."

Quickly, I regained my footing, but still there was no sign of my partner.

"Where are you?" I called. "Confound it, man, I hear you but I cannot see you!"

Before I could issue another comment, a large patch of gorse began to shake, exposing a very disheveled Sherlock Holmes.

"Look at you, Holmes," I laughed, "it looks as though you've been roughed up by a bear. . . What has happened to you?"

"Never mind my appearance, Watson," he continued, pointing to a fissure in the rock face. "Look what I've uncovered! It's the opening to the Daddyhole cave that Wiggins found, and it's exactly where he said it would be in the note I received earlier. It's hard to believe how well it is concealed by the vegetation!"

I promptly followed him into the opening of what appeared to be another cave. The only light available to us was the daylight which filtered through the sharp thorns of the gorse covering the entrance to this hollowed out area.

"Watson, if you would be so kind, please go back to the carriage for a lantern," Holmes requested.

I quickly returned to the opening and we proceeded down a very precarious pathway, deeper and deeper into the interior of the Babbacombe cliff wall. Light from our lantern flickered brightly, casting bizarre shadows along the sides of the cavern walls on our perilous descent. Down and down we went, finally reaching a huge hollowed out dome, framed by tons of rock above the cave floor.

"Ah, this looks familiar," he whispered.

We stood there quietly observing the magnificent stalactites that seemed to be hanging everywhere in that immense open space. Holmes was about to speak when we heard footsteps which seemed to be coming our way. The sounds were accompanied by reflected light. Spying a rocky outcrop, we extinguished our lamp and hopped behind a large boulder with seconds to spare!

"Here's the other way out," came the voice of a tall man pointing to the worn pathway that led upwards and out of the cave.

"When we've finalized our work, we shall exit here," he continued, a broad smile showing his pleasure at the thought.

"But, Terra," one of his followers implored, "What will we do with the evidence, if you know what I mean?"

"Evidence," Terra thundered angrily, "if you don't have the stomach for it, I'll have to find another to take your place. Do you understand, Brother Roachman?"

At that remark, the fellow known as Roachman, knelt before his leader and recanted, "Please, Terra, forgive my insolence. Of course, I'll do the job. Haven't I always done your bidding? You know that you can always count on me."

In response, Terra issued a bone-chilling, "That's what had better happen. . . or else. . . "

There was absolute silence after that icy altercation, and soon thereafter, the band disappeared, turning back on the same pathway from which they came.

Holmes and I waited for the light from their lanterns to disappear. Clearly, Terra was involved in something very, very evil, for we could easily see how fearful his followers were of him.

Before I could voice my own feelings on what we had just witnessed, Holmes whispered, "Well, Watson, we've now identified a major player in this convoluted mystery. Perhaps we should follow them and see if this tunnel connects to Kents Cavern or any other subterranean byway."

"Holmes," I voiced, "I forgot to tell you about the terrible dream I had only recently."

"A dream, a dream you say?" his voice sounded most dismissive. "I hardly think I need to hear another one of your inane nightmares, Watson. My good fellow, we've no time for such nonsense!"

Angrily, I grabbed him by the shoulder, scolding, "Listen, you, you consulting detective. This dream concerns our investigation and you must let me get it off my chest."

"Easy, there, Watson," he softened. "If you feel it that important, please tell me now so that I may reflect upon all that you may have experienced."

For the next several minutes, I related the horrible tale, sparing no detail, as was his request. For his part, he seemed to be listening, but I only heard an occasional "Ah. . . Is that so?"

I concluded my recollection, issuing, "Holmes, this huge cavern in which we find ourselves is very much like the one in my dream. I truly believe that my dream has some connection to this case! Of course, I don't know how it could, but I feel it. I feel it deep inside of me."

There was no immediate response from my companion, and we went back to trailing Terra and his men along the underground pathway. One could easily hear them plodding along ahead of us, and we took special care approaching every twist and turn, every nook and cranny. It would not do, if we were discovered following this cult leader and his flock, particularly in this dank, secluded locale.

Holmes began to slow his pace and suddenly stopped in his tracks! Holding his finger to his lips, he signaled me to follow his lead. We quickly dropped down out of sight behind a huge stalagmite to our left and remained motionless.

"Did you hear that?" he questioned.

I had to reply, barely whispering, "No, Holmes. I can only just make out the sounds of the group that we have been recently tracking."

"There," he continued, raising his finger to his lips, suggesting that I keep quiet. "There, now, there it is again!"

After a short pause, Holmes slowly made his way to the other side of the wall, issuing, "Miss Miller, would you be so kind as to come out from behind that wall and join us, please?"

Before I could voice my surprise, a very timid, embarrassed, young Aggie Miller sheepishly rose from her hiding place and tip-toed her way to our side of the path.

Our young friend was about to say something, but Holmes raised his hand, whispering, "Tut, tut, Miss Miller, I won't ask you to explain your presence at this time, due to our dangerous position. Just follow along quietly and we may yet escape the awkward predicament in which we now find ourselves."

Aggie merely shook her head, looking down at her feet. I knew that she realized her mistake, but now was not the time to chastise her. Our primary concern had now become her safety as well as our own, and that necessitated retracing our steps back up the winding path to the cave entrance atop Daddyhole Plain.

Before we could stop her, she whispered, "Gentlemen, where are you taking me?"

"You, young miss, are leaving this cave, and the sooner the better. We are all imperiled by your lack of judgment," scolded the world famous sleuth.

Aggie slumped her shoulders, obviously validating Holmes's livid retort. She obediently followed us as we stepped gingerly along, when suddenly, she regained her composure and voiced, "I know that I was wrong, but let us at least take the short way out of here..."

"What? What are you saying, young lady?" Holmes angrily responded. "Do you know of another means of egress?"

Aggie now began to strut away from us, disappearing around a corner that we had somehow missed in our earlier explorations.

"Here it is, gentlemen," the young detective-assistant announced, pointing to a tiny gap hidden in the shadowy darkness.

"Once through this fissure, the path widens and it will take us directly into Kents Cavern," she politely offered.

I looked at Holmes but he could only shrug his shoulders and whisper, "Come Watson, Miss Miller has, perhaps, given us a better option."

We followed the young girl through the tiny aperture and with the help of our lantern, found our way through another hidden passageway that took us into a remote corner in one of the many chambers in Kents Cavern. Once there, Holmes raised his light to better illuminate that space. He scratched his head, voicing quietly, "I don't know how I could have missed this opening."

Aggie paused, reaching up and loosening a large, dark greyish-black drape which was fastened to a hidden beam positioned above her head, "Perhaps this might be the reason, Mr. Holmes."

She quickly placed one end of the curtain-like material on one stalagmite and stretched it across the opening to another stalagmite, virtually making the cave opening invisible to all but the sharpest eyes.

"Wonderful work, Aggie," I chimed. "What say you, Holmes?"

Ignoring my remark, my friend quickly signaled us to follow, whispering, "Not now, Watson, we must quickly leave this cave before we are discovered."

Several minutes later, we found ourselves emerging through the main entrance of the underground cavern into the fading sunlight.

Luck was with us, for the property owner, Powe, must have left for home. We could only hope that we had not been seen.

After returning to Daddyhole Plain to get our carriage, we headed back to Ashfield. The silence was deafening, for Holmes knew he had to chastise our young detective, but he didn't want to hurt her feelings. After all, he was the one who had decided to bring her into our confidence.

While the horses clip-clopped their way along Babbacombe Road, he delicately began to preach, "Miss Aggie, I first want you to know that I understand how naturally curious you are. That is part and parcel of your personality, and that is all well and good. I also must compliment you on your clever ways. It was very good work to have found that hidden passage. However, be that as it may. . . "

After a brief pause, before he could continue, the young girl whimpered, "Please don't scold me, sirs. I'm so very sorry, Mr. Holmes and Doctor Watson. I'm ashamed of my behavior. I know Mum will be extremely cross with me when she learns of my actions. I sincerely hope that you can forgive me, for I know that I could have jeopardized elements of your investigation by my carelessness."

"Miss Miller," Holmes responded firmly, "while it is true that you had only the best of intentions, you were clearly in the wrong. Heaven only knows the kind of danger in which you could have placed yourself! Think of what might have happened. How could you not think of your Mother? How could we ever forgive ourselves if something had happened to you?"

Aggie bowed her head. She had once more crossed the line.

She had disobeyed her superiors, again. There was nothing more to be said, so she just sat there until we had pulled our carriage up to her house.

As the young girl started for her front door, Holmes called to her, "Aggie, your mother need not learn about your day's adventures unless you wish to tell her. But, Miss Miller, I do not want to find you interfering any further. Is that clear?"

"Yes, Mr. Holmes," she whimpered, disappearing through the front door of her home as our carriage headed back to our lodgings.

In no time at all, we were back in our comfortable hotel suite, savoring the soothing effects of a warming toddy. Holmes was still busy organizing notes he had made earlier in the week. For my part, I was much too fatigued to pay attention to the occasional mumbled whispered outbursts that often accompanied his subconscious analysis of information gleaned over the past several days.

It had been a most tiring morning and, like most people, I was content to merely close my eyes hoping to restore my strength, which I might add, had been truly sapped. Not my friend, however. When he was totally engaged, sleep was anathema to his methods. A good night's rest was a waste of time in his logical mind, for Holmes believed that seconds lost could result in tragic consequences.

"Confound it," he sputtered, brusquely filing his papers back into his briefcase.

Shaking his head back and forth, he walked past the bureau and pulling back a curtain, peered out over the rocky coastline below. After pausing there for a brief time, he struck a match to his briar. Slowly, he shuffled over to an armchair near the glowing fireplace and took his seat. He seemed deep in thought as he sat there. The furrowed brows and voluminous puffs of smoke indicated a serious problem had arisen; one that was obviously most troubling.

I sensed his frustration and, normally, I'd avoid striking up any conversations while he languished in this malaise.

This time, though, I felt compelled to ask, "Holmes, might there be any way that I could be of assistance?"

At my request, he smiled and mildly chided, "Good friend, I appreciate your kind offer, but now is not the time."

Well, I had made the offer and it had been declined. Perhaps it was just as well, for I was beginning to feel very weak. That was it, I needed nourishment! I realized that it was nearing midday and I was famished.

" I say, Holmes, how does a brief afternoon meal sound to you?" I inquired.

My questioned went unanswered, and while waiting for his response, suddenly a cadenced series of raps came from outside of the door to our suite.

"Whom do you suppose that might be?" I asked my colleague.

While reaching for the knob I was startled to observe Holmes, pistol in hand, standing near one of the hotel room dressers. Holding his hand over his mouth, he signaled for me to remain where I was. Momentarily stunned, I did as I was told. While we waited anxiously, there came a low whistle from the hallway beyond.

Much to my surprise, Holmes lowered his weapon, and opened the door voicing, "It's all right, Watson. It's only Wiggins and Mr.

Roberts come to call."

The two men quickly entered the room offering, "Good day, Mr. Holmes and Doctor Watson. We thought you would want to learn of our most recent findings as soon as possible."

"Indeed we do, gentlemen," Holmes replied, suggesting, "please take a seat" as he pointed to the hotel room chairs.

Turning to me he ordered, "Watson, call down for some lunch for us. There's a good man."

Several minutes later found our group enjoying some delicious luncheon items.

Between bites, Roberts and Wiggins took turns explaining their latest discoveries.

"I'm glad you had a chance to examine our cave findings, gentlemen, but we have more information to share with you," Roberts remarked. "Please continue, Wiggins."

Wiggins began, "Mr. Holmes, Bobo and I did find several interesting bits of information about several of those individuals that you wanted us to investigate."

"Well," implored Holmes, rubbing his hands together with much excitement, "come on, lads, let's hear it!"

Wiggins smiled as he continued, "As you have learned from our earlier report, Mr. Holmes, when we first arrived in Torquay, we spent several days acquainting ourselves with the businesses, buildings, streets, some of the citizenry, etc. By sheer luck, we happened to be present at a town gathering that was to become terribly disruptive.

We learned that many of the town residents were naturally upset when it was reported that yet another council member had been killed. There was much turmoil and agitation at the news, with many of the citizens ready to riot over the lack of results in the police investigations. No one had yet been charged for any of the murders that had occurred over the last several months, and the community was rightfully concerned.

Bobo and I quietly observed the actions of the group, and noticed that it had begun to act very much like a hostile mob, growing in size and fervor. Both of us believed that were it not for the intervention of a local minister, there could have been a great deal of trouble. This man, Vicar David Prentiss, made his way to the top of the steps of the town hall, waving his arms wildly. He immediately called upon the boisterous crowd, demanding proper civility. After some calming words, he bade the residents go home and care for their loved ones. He tried to allay their rising fears, insisting that the proper authorities were doing their very best, and would continue to do so until justice was done.

Well, while Bobo and I listened to him address his fellow citizens, we were intrigued by his calm demeanor. We could sense that there was something about him, I don't know exactly what, but he seemed to possess some type of special charisma, I suppose you might call it. His words to the angry gathering had a remarkably soothing effect upon them. When he had finished, the group disbanded and quietly returned to their homes and workplaces, just as he had requested. Although there were still some individuals mumbling their dissatisfaction, most seemed much more subdued.

At any rate, Bobo and I decided to call upon the good Vicar and looked for an opportunity to do so. Initially, we lost sight of him but as the crowd thinned we were able to catch him as he neared his manse.

After introducing ourselves, we requested to speak to him. He seemed a bit timorous at first, but welcomed us into the simple dwelling, just the same.

We began our conversation identifying ourselves as tourists from London, here to enjoy the Christmas season in historic Torquay. We further remarked that it must have been Providence that placed us here to witness his address to the frenzied gathering. We articulated our need to compliment him for his extraordinary efforts in quelling a most dangerous situation.

He seemed to relax a bit after our praise, but he again pressed us as to why we felt the need to talk to him. Bobo restated how touched we were with his remarks, once more stressing how impressed we were at the calming effect they had had on the townsfolk. After Bobo had finished, Vicar Prentiss softened even more. For, as you might have surmised, the more we complimented the cleric's impassioned speech, the more comfortable he became in our company.

After several more minutes of pleasant conversation, the Vicar thanked us for our kind words, promising that he would continue to speak up whenever he could help maintain order in his community. He then apparently felt the need to provide us with another sermon emphasizing the importance of all the town residents to change their evil ways. 'Only then,' he concluded, 'would the murders stop.'

We thanked him for his time, explaining that we would soon be returning home to spend New Year's Day with our loved ones. And that was that!"

"That is, until we ran into the Vicar again, yesterday afternoon," interjected Bobo.

"Go on, my good man," Holmes pleaded. "Pray tell us what else you have uncovered."

Bobo smiled, then began again. "Of course, both Wiggins and I were keen to learn more about the man since his was the first name on that list you gave us the other day."

As Wiggins swished a sip of tea, he motioned Bobo to continue talking.

"Well, gentlemen," the tiny investigator spoke in a most calculating, ponderous manner, "Wiggins and I were on our way to an early dinner when we spied himself walking very quickly down Torbay Road. Upon seeing us, he politely doffed his cap and proceeded on his way, but it seemed to us that he had suddenly increased his pace.

Naturally, we had planned to follow him, perhaps to get another interview, but to do so, we would have to walk much faster. We were closing fast, calling out to him, but upon arriving home, he unlatched the door and quickly disappeared, pretending not to have heard us.

I reached out for Wiggins and directed him quietly down an adjacent street. When we were out of sight of the Vicar's dwelling, we discussed our next move. Should we simply knock on his door and try to start up another conversation? Surely, he might find that to be highly suspicious. Then, we thought about stealthily sneaking up along the exterior walls of the house and try to sneak a peek through the windows. Maybe we could gather some information in that way. But, how much information could be gained from so great a distance?

After a short discussion, we agreed that the best form of action would be to walk directly up to his front door, ask to see him and, if he were agreeable, discuss what he thought about the murders. And that is exactly what we did.

Prentiss, while acting civilly toward us, seemed extremely anxious. He offered to brew some tea, but we told him we didn't want to trouble him. We said that we were curious about what he thought of the most recent murder.

'Have you learned any more about the last murder victim, a Mr. Fenwick, I believe?' Wiggins offered.

Prentiss scowled and remarked, 'Yes, another poor soul has been taken from our community, and another member of the town council.'

'Gentlemen, I'm afraid that I have no answer, but surely there must be some connection, all of the victims members of our local governing body,' the religious leader stated sadly.

The Vicar continued, 'For some reason, our constabulary continues to move very slowly with these investigations. Why that should be, I cannot surmise.'

'What about the Druids?' I questioned. 'Though we've only been here for a few days, we've overheard many people mention their names as possible suspects.'

The Vicar shrugged his shoulders, issuing, 'You know, gentlemen, I have not had the time nor inclination to meet their leader, Terra, I believe that is how he is addressed. Why I wouldn't recognize him if I tripped over him. I don't know what else to say about these crimes. I certainly have no knowledge as to who would want to kill those gentlemen.'

It was obvious at that remark that Prentiss did not want to say any more, so we slowly rose from our places and thanked him for his time. He courteously walked us out to the hallway, and wished us well.

Then, before we were out the door, Wiggins, here, stopped suddenly, raised his hand, turned and faced the minister and said, 'Thank you again for your time, Vicar Prentiss, you have been most kind indulging our curiosity and we do appreciate it.'

Prentiss bowed his approval in a seemingly embarrassing manner.

Suddenly, something seemed to jog Wiggins's mind and he called back, 'Oh, Vicar, I was just wondering where you might have attended seminary? If you don't mind my asking. Judging by the way you handled Torquay's rebellious town folk, I'm sure you must have attended one of England's finest institutions. Might I inquire where you received your ordination?'

The question seemed to have caught the man completely off guard, for he paused, thought about it for a moment and mumbled something to the effect that he had received a wonderful religious education! And with that, the door was closed and we left the Reverend David Prentiss."

I looked at Holmes, waiting for some kind of remark, but he seemed totally preoccupied, tapping the ash from his pipe.

"Hmmm... Mr. Bob-o," I spoke, adding a suggestive remark, "If Holmes and I had had that same experience, we would most certainly have followed up on the Vicar's deliberate evasiveness! Gentlemen, we would have searched until we had located the seminary."

Mr. Roberts gave me a strange look, "Dr. Watson, that is exactly what Wiggins and I did... And, please try to remember, it's Bo-bo, not Bob-o..."

Realizing that I had mispronounced his name yet again, I apologized. "Mr. Bo-Bo, I'm very sorry. I just can't seem to remember how to say your name."

Wiggins smiled at my remark and took over, relating, "Gentlemen, there's more. After checking with all of the seminaries in England, nowhere, nowhere did the name David Prentiss appear!"

Holmes smiled, "You might have suspected as much, for our Vicar Prentiss could have chosen to use an alias!"

"Hmm, an alias, Holmes?" I queried.

"Yes, Watson," he added to his previous remark, "Vicar Prentiss may have been ordained using another surname, or for that matter, not at all. He may merely be posing as a minister."

Then Holmes turned back to Bobo and Wiggins, "Tell me, what else have you to report."

Bobo suddenly became very animated, and after hopping up on a hotel wing chair, opened a valise he had earlier placed on a table. Lifting it high above his head, he smiled and bid us to pay close attention.

"What else, gentlemen? Why we've quite a bit more for you to consider," Roberts teased, shaking the case.

"Gentlemen, Wiggins and I left the town square after talking with the Vicar and promptly took our landau to the site of the most recent murder, deciding to delay our evening repast. When we arrived at the scene, there were still a few curious onlookers standing around along with some police presence, all waiting for Chief Inspector Davis to make his entrance.

After his carriage arrived, he signaled for us to join him. We quickly followed him to a sectored off plot along Babbacombe Road where poor Dennison's body had been found. Davis seemed pleased to see us, whereupon we were informed that the poor man had been strangled. The type of device used by the murderer had yet to be identified, but Davis believed it to have been a laqueus used by the Romans who invaded England. Davis had seen a similar implement while searching through a list of ceremonial items used by Druid priests. He had learned that it was a tool used to strangle small animals as sacrificial offerings to Mother Earth.

Wiggins was curious as to why the lawman was proceeding along those lines, and Davis responded rather pointedly, 'Why Mr. Wiggins, the first two atrocities were performed following ancient Druid ritualistic procedures. I thought it would be valuable to delve deeper into their culture!'

By the look on our faces, the Chief Inspector knew we were somewhat confused by his remark.

Smiling sheepishly, he elaborated, 'Obviously, the clues are simple enough to understand, are they not? Terra and his followers must be behind all of these murders. Surely, you must come to the same conclusion. . .'

Wiggins and I shook our heads to the affirmative, pretending to agree with his findings, but Davis was looking for some comment from us, any comment.

'Well, gentlemen?' he asked.

'Why, yes, certainly seems that way, doesn't it, Wiggins?' I urged, nudging my friend.

Wiggins seemed confused by my response, but caught my drift

and offered, 'Of course, Mr. Roberts. Chief Inspector Davis appears to have enough information to make an arrest.'

Davis smiled proudly, issuing, 'Well, kind of you to say, gentlemen, but I'm not quite ready to issue a warrant. There are a few more details I need to investigate.'

And the lawman quickly bid us adieu, hopped back into this carriage, and left the scene to his fellow officers."

Holmes sat quietly for several minutes while Wiggins and Bobo looked anxiously for his response to their findings.
I, too, was most interested in what my friend might have to say, but he remained quietly smoking for several more minutes.

Finally, the silence was broken when Holmes remarked, "Gentlemen, well done. However, there are still so many questions left unanswered. We have come a long way in our investigation, but there is still much to discover and it will be increasingly more difficult to proceed as we have done in the past. It has become readily apparent that our foes are watching our every move."

"Yes, Mr. Holmes," Wiggins agreed. "Ever since our fiasco at the pub and our visit to the Druid encampment, Bobo and I have seen many of the same characters shadowing our every move."

"I'd like to have a go with them, Mr. Holmes, if you thought it might help," offered Mr. Roberts.

Trying to conceal his smile, Holmes quickly responded, "No, No, Bobo. Now's not the time to tip our hand. It'll be better for us if they think we don't know they're being seen."

"Besides, you and Wiggins have all of the necessary skills to disappear if necessary," Holmes suggested.

Both gentlemen smiled proudly at the comment with Bobo concurring, "Yes, of course we do, Mr. Holmes. I get your meaning, sir. . ."

"Tell me, Wiggins and Bobo, do you believe that it is an open-and-shut case against this Terra fellow, or have you other suspects in mind? I would like to hear what you have to say."

Wiggins started to respond to the question, when Holmes suddenly rose from his chair and shrieked, "Egad, what time is it?"

Glancing at his timepiece he voiced, "Fool that I've become, quickly, we must get to Daddyhole. It's the solstice, the day of the Druid gathering."

Chapter 16 Too Late

Our trip along Babbacombe Road to Daddyhole seemed to take forever and, to add to our mental discomfort, the carriage rocked and rumbled the entire way from our hotel to the clifftop overlooking the English Channel. It was almost 1:15 PM, and the ceremony had been scheduled to begin promptly at 12:03 PM, the beginning of the winter solstice.

Holmes continued to chide himself for his loss of focus, and he spent the entire trip mumbling and shaking his head.

"Gentlemen, I'm afraid that I'm losing whatever skills I believed that I once had. All morning I've been planning to attend this ceremony," he moaned, "and now I'm afraid that we may have missed it entirely!"

"Don't worry, Holmes," I spoke in an effort to encourage him, "they may still be celebrating. From what I've heard, they carry on for hours!"

"I've heard the same thing, Doctor Watson," Wiggins agreed.

"Yes," Bobo added with a smile on his countenance, "I'm quite anxious to see what they'll be doing.

Sure enough, as we pulled our conveyance up to the broad expanse, we could see the revelers dancing all about the clifftop, singing and waving banners, holding sticks and bowing toward the sun. A huge fire had been lit and the tribal members, each in turn, approached the burning branches and tossed small packets of incense into the flames. Musicians playing lutes and rhythmical drums accompanied their strange singing and dancing, and clearly, much wine had been consumed by members of this Druid community.

"Well, what have we here?" Wiggins observed. "It looks like we may have made it in time, Mr. Holmes, adding, might I inquire what you expect to find here?"

Holmes jumped out of the carriage, tied the team to a nearby post and signaled us to follow him as he disappeared behind a tall thicket. Quickly, he pulled out a small telescope and began to examine the noisy gathering.

Wiggins, Roberts, and I could only watch and wait to see what Holmes would do next.

"Gentlemen," he offered, "I think we should split our resources and move along and through these celebrants in an effort to locate their leader, Terra. He should be wearing the traditional deer antler headdress which is symbolic of the sect's chief."

"If you are able to locate him, try to follow, but whatever you do, don't let him see that he is being watched," continued the world's foremost consulting detective. "If he sees that he is being observed we may never be able to bring him to justice."

Bobo queried, "Mr. Holmes, with all due respect, I have to ask, what would you have us do when we've located this man? Should we seize him and hold him until the constables can charge him? As to that, what crimes has he, in fact, actually committed?"

In response, Holmes merely stated, "Mr. Roberts, at this point it is only a case of circumstantial evidence that could lead to his arrest.

Chief Inspector Davis confided that he was going to arrest Terra at this very event, but I convinced him that he didn't have enough evidence to prosecute the man."

"So, to repeat Bobo's question," Wiggins interjected, "What should we do, besides locate the man?"

"Watson," Holmes offered, "would you tell these gentlemen what we're going to do next?"

At that remark, I was momentarily flabbergasted, lost for any response to my friend's directive to me. I bowed my head and turned away for a brief moment, trying to imagine why he had put me in such a position. I could feel pressure building up within me as I searched for what I might do next. Just when I was about to embarrass myself, the answer came to me. I realized what he wanted me to say, and I happily related what next we needed to do.

"Why, gentlemen," I replied, "it will be our place to try to catch this fellow, Terra, in the act of committing a crime. At that moment, we will have become witnesses to the law-breaking, and any arrest after that would result in successful prosecution of the perpetrator."

I quickly looked in Holmes's direction and found his smile to be one of complete approbation.

"Watson, old man, that is exactly what we need to do. Bravo!" he offered. "Now let's get to it!"

Following my friend's earlier directive, Wiggins and Roberts walked through one section of the large gathering, trying to blend in as best they could amidst the joyous crowd. After watching them weave into the mob, Holmes led me slowly over to the edge of the cliff and together we disappeared down the path through the thicket leading to the cavern below the plain of Daddyhole.

"Holmes," I whispered as he lit the small lantern he had hidden behind one of the boulders near the opening, "shouldn't we be searching for Terra with Bob-O and Wiggins?"

"We are, Watson," he responded. "It's my belief that we will find them down here, gathering the Roman coins that they've been able to discover and preparing them for removal."

"Do you remember when you and I visited Kents Cavern and I began to gather information?" he inquired as we made our way downward to the floor of the cave.

"Why, certainly, Holmes," I replied. "I remember the look on poor Mr. Powe's face as you speedily moved from one area of the digs to another, jotting down information and drawing sketches of the surrounds. Why do you ask?"

"Well," he went on, "I never did get around to showing you what my findings indicated, and I believe they have a major bearing on our investigations."

"You see, Watson," he continued, raising the lantern over his sketches, "if you look closely on the side of that huge stalagmite, I've depicted there, preserved by a glaze of dripping limestone, you will see what appear to be scratches."

"What do you mean scratches?" I asked as I tried to make out his drawing.

"Well, upon examining those markings more closely, I found that they were not mere imperfections but rather words, carved by a knife," he whispered solemnly. "And, Watson, the words were written in

Latin. . ."

"What? Latin you say?" I spoke with genuine curiosity. "Well, what did they say?"

Holmes began, "Invenietis enim thesaurus vester est. Protegentur ab unguibus quae imminent."

I just stood there, staring at my friend, very much agitated by his response.

Holmes I slowly mouthed, "Latin? Latin? Do you seriously believe that I have complete mastery of one of the dead languages of antiquity? Pray translate, if you would be so kind."

His expression quickly changed and he offered, "Oh, of course, my good fellow. That was rather presumptuous of me. Why, I most assuredly meant you no insult."

"The message would translate to, 'You will find your treasure here, protected by claws which threaten."

By the look on my face, he knew he had to explain further.

"Watson," he continued, "I believe that those words were instructions to locate the Roman coins left by the Druids who had been colonized by the armies of Roman emperor Vespasian or perhaps, Hadrian's Legions!"

"Don't you see, Watson," he implored, "Terra and his Druid followers must have found references to a treasure of golden Roman coins that were secretly stored in the coastal caves near modern day Torquay."

I had to admit it made perfect sense, and replied, "Ah, yes, I see. But do you believe that this treasure remains buried in the caves or do you suspect that it has already been removed?"

"That is what we have to determine, my good man," he concluded.

We had barely finished our conversation when we began to hear footsteps coming closer and closer to our location. Thankfully, we spied another alcove and speedily sought refuge there. Once positioned, we saw reflected lights bouncing off the sides of the moist cave walls as a band of men made their way into the spacious domed cavity.

Holmes and I quietly observed the group, wondering what would happen next. I had no idea what Holmes and I would do should we be discovered, for we were greatly outnumbered. It was true that we had both brought our revolvers, but that gave me no real comfort.

Just as I was coming to terms with our perilous situation, a deep voice called from the depths of the cave, "Mr. Holmes, Dr. Watson, you can come out now. We saw you enter the passageway and we know that you are here."

Holmes grabbed my arm and whispered, "They're bluffing, Watson. Don't make a sound."

Time seemed to stand still while the tall Druid leader began to walk about the perimeter of the cave. As he moved from one alcove to another, he continued to speak, "Come out, Holmes. You know that you are outnumbered. There is no way out... You are only delaying the inevitable..."

A chill ran down my spine for I knew that there was no escape for us.

Holmes broke our silence as we moved toward our adversary, issuing, "Terra, tell your men to fall back for as you can see Doctor Watson and I have our revolvers trained on your head. Let me further assure you that we are quite prepared to send you to the hereafter."

"Ah, there you are, gentlemen," the Druid chieftain calmly spoke. "We appear to be at an impasse, as it were."

"I see no impasse, Terra," stated my companion. "We will be placing you under arrest and your days of pillaging and looting will soon be over."

Holmes's remark, incredibly, was met by group laughter.

"Mr. Holmes," our opponent slowly pointed to the cave passageway, "Look what we found on our travels!"

With that comment, we saw a shrouded figure being led into our midst and positioned next to the Druid leader.

"Oh, no, Watson," my friend whispered, "I now fear the worst."

As Holmes was finishing his confidential remark, Terra quickly removed the cloak. There, bound and gagged, shivering in the dank surroundings, was a young and terrified Aggie Miller. . .

Several seconds passed and Holmes and I lowered our weapons as Terra strutted around the young detective.

"Impasse Mr. Holmes? I think not!" the leader of the cult voiced.

At this point, the young girl began to shake nervously and when she saw Holmes and me being bound and gagged, she burst into tears. Before we three were led away, another figure appeared at the passage entrance. A wicked smile on her face signaled the presence of the evil Lucretia Bedlam, and she quickly made her way to her co-conspirator.

"Well, we've captured the meddlers, Terra," the evil Bedlam issued, shaking her head in apparent dismay.

"Yes, Bedlam," sneered the Druid leader. "It would seem that the great Holmes-Watson team has underestimated their opposition this time."

"Ha! They snooped and snooped and succeeded in making our jobs most difficult, but we will have the last laugh when all is said and done," Bedlam announced.

"What to do. . . What to do?" a pompous Terra pondered, placing his open palm on his pronounced chin. "You have presented us with quite the dilemma! Had you minded your own business, it may never have come to this moment."

"Take them to the storage room," he boomed. "We'll tend to them after we've removed the Spanish doubloons and Roman booty."

After being led through one of the side alcoves of the huge cavern, we soon found ourselves hanging by our outstretched arms, tied to a beam spanning a narrow section of the storage room. It was most painful and I cursed the villains who would think of doing such a thing to a mere child. Clearly, Aggie Miller, no matter how brave, was in great discomfort.

The small room was located behind a sturdy door which had been securely fastened from without. We still had our mouths gagged, barely able to breathe, let alone talk. I was convinced that we would soon learn our fate with these killers. After all, they apparently had no qualms about killing four councilmen!

Suddenly, Holmes opened his mouth and expelled the nuisance silencer, having long ago mastered a technique which would free him from that type of vocal confinement.

"Miss Miller, Doctor Watson," he whispered. "Don't worry. . .

we'll soon be up and out of this mess!"

Holmes's encouraging words sounded good to me, but I couldn't imagine how we could ever escape from this situation.

Seconds later, I heard a loud, unworldly snapping sound followed by a rather ominous stifled groan and found that my partner had somehow wrested one arm from the beam. With the agility of a Sumatran orangutan, Holmes swung his body up and atop the beam, quickly freeing his other arm. In no time at all he had freed both Aggie and me. Next, he began to tiptoe closer to the door that kept us from freedom.

"Thank you, Mr. Holmes," a very weepy and exhausted Aggie Miller whispered to my friend. "I'll not attempt to tell you how I got myself into this fix. Sadly, I believe it to be genetics!"

As angry as he was, I thought I observed a little smile at the corners of his mouth, but he had to chastise the young girl, "We don't need to know how or why you're here, young girl, at least at this moment. What we need to do is get out of here safely!"

After he had spoken, I noticed that his left arm was hanging unnaturally by his side,

"Holmes," I whispered, "that arm appears dislocated!"

"Brilliant, Watson," he replied hastily, and before I could reach over to him, he grabbed the injured limb and quickly snapped it back into place.

"Oh, my," I offered nervously, shaken by what I had just witnessed, "can I do something to help?"

Of course, there was nothing left to be done without proper tools and medications.

"I'll be fine," he voiced, "I've had to do that 'trick' before and I'll be fine in a few days."

That having been said, Holmes pulled a matchstick from his vest pocket and used its light to peer out through the keyhole.

"Excellent," he voiced as he unraveled a folded copy of one of his sketches and carefully slid it under the bottom of the cell door. "We are in luck, the key is still in the lock!

"Watson," he offered, "If you would, please hand me that slender piece of chopped firewood. Mind the slivers, old man."

I did as he suggested and passed the tiny shoot into his waiting palm.

Aggie, sensing what he was about to do, voiced, "Oh, I see what you're doing. It's simply marvelous, Mr. Holmes!"

Without bothering to reply, Holmes pushed the stick into the keyhole and listened as the key dropped outside the door. landing on the paper he had placed there.

The soft "kerplink" indicated that the key had dropped, and immediately, our means of escape was now in the hands of Sherlock Holmes.

There was no time to spend on checking the whereabouts of the cult members so the three of us simply burst through the door, unaware of the guard who had just then returned to the doorway.

The impact was powerful enough to knock the man senseless and we watched him as he collapsed to the ground. Holmes and I quickly threw the man into the cell and locked the door. Immediately afterward, we hurried along the narrow corridor and through Aggie's shortcut into Kents Cavern before finally slowing down.

As we tried to catch our breaths, I wondered what our next step would be. I didn't have long to wait for my thought to be answered.

"Aggie, we're going to find Mr. Powe and have him take you home immediately," Holmes slowly dictated his wishes to young Miss Miller.

She said nothing, but shook her head to the affirmative as we started for the workshop of the owner of Kents Cavern.

As our group left the cave interior and moved into the afternoon sunshine, Francis Powe almost keeled over as he watched us emerge from the darkness.

"What in the world? How in the world? Why? Why?" the stunned carpenter issued.

"Mr. Powe, we haven't enough time to explain right now, but we would appreciate it if you could be kind enough to accompany Miss Miller back home as soon as possible," Holmes suggested to the still flustered Powe.

"Miss Miller," Holmes continued, "I would ask that you refrain from disclosing any information to Mr. Powe and your mother at this time. Do you understand? Can you keep your promise this time?"

Mr. Powe seemed most anxious when he heard these demands from my partner, but when Holmes promised to divulge all of the facts the following morning, he indicated his willingness to abide by my partner's unusual request.

As soon as the two of them had disappeared on their way to Ashfield, Holmes warned, "Watson, we must hurry to Torre Abbey, post haste! Now that they know that we've been able to elude them, they'll be heading back to complete their pact with James Cary. And you know what that will mean. . . "

On our way back to the Cary residence, I wondered what role, if any, Mr. Randolph had in this matter, asking, "Holmes, do you suppose that Malcolm Randolph had any knowledge of this elaborately orchestrated robbery?"

"Of course he did," Holmes answered.

Holmes then turned to the butler's role in this mystery.

"When Cary received that threatening letter, he confided in Randolph, requesting that the butler not tell any of the other members of the household staff. It would be their secret, Cary not wishing to alarm his family and their faithful servants. He came up with a plan to move his family away from Torre Abbey until the threat had been removed. His next step was to contact us, having become aware of the several successes you were kind enough to document. Many of which, he must have noticed, had been resolved with the utmost discretion.

Shortly after, Cary informed the staff that the family would be visiting relatives for several weeks and that he would be placing them on hiatus until their return. At that point in time, Malcolm Randolph may have been totally unaware of Bedlam's plans. It would seem that at the beginning of her employment at Torre Abbey, the woman had been performing her duties adequately. While not overly friendly, she had been following the butler's directives to the letter. Still, he must have sensed that something was not quite right, and as we both now know his suspicions proved to be correct.

Randolph noticed that Bedlam always seemed to be nearby whenever Cary and he would converse. He became further concerned when he caught her skulking behind the staircase which led to the tunnels below the Abbey. According to one of his comments to us, when he confronted the woman, accusing her of secretly eavesdropping, she repeatedly denied such actions vehemently, attributing it to mere coincidence.

I sensed that Randolph began to shadow the housekeeper. Ever careful to avoid being seen, the butler learned of the many secret passageways that existed below the family home."

When Holmes briefly paused his explanation, I found that I simply had to interject, "Holmes, why didn't Randolph disclose this information to us? Surely, it would have saved us a great deal of wasted effort, not to mention the danger in which we were placed."

"Watson," Holmes smiled at my comment, then asked, "do you remember when we interviewed Randolph? Do you recall me asking him if he could tell us anything that might help us in our investigation?"

"Why, yes, Holmes," I responded, "I didn't realize that he knew more at the time."

"Well, my good friend," Holmes continued, "I distinctly remember his response. Don't you recall him saying, 'I would like to help you, gentlemen, but **I can't**'."

The look on my face betrayed my confusion, I began to spew forth gibberish, "Well, er, oh, I believe so. . ."

"Watson," Holmes began to chuckle. "What a dunderhead I was. Randolph was giving us a clue after all. When he said **'can't'** he was referring to Kent, as in Kents Cavern."

"Oh, I see now," I bowed in embarrassment, continuing, "so that's why you became so interested in the caves."

"Of course," Holmes replied, adding, "Watson, don't you see that with Bedlam always within earshot, the butler had to be careful not to put Cary and his family at risk. If Lucretia Bedlam heard Randolph actually tell us where to look, she could certainly have done grave harm to the Cary family."

Holmes was in the process of finishing his remarks as our carriage entered the grounds of the old Abbey. We imagined that we would run into the brigands removing their treasures out through the rear entrance of the lower levels of the estate. Holmes believed that they would store their findings near the old catacombs. Our revolvers were at the ready, fully loaded, as we moved ever closer to the Spanish Barn.

"Hello, Mr. Holmes, Doctor Watson," came a most familiar voice.

I was about to empty a round into the shadows from whence the voice came, when Holmes calmly said, "Relax, Watson. All is well! Our work is done here, my friend."

Putting his weapon away, the world's greatest consulting detective reached into the darkness and offered, "Chief Inspector Davis, so nice of you to drop by. . . Did you get to meet the lovely Lucretia Bedlam?"

Both men shared a laugh while I nervously scratched my noggin, offering, "Gentlemen, what is the meaning of this? We should be on about our business with these dangerous killers on the loose. Someone else might be being murdered!"

"Shall I tell him, Holmes?" the Chief Inspector offered.

Holmes nodded to the law official, stating,, "Davis, please educate the good Doctor. . ."

What followed was Chief Inspector Davis's summary of the afternoon's events. Briefly, he said that he was informed by Mr. Holmes that a major crime was to commence on the afternoon of December 22nd, the date of the winter solstice. Mr. Holmes had further suggested that the Chief Inspector should surround the Torre Abbey grounds and be ready to arrest all of the individuals who would be seen carrying bags or boxes from either the main building or the Spanish Barn.

Davis was urged to bring a large number of constables with him, and to be ready for any possible altercations coming from the suspects. He was informed that particular attention should be given to a certain Lucretia Bedlam, whom Holmes had believed to have been one of the ringleaders of the operation. She and the Druid leader known as Terra were to be interrogated as to the threats made to Mr. James Cary, owner of Torre Abbey.

As it turned out, Davis followed Holmes's plans to the letter, resulting in the arrest of one of the most dangerous crime organizations in England and, indeed, the entire European continent.

Having listened to Davis's description of the day's events, I was greatly mystified. I had to admit that I was totally unprepared for such a resolution to the threats that had terrorized the Carys over these past several months.

I turned to my friend, "Holmes, I must say that I am greatly relieved by what has recently transpired, but I still don't understand the need for the killings. Why did those people need to be killed?"

Before I could get an answer from him, a wagon pulled up to the Torre Abbey household. It was now completely dark except for the lanterns that adorned both sides of the main entrance. The light cast by these devices was bright enough for us to identify Mr. James Cary accompanied by Wiggins and Mr. Bobo Roberts.

Upon seeing us, they cheered loudly. "Mr. Holmes, Doctor Watson, we're so glad to see you are safe."

Quickly, they hopped down from the carriage and made their way over to us. Cary also walked over and he was the first one to talk.

"Mr. Holmes and Doctor Watson, words cannot describe my gratitude for what you've done for me and my family. I knew not where to turn. I knew not what to do." Clearly, he was speaking from the heart.

"As a matter of fact, had I not taken a look at my daughter's copy of "The Sign of the Four", I don't know what I would have done," Cary admitted. "It got me thinking that here was a man for my situation!"

"By Jove," he continued, "you both proved worthy of your outstanding reputations."

"Ah, thank you, Mr. Cary," I bowed, continuing, "but you should also be thanking your own village constable, Chief Inspector Miles Davis, and the newest members of our crime-fighting fraternity, Mr. Bill Wiggins and Mr. Bob-O Roberts."

Cary shook his head in approval and was about to continue praising those gentlemen when Mr. Roberts spoke out.

"Ah," Bobo Roberts felt the need to speak. "Dr. Watson, it's

Bo-Bo...Bo-Bo..."

"Damn it all," I suddenly blurted out loud. "For the life of me I can't ever remember how to say your name! Please excuse my outburst, Bobo. Also, Mr. Cary, I didn't mean to interrupt."

"Of course, doctor," Cary replied, and once more facing the other three men and issued, " Gentlemen, thank you one and all. I can assure you that I am eternally grateful for your work in protecting me and my family. Please be assured that I am at your disposal if ever you need my counsel. Now, if you'll excuse me, I must attend to the needs of my family."

We must have looked as weary as we felt, for when Chief Inspector Davis suggested we join him for a pint, he was quickly taken up on his kind offer. Our group agreed to meet later that evening at 7:45 PM at an establishment called Davey Jones Inn. Holmes and I received transportation back to the Imperial Hotel from one of Chief Inspector Davis's constables and it wasn't long before we were back in a hotel landau heading for our rendezvous. As the drinks and steamed cod were being served, a conversation started up in a most peculiar manner.

"Say, Mr. Holmes," Wiggins began, "we've all been so busy the last several hours, I forgot to tell you what Bobo and I were able to discover after we split up on the Daddyhole plain."

Holmes just looked at him for a moment and then, inquired, "Ah, Wiggins, please excuse me for my lapse of concentration. I'm afraid that it skipped my mind completely due to the day's excitement. Pray tell us all about your findings."

"Wait just a minute," Bobo suddenly spoke out, "Wiggins, I think we should warn Mr. Holmes and Doctor Watson, that what you're about to tell them might perhaps, serve to diminish their excellent day's success."

That brought everyone to attention with Holmes, now very much interested, inquiring, "Oh, my, you two are about to tell us about your run in with the Reverend David Prentiss, are you not?"

You could have heard the proverbial pin drop when Holmes made that remark. Chief Inspector Davis was as mystified by Holmes's comment as were Wiggins and Bobo. All exchanged glances with each other wondering how Holmes could have found out about their remarkable good fortune.

"Hold on now," Wiggins started, "Mr. Holmes, Doctor Watson, how could you have learned about our meeting with the Vicar? Why it was only Bobo and me that had the experience. We only just confided the event with Chief Inspector Davis, for proper legal enforcement procedures."

I couldn't believe what I was observing. Holmes and I had been together all day long. I didn't know how in the world he could have learned about the activity of Wiggins, Bobo and the Vicar, whatever it was.

Holmes was now smiling broadly, laughing his haughty laugh, the laugh usually reserved for those with whom he was jousting.

"All right, Mr. Holmes," Bobo teased, "if you think you know what happened to us this afternoon, please go ahead and tell us. But, be sure you tell us how you learned of these exploits."

I must say that I always looked forward to others experiencing

Holmes's unusual deductive skills. Tonight promised to be one of those moments!

"If you insist, gentlemen," Holmes replied in a very deliberate manner and then he began his explanation.

"Wiggins, when you and Bobo arrived back at Torre Abbey with Mr. Cary, I sensed from your smiling faces that something wonderful must have occurred that afternoon. When you learned of Doctor Watson, Chief Inspector Davis and my accounting of the capture of Terra and Bedlam, along with their thugs, there seemed to have been very little interest on your parts. Oh, you both congratulated our success, but I would have expected much, much more in the way you reacted.

Hmmm. . . what could that mean? Only one thing, one thing as far as I could determine. The Wiggins-Roberts duo must have achieved something far better. Now, what could be more important, more meaningful than removing a large, dangerous bunch of international thieves from the streets of Torquay, England?

Well, now it becomes rather simple to deduce that some how, some way, the person or persons who murdered Torquay's four councilmen has or have been captured. Certainly, that would be something to crow about, wouldn't it?

Congratulations are definitely in order, Wiggins and Bobo. . . Great work!"

The looks on our companion's faces indicated how fascinated they were at Holmes's commentary, and soon, could be heard some muffled laughter.

When he had finished, I again thought of how simple he always made it seem. It always seems simple when the magician shows how "leger de la main" is unmasked for all to understand. Still, it continues to boggle one's mind.

But Holmes was not finished...

"Gentlemen, if you will continue to indulge me for a few minutes more," offered my partner, "I will endeavor to describe how this capture came about."

"I, for one, cannot wait to hear your depiction," spoke Mr. Roberts, who appeared slightly put off by Holmes's apparent braggadocio.

"When Watson and I last saw you, Bobo," Holmes continued, "you and Wiggins had blended into the crowd of singing, dancing Druids. At that point, Doctor Watson and I headed down into the caves. So, what I am able to tell you about the capture and successful arrest of Vicar Prentiss may seem like a lucky guess or some mystical ability, but let me assure you it was neither.

I believe that while the two of you were pressing through the crowd, looking for the antlered leader, Terra, you saw Vicar Prentiss and decided to follow him for a while. Having witnessed some of his peculiar actions earlier in our investigations, it would seem logical to trail him and see what he was up to. Now, somewhere along the way, you must have witnessed him doing something strange, something out of the ordinary that captured your interest. My theory is that Prentiss had been following someone, and after accosting that person, forcibly led that person down the pathway to the shoreline below Daddyhole Plain.

The two of you, fearing the worst, confronted the evil Prentiss who was about to claim another victim of his blood lust. A fierce struggle ensued, and the two of you were able to subdue and arrest Vicar David Prentiss, the serial killer of Torquay."

Bobo, unable to control his emotions, raised his voice, "Mr. Holmes, you had to have been there to describe the event so accurately! Or, else, someone who had witnessed our actions reported back to you. That's the only way you could have known what actually happened!"

Holmes, smiling as he added his favorite blend to his briar, responded calmly, "So it would seem, Bobo, so it would seem. But, alas, you are wrong. . . "

"I will continue," my friend offered to all of us. "Mr. Roberts, when you and Wiggins approached us at Torre Abbey, I could not help but see sand in the folds of your partially soaked pant cuffs. Your shirt was badly torn, and the fresh scent of Channel fish was, dare I suggest, quite telling! Wiggins's coat likewise showed signs of wear, and clearly, fabric tears and pulls were most noticeable. From those clues, I deduced a mighty struggle."

At that point, a very audible silence was most apparent in our group as Davis, Roberts and Wiggins all reviewed what Holmes had logically put forth.

Suddenly, we all began to laugh with unbridled delight at what had just occurred.

"Holmes," spoke the law officer with great affection, "that was incredible. I had heard of your skills and read about them through the efforts of Doctor Watson's writings, but I have to say that to witness them, firsthand, is particularly satisfying. I applaud you, sir, and I will never forget what I've just seen and heard."

"You know, Mr. Holmes, I am also stunned by what I've heard," Bobo Roberts expressed with deep admiration. "Wiggins had shared many of his experiences with you and the good Doctor, but they seemed difficult to fathom. Now, having witnessed your skills, personally, I will never doubt your worth."

Wiggins just bowed in silent agreement with his detective partner. I, for my part, smiled contentedly, happy that others had been privy to some of the skills that I had seen over so many years and so many adventures.

Holmes sat at the table, his smoke filling the tiny pub, quietly relishing the laudatory comments that had been put forth.

"So," he inquired, "while you gentlemen were impressed by my mere ability to put puzzle pieces together, I have to admit that I'd really like to hear about Prentiss."

"Perhaps, tomorrow gentlemen," suggested Chief Inspector Davis. "I would like all of you to meet me at Torre Abbey at 10:00 AM."

The "Spanish" Barn at Torre Abbey

Chapter 17 All Is Explained

December 23rd

At 10:00 AM, Sherlock Holmes and I once again entered the main hall of Torre Abbey. The building was very much alive now that the Cary family and full staff had returned to their stately home. It was so good to hear little feet running up and down the polished stairway, doing what children are expected to be doing. Randolph smiled broadly, as he welcomed us back. These were once more happy times in the Cary household, and this was how it should always be.

After a warm greeting, we were quickly ushered into Mr. Cary's comfortable study. There were smiles all around the huge conference table and we quickly joined our friends.

"Well," joked the Chief Inspector, "I'm glad to see all of you are here on time. As you are about to learn, there are many, many loose ends that need to be tied up and I'm certain that all of us have questions that still need to be answered. Who would like to begin?"

It came as no surprise to anyone that Holmes stood up, offering, "Why don't I start?"

"Gentlemen," he paused dramatically, "like the rest of you, I want this case to be closed as soon as possible. It has been a busy several days for some of us, and sadly, weeks and months for a few more of you."

"And so," he continued, "I would like to answer the first question which I will also take the liberty of posing."

All of our party found Holmes's clever comment most amusing and bade him continue.

"Now I'm sure that many of you are curious about Lucretia Bedlam," he paused briefly. "Well, there is much to learn about this woman. Who she is? From whence she came? How did she become a member of the Cary household?"

"Certainly, we're all in agreement that she was a miserable scoundrel, though I hate to make that type of a remark about a person of the fairer gender. But we need to know more. . ." Holmes stopped again to strike a match to his ever-present pipe.

"Here is what I've learned about the woman, Lucretia Bedlam," Holmes began, having set the stage for his report.

"When the threatening note first arrived at the Cary household, it was believed by all to have come from the same person or persons who had been executing the councilmen. Mr. Cary and the rest of us were unsure from whence it had come, but the message was certainly clear enough. The Cary family, because of Mr. Cary's position on the Torquayian town council, was now in real danger. Like any caring individual whose family had been placed in harm's way, Mr. Cary moved his loved ones out to their country home, purportedly for the purpose of spending time with other family members, but in actual reality, for their own protection.

We found out later, that Mrs. Bedlam had written the letter. She did so to make it easier for her gang to search for a treasure she believed to have been hidden somewhere on the vast Torre Abbey grounds.

Bedlam, we later discovered, had been a devout member of the Premonstratensian Order and had been residing in Paris. While there, living the monastic life, she realized that she had lost her calling. Leaving the abbey, she set out to find another career. Soon thereafter, Bedlam began to spend time in the company of some shady characters. Sadly, she became enamored of their decadent lifestyles and quickly gained favor, rising in their ranks to become the leader of a notorious band of brigands known as the Grenadier mob. For years that group terrorized France and many other European countries, specializing in bank robberies and extortion. Interesting to note, her gang has not yet been implicated in any murders, though I've only been able to make the most rudimentary inquiries.

She must have learned about Torre Abbey and the story of the Spanish treasure while still serving at the Parisian Abbey of St. Norbert. While there, it is reasonable to conclude that she probably came across historical records dating back to when Torre Abbey was still operating under the Premonstratensians. Surely, she must have found a crude map of some sort which made reference to the hidden location of the silver bullion lost during the capture of the Spanish ship, Nuestra Senora del Rosario, in 1588.

An aside, gentlemen, if you wouldn't mind, Doctor Watson and I had discussed this very interesting historical event on our way to Torquay. According to local history of this region, the Spanish vessel had sailed near the coast of Falmouth, initially avoiding notice by the British fleet. Word came from Spanish spies that the Nuestra would soon be discovered, and its capture would mean British seizure of the huge amount of silver in its hold. Under cover of darkness, the Nuestra slipped by the British fleet near Torquay, and sent a landing party ashore to carry the bullion and bury it in a hidden cave, called Caverna del Diablo, and there, it was believed, the treasure was buried.

Legend has it, that soon after, the vessel entered battle. Despite valiant efforts, it was captured by the British fleet and the entire crew of the Nuestra was remanded to a tithe-barn belonging to the Torre Abbey estate. There, for fourteen days, the imprisoned sailors languished in crowded quarters, many eventually succumbing to the terrible conditions. It was believed that one of the Spaniards, who had been a member of the landing party, escaped from the barn, and somehow made his way back to the location of the treasure. With him went the actual location of the silver, its whereabouts unknown, until Mrs. Bedlam found the map.

Once she had it in her possession, the Cary's new housekeeper fixated on finding the treasure, planning a strategy that might give her and her band access to the Cary estate and the entire grounds of Torre Abbey. She sensed that there must have been some type of underground passageway to the Cavern of the Devil.

All she lacked initially was the opportunity to search for the bullion, unencumbered by people who would, naturally, become aware of her actions. If she could only find a way!

Fortunately for her, as we have learned, Mr. Cary had advertised for additional personnel to staff his large estate. And so it was that Lucretia Bedlam approached Mr. James Cary with a forged letter of recommendation that supposedly came from one of Cary's former associates who had recently moved to Paris.

Of course we all realize that Bedlam had received an excellent education while serving as a postulant in the Premonstratensian abbey in Paris. She easily gained Mr. Cary's approval and confidence. It only became a matter of time for her to hatch her plot to gain total control of Mr. Cary and the entire estate."

All eyes turned to James Cary when Holmes had completed his background information on the infamous Bedlam.

"Mr. Holmes has done well in articulating the doings of that Bedlam woman," Cary whined. "I am ashamed of the way that I handled my predicament. I feared for the safety of my family, and so, with the help of my good friend, my valued butler, Mr. Malcolm Randolph, we agreed to virtually every request she made of us."

"No one here would have done anything other than what you were forced to do," Chief Inspector Davis spoke, trying to assuage the guilt that Cary must have been feeling.

Cary thanked the lawman and continued, "Mr. Holmes, as you probably discovered when you arrived here, Bedlam never suspected that I had contacted you about the threatening note. However, with your sudden appearance at Torre Abbey she realized that I had asked for your help. Subsequently, her threats to me and my family became ever more vile. Randolph wanted to help you, but he couldn't risk what could happen to my family."

"I understand fully and you had every reason to trust him," Holmes added, "he had a great responsibility resting upon his shoulders and he handled himself properly."

"What can any of you tell me about this Druid, Terra?" the Chief Inspector voiced.

"Ah, Terra," sighed Wiggins, "I can tell you a few things about the man, but I've a feeling Mr. Holmes and the good Doctor Watson will be able to fill in any of the items I may skip."

And so Wiggins began his informative narration.

"Well, when we were first contacted by Mr. Holmes, he invited us to help with an investigation he was soon about to conduct. Early on, he suggested that Bobo and me take a trip to a Druid encampment a few miles out of Torquay. There had been much talk about these strange people and their ways and many of the town's inhabitants began to associate the murders that had been committed over the last several months with them. As we all came to learn, the weapons used included many of the devices utilized by the followers of Druidism. You know, the noose known as a laqueus and the like. Also, druid signs like triskels, awens, torcs and sigils began to appear near each of the killings.

Anyway, we reported what we had observed to Mr. Holmes and Doctor Watson. Soon it became evident to us that someone wanted the Druids to take the blame for the murders. From what Bobo and I had seen, the tribe seemed like a harmless group of lost souls, looking for something they could see and believe in. The leader, Terra, did not pose any threat to anyone, at least as far as we could tell. Still, there was something going on out there that was a little disturbing. For instance, the entire Druid settlement had guards all about their village. We saw no reason for that, but it was a new experience for all of us. We could only judge by what we observed.

Bobo and I did observe several among them searching the grounds, apparently keeping an eye out.. I remember asking one of their folk what they were seeking and he pulled out some strange looking coin. He explained that this entire area had been colonized by the ancient Romans, hundreds of years ago. Members of this Druid community had found some of these golden coins here and there and they said that their leader, this Terra, sent them all over the southerly coast to look for more of the coins.

Well, Bobo and I reported what we witnessed and Mr. Holmes seemed very interested. It wasn't two days later that we received a brief message from Mr. Holmes. We were advised to keep an eye on the sect, and that Mr. Holmes had learned that the area had, indeed, served as a Roman outpost during the reign of Hadrian, the ruler responsible for the construction of the famous wall that divided England for many, many years.

Holmes further informed us that the cult leader was certainly no fool. It would have been easy for a man of his purpose and intellect to determine that the abbot of Torre Abbey and his friars might have discovered a repository for the Roman golden coins on or about the surrounds of the abbey.

In conclusion, the last time we were in contact with any of the Druids was yesterday when we became involved in the solstice celebration."

Bobo was the next to speak out, "Mr. Holmes, have you any

idea how Bedlam and the Druid leader came to work together?"

Holmes looked over at me and offered, "Watson, why don't you field this interrogative?"

I was glad to have been invited to share my knowledge of the situation, which had been greatly clarified after a recent talk with Holmes.

"Certainly, Bo-Bo," I teased, for I had finally gotten his name correct. "Holmes and I analyzed the strange alliance over several conversations and we agreed that their collaboration was one of those bizarre serendipitous events that one hears about from time to time. Did we believe that the two search parties were searching for two different commodities? Yes, at least at first.

The Druids, upon finding the cave at Daddyhole, entered the caves for the expressed purpose of finding ancient Roman gold coins, which were supposedly buried beneath the bones of an ancient cave bear. Bedlam, as you already have learned, sought the Spanish silver bullion from the Nuestra.

Was it possible that one of the two treasure hunting parties may have passed through the cave tunnels without knowing another group was also searching in the same locale?

Holmes and I agreed that it could only have been an extremely remote possibility for that condition to have existed. The laws of probability would dictate that the two groups had to have discovered each other. At that point, the two leaders decided that it made more sense to work together rather than become embroiled in a knock-down, drag-out altercation. Both groups had become aware that they were being watched and knew that time was running out on them.

Additionally, working together, both gangs would be able to work harder and faster, and so, share two treasures instead of one!

Our theories on the matter proved to be correct as you know, for when both parties were captured as they emerged from Torre Abbey, they were all working together."

"Gentlemen," Davis responded with modest gratitude, "it was only through your careful investigative skills that our lawmen were able to make those arrests."

"That leaves us with one last mystery," Holmes stated, looking directly at Wiggins and Roberts. "Would you detectives please provide us with the details as to how you were able to capture the person responsible for terrorizing the peaceful little community of Torquay?"

Bobo smiled and turning to his partner, Wiggins, suggested, "Wiggy, why don't you present the details of our adventure?"

"Certainly, Bobo," the tall quiet Baker Street Irregular replied. "I'll try my best to tell the story exactly the way it happened."

"As you correctly surmised, Mr. Holmes, Bobo and I were very active in our search among the Druid celebrants on Daddyhole Plain. We followed your advice looking for an antlered individual, Terra, whom we believed would certainly be conducting the solstice rituals for his devoted followers. I must tell you we were both very uncomfortable moving through the noisy gathering, many of whom were well-along on the road to the land of drunken stupor.

At any rate, the crowded revelers made it most difficult to observe the goings-on, but good fortune was with us, for a path opened up leading to the edge of the cliff overlooking the Channel. Bobo and I began to walk along that pathway to take a rest from the pushing and shoving that we had been experiencing as we searched the crowd. We paused along the precipice and scanned the horizon, enjoying the marvelous view out to sea from such a favorable vantage point.

While there, Bobo pointed out two individuals walking down the steep path to the beach below. At first, we thought nothing of it as they reached the rocky shore. Suddenly, we witnessed one of the men push the other and a fight broke out. Ordinarily, we would have ignored such actions, for arguments are frequently settled with fisticuffs, but for some reason, we sensed that this brawl could lead to serious consequences.

We charged down the trail, yelling and screaming in an effort to stop the fight before any serious damage could occur. Fortunately, both men saw us approaching and the fighting abruptly stopped. As we were nearing the site, suddenly one of the individuals picked up a good-sized rock and hit the other man on the side of the face, knocking him to the ground. Immediately, I took after the scoundrel while Bobo tried to help the felled man.

After a brief chase, I was able to tackle the individual who began to put up a hell of a fight. He reached in his coat pocket and tried to slip a laqueus over my head. Blocking his effort with my left hand, I quickly landed a solid left to his chin and the fight was over.

Imagine my surprise, gentlemen, when I recognized that the face I had newly punched, belonged to none other than Vicar David Prentiss!

I quickly secured his hands and arms with the very weapon he had tried to use on me and I also located additional cord in his winter coat. While he was still unconscious, I searched his pockets and found an ancient dagger, torcs and other Druid signs and paraphernalia. I wondered if Prentiss was somehow involved in the series of murders of the town's councilmen. Could this be the one? It certainly would call for an investigation of some kind, for Bobo and I could certainly attest to having witnessed an attempted murder.

The gentleman whom Prentiss assaulted seemed to be recovering, but the rock had left a deep gash below his left eye that would surely require medical attention. After Prentiss had regained consciousness, the four of us made our way to the top of the cliff where two constables were located. They cuffed Prentiss and led him back to police headquarters. Bobo and I were required to accompany the prisoner to submit statements as to what had taken place. The injured man, we learned, was yet another Torquay councilman by the name of Donald Dunhill. After some minor attention at the local infirmary, he too appeared at the station where formal charges were made against Vicar Prentiss.

"Well done, men," Chief Inspector Davis congratulated Bobo and Wiggins, adding, "I'll finish the rest of the story of Vicar Prentiss."

"Immediately after Prentiss had been charged," Davis began, "our officers obtained a court order allowing them to search the vicar's properties. It became readily apparent after examining all of the Druid tools, weapons, symbolic artifacts, etc. found there, that Prentiss had somehow been trying to influence public distrust of the Druid cult. Upon further examination, and it didn't take long, Prentiss was placed under arrest for the murders of the four councilmen and attempted murder of the fifth.

Yesterday afternoon, before Wiggins, Roberts, and Cary arrived at Torre Abbey, David Prentiss pleaded guilty to all of the murders of the councilmen. He also identified his fellow conspirators who are currently still at-large."

"Gentlemen," the Chief Inspector voiced as he slowly rose from his chair, "I wish to thank you, one and all, for your roles in bringing these tragic events to a sound conclusion. Mr. Cary, we're glad to have you and your family, safe and sound back at Torre Abbey. Mr. Wiggins and Mr. Roberts, let me say that it has been a real pleasure making your acquaintances and I must commend you both on your fine investigative efforts. I'm sure you both will have excellent careers."

"Mr. Holmes and Doctor Watson," he addressed them with great respect, extending his hand, "I cannot say enough about the incredible skills you both have displayed in your efforts to help solve these crimes. Like many residents of our fine country who have heard and read about your many successful adventures, I, too, am duly impressed by what I have witnessed and learned."

Holmes thanked the lawman for the kind words and added, "Chief Inspector, your modesty obviously prevents you from saying it, but I would like you to know that I believe your town is extremely fortunate to have such a dedicated, competent detective in charge of peace-keeping. Your professionalism has been on display in all of our dealings with you and it is no wonder that we were successful in bringing those criminals to trial. On behalf of Mr. Wiggins, Mr. Roberts, Doctor Watson, and me, I wish to congratulate you on your handling of these investigations."

After shaking their hands and bidding all a good day, the Chief

Inspector left the room and headed back to his office. Wiggins and Roberts were still smiling broadly and would soon be taking their leave. It had been a most successful conclusion to their first investigation.

Holmes and I slowly walked into the wide hallway in time to see Mr. Cary re-entering the building. "Mr. Holmes, Doctor Watson," he began, reaching into his pocket, "here is payment for your outstanding work. I trust that you will find it suitable."

Holmes never even glanced at the envelope as he placed it in his pocket, issuing, "Mr. Cary, I have no doubt that your generosity will be most acceptable to Doctor Watson and me; furthermore, I wish to thank you for . . ."

My friend stopped mid-sentence at the sudden appearance of two young ladies who were making their way down the Cary home's majestic staircase.

"Mr. Holmes, Doctor Watson," the young girl spoke most cordially, "I would like to introduce you both to my best friend, Miss Margaret Cary."

"We are delighted to make your acquaintance, Miss Cary," Holmes politely offered. "Miss Miller has told us so much about you and how much she values your friendship."

"Thank you, Mr. Holmes," the young Cary girl replied, mildly blushing at the compliment.

I couldn't miss the opportunity to add, "Yes, Miss Margaret, Aggie had only the most wonderful things to say about her favorite friend."

"It was nice meeting you," I added, "but I'm afraid that we can't spend more time chatting. You see, Mr. Holmes and I have a carriage waiting and we must hurry if we are to catch our train at Exeter."

"Sadly, Doctor Watson is correct," Holmes offered, "we are on a schedule and it must be followed."

"Miss Cary," he continued, "would you please excuse Miss Miller for a few minutes?"

"Of course, Mr. Holmes, the young Margaret Cary replied, turning to Aggie, "Aggie, I'll be in the pantry with Mr. Randolph."

"Aggie," Holmes suggested, "can we talk? How about the library?"

All three of us entered the spacious room and sat in three of the most comfortable wing-chairs I had ever enjoyed.

"Before you begin," Miss Miller started, "I am sorry that my part in this adventure ended the way it did. I was careless when I thought I could spy on those horrible criminals without being caught. I know that you and Doctor Watson had given me plenty of warnings about my level of involvement, and I disobeyed you, time and time again. I should have known better and there is absolutely no excuse for the way I behaved, especially, the way I put you and Doctor Watson in great danger. If something had happened to me, that would have been tragic, but I now know how much pain it would have caused you both, had something happened to me. Please forgive me!"

There was silence in that room and, for possibly the first time, my friend seemed at a loss for words.

Finally, he spoke, "Aggie, there are any number of things you need to hear from me and the good doctor, but I'll not tarnish your emotional apology with additional admonitions. I believe that this last episode may have been all that needed to happen. Please thank your wonderful mother for allowing us to get to know you both and for permitting us to have the pleasure of working alongside one of the finest young detectives I know."

With that remark, the teary-eyed young girl quickly rose, ran to hug Holmes and me, and started for the hallway.

She stopped, turned and offered, "Thank you, Mr. Holmes and Doctor Watson. I shall never forget you both."

Chapter 18 Heading Home

Our work in Torquay having been successfully completed, Holmes and I were on our way to catch the train from Exeter to London. We had been away since December 18th and we were both ready to return to our hectic, noisy, London and our Baker Street residence. Another adventure had come and gone, and once more we had been able to thwart the nefarious plans of some of Europe's worst criminal minds. We saved the Cary family from harm and aided in the arrest of two gangs and a serial killer. To my way of thinking, we had done well, very, very well indeed!

"I see by your contented smile that you're enjoying yourself, Watson," my friend teased as our carriage driver moved our luggage to the baggage portal.

"That was not such a difficult deduction," I replied as our London train pulled into the Exeter station, adding, "you know how much I have grown to love re-living our escapades!"

"We certainly had very little time to rest in Torquay," I began again. "From the moment we arrived until we parted company with our fellow detectives, we seemed to be on the go. Wouldn't you agree?"

My friend had little to say, for he was busy directing me into our compartment on the London Express. Luckily, this route had no stops on the way to Paddington Station, saving us at least fifty minutes on our return trip.

"Holmes," I suggested, "you must agree that this was one of our most interesting cases. I mean, with the capture of Vicar Prentiss, and the two gangs, seeing how well Wiggins and Roberts handled themselves, and meeting that young girl, Aggie Miller, and her mother. also, the quaint little town of Torquay. I say, it was quite the whirlwind experience!"

"Quite," my partner tersely responded.

Sensing some mild irritation in his reply, I ventured, "Holmes, is there anything troubling you?"

"Why, no, Watson", he stared at me as he adjusted his reading glasses, "whatever gave you that idea?"

Staring right back at him I raised my voice, "Now, listen Holmes, you can't deny that you are not in a very talkative mood. Simply tell me and I'll say no more!"

"Watson, Watson," he warmed, "old friend, you who know me so well, sometimes know me not at all. I meant nothing hostile in my tone. Your reverie simply interrupted my train of thought. My reflexive response, I do admit, may have seemed a bit caustic. That was all it was. Forgive me."

"Fine," I replied, turning my attention to the winter scenery as we slowly moved up a mild grade.

Holmes had picked up a copy of the Exeter newspaper and was quickly turning page after page, clearly searching for a particular topic.

"Ah, hah," he muttered softly, "Watson, how quickly the news travels. Why only yesterday the arrests and charges had been made and now, this little local paper has the information in print."

He went on, "Listen to this, my friend." Holmes began to read:

Headlines: Happy Christmas for Torquay Residents

"It would appear that residents of the lovely coastal town of Torquay will get to enjoy a Merry Christmas season after all. The town had been the focus of attention since October after one of their councilmen, a Mr. Henry Dinsmore, had been found murdered. The following month brought another councilman murdered, with evidence in both cases pointing to members of the Druid cult that had camped nearby. Citizens had been up in arms over these two deaths, accusing the local authorities for the lack of progress in their investigations.

Things went from bad to worse when two more councilmen were found murdered within two days of each other, once again with evidence indicating Druid involvement. When reporters tried to elicit answers from the officials, Chief Inspector, Miles Davis, could only reply, 'these events are still under investigation. We still haven't enough evidence to arrest.'

Residents had been locking themselves in their domiciles, afraid to work, visit the shops, go to local eating establishments, etc. The entire community had virtually been shut down out of sheer terror!

All of this changed dramatically when Chief Inspector Davis and his excellent fellow law officers were able to capture a prime suspect in the murder investigations. This individual, a Vicar by the name of David Prentiss was caught in the act of attempting to murder Mr. Donald Dunhill, another Torquay councilman.

According to reports, Prentiss was seen attacking Mr. Dunhill along the shoreline of Daddyhole Plain. Two men who witnessed the attack contacted constables in the area who were successful in subduing the perpetrator, Prentiss.

It was further discovered that when charged with attempted murder, Prentiss decided to plead guilty to murdering the other town councilmen. At that time, no further information was made available to our team of reporters."

"Why, I'm stunned, Holmes," I complained. "I can't believe that Chief Inspector Davis said nothing about our assistance in the case."

Holmes snickered at my remark then added, "Watson, our case didn't directly lead to the arrest of Prentiss. It happened while we were trying to protect the Cary family. Still, Detectives Wiggins and Roberts were not mentioned by Davis, and they were the very ones who saved Dunhill's life and captured Prentiss!"

"Oh, my, Holmes," I sighed, angrily, "it would appear that Mr. Wiggins and Mr. Roberts are receiving the same treatment that you and I have received from the local police in our investigative efforts. We do all the work in helping them solve the crimes, but they claim all of the credit for themselves."

"Sadly, that seems to be the case in most instances, Watson," my friend replied. "I've told Wiggins as much when we discussed his career choice."

As our locomotive moved ever closer to its destination, Holmes and I began to discuss many of the questions in our Torquay investigation that we had left unanswered.

One of our discussions dealt with the Ghost of the Spanish Lady.

"I must say, Holmes," I began, "what about the legend of that spectral sighting? I remember we had read an article about a supposed recent appearance witnessed by one of the residents, I believe her name was Spenser. What do you make of it? Also, It's too bad we didn't track that mystery, as well."

Holmes gave me a strange look and then confided, "Watson, you may remember as we discussed this 'ghost' apparition, you teased about how I didn't believe in such things. Well, let me assure you, it wasn't a ghost. As a matter of fact, I forgot to tell you what I discovered in that regard."

"What?" I spewed forth my disappointment. "Do you mean you know that it wasn't a ghost that the woman had observed? Well, what do you believe it was that you saw?"

"Watson, at the time we had more on our minds than some local woman's vision, and we moved on with our own work," Holmes stated. "But, just the other evening when we had returned to the Abbey in our effort to find Cary at home, I observed a strange lighting effect which could be seen moving back and forth across the upper walls of Torre Abbey and the Spanish Barn."

"If you remember, Watson" he continued, "there is a tall pole positioned in front of the house, that has some kind of reflective plate attached to it. I had not given it much attention when first we had explored the grounds, but that evening, the wind was gusting, and every so often, when light reflected from its surface, a strange shape would be cast up on the upper levels of the Abbey and the barn!"

"Watson, the image I saw was that of a dark, shrouded figure," Holmes confided, further issuing, "and, Watson, I noticed that as the pole swayed it produced a most unusual sound that actually did sound like some person moaning. . ."

After letting his words stew for a few seconds in my own mind, I offered, "Holmes, good fellow, that must have been how all of these ghostly appearances had occurred! Why there's another mystery solved."

I continued, "I only wish you had told me when you had seen and heard it."

"Watson," he apologized. "Yes, I should have, but if you remember, that's when we heard Bedlam and Cary arguing."

Next, our conversation moved on to the vicar.

"Watson," Holmes sighed, "I'm glad that we were able to help Cary. I'm also happy that the two mobs were captured as well, but I have to say that upon looking back on the whole series of events, the one thing that I'm disappointed about was not having had the opportunity to meet Prentiss."

"Really, Holmes," I voiced, completely baffled by what I had just heard. "Please tell me why you would you ever want to meet with a murderer?"

"First of all," Holmes began, "I would try to find out why Prentiss had chosen council members. I mean, why them? I would also like to have validated my belief that he was trying to implicate Terra and his clan, although it seems rather obvious. Additionally, I would like to have delved deeper into the man's mental condition. Was he simply a psychopathic killer, or did he have some serious brain damage which led to his compulsive actions?"

"Well, Holmes," I replied, "my friend, you are in luck."

"What do you mean, Watson?" Holmes inquired. "Do you know something about Prentiss that I don't?"

"Actually, I do," I spoke most deliberately, removing a folder from my valise. "Holmes, I was saving this as a surprise until we were back in London, but I sense that you would like to read this report now. Would that be a correct assumption?"

"Why you old. . . " he began as he took the folder from my outstretched hand.

A brilliant smile came to his countenance as he quickly perused the document. Immediately, he replaced his glasses and before we had reached Winchester, he had completed his reading and had returned the information to the folder.

"Watson," the great detective asked, "when did Wiggins give this to you?"

"Holmes," I responded, "as you now know, Wiggins and Roberts were at the police headquarters when Vicar Prentiss was being charged. Chief Inspector Davis allowed them to observe the initial interrogation and they were also allowed to take notes. Wiggins knew how detail oriented you were, and slipped me the folder before we had left Torre Abbey."

"You know, Watson," my friend offered, "those two young men are going to be fine detectives some day. I am most impressed with the way they handled their end of our investigation and I will most certainly let them know about it."

Almost as soon as these words were out of his mouth, Holmes inquired of me, "Say, old boy, did you have a chance to look over this report? If not, I would be only too happy to summarize."

"Go ahead, Holmes," I urged, knowing full-well how much he wanted to attach his own opinions to the events.

Treachery in Torquay

"Well," he began, "in answer to the questions I had posed earlier, according to the interrogation, Vicar David Prentiss is, in fact, no vicar at all. His real name is Matt Kramer, an escapee from the prison at Dartmoor, where he was serving time for the attempted murder of a London politician. He was able to hide beneath the framework of the prison milk wagon when it left the facility having completed its daily delivery.

His disguise as a minister was a brilliant scheme, for no one would have dreamed that a convicted felon could ever assume the behavior of a Man of God. Also, most individuals who had escaped captivity would most certainly have tried to put as much distance as possible between themselves and the prison in which he had been housed. Kramer decided to hide in plain sight, sensing no one would suspect him to be the escaped convict.

As to why he chose to murder councilmen, his response was a simple maniacal, why not. While that answer would suggest Kramer's mental instability, the fact that he was able to come up with a plan to place the blame on a cult of Druids does indicate some level of competence.

Finally, in answer to my desire to delve into Kramer's mind, I'm afraid that would serve no purpose. According to his psychiatric evaluation, the man was nuttier than a mad hatter.!"

When he had finished his summary of the official interrogation, we both settled down for a short while, resting our eyes as our locomotive continued along the rails, each second bringing us closer and closer to our stop. I was content in the knowledge that we had succeeded in helping so many people to resume their ordinary daily work and joys. Christmas would once again be a happy occasion for the lovely resort community.

I tried to rest my weary mind, but there was still something that I had to exact from Holmes. This was the first time that I had seen another side of him. In the course of this investigation there appeared a more caring, compassionate, even paternal Holmes, and I wanted to know more about these alterations.

"Holmes," I inquired with great sincerity, "I have noticed a change in your demeanor during our trip to Torquay. I'm curious as to why this may have happened. You have always been, forgive me, the stern, unemotional, problem-solver whose only concern was to effect a proper solution to a difficult situation. I wish to know if you are aware of these changes."

"Utter rubbish, Watson," he replied. "I'm the same as I've always been: concise, demanding, with very little emotion, skeptical, sarcastic at times, and don't forget egotistical!"

"You must be imagining things, old friend," he suggested.

Changing the subject, he offered, "Watson, old chap, what would you say to a trip to a local pub when we disembark? I'll join you for some fish and chips."

Saying nothing, I simply stared at him, waiting for him to continue our discussion.

"Well, my good man," he answered his own question, "you may not be hungry, but I am. Should you change your mind, you are most welcome to join me."

Again, I chose to say nothing. Instead, I picked up the Exeter newspaper and slowly leafed through the agony section.

A short time later, he softened, "Well, perhaps I have changed. I'm not sure why or how much, but as we became more fully aware of the possible dangers in which we had unwittingly placed Miss Aggie, I grew very concerned about her welfare. She is a brilliant young girl; extremely intelligent, kind, observant, careful in her conduct. Those are all laudable qualities, to be sure. However, we were also witnesses to how dangerously inquisitive and terribly headstrong she can be."

"So, what are you saying, Holmes?" I teased.

"You bloody well know what I'm saying, Watson," he returned, somewhat harshly, "she touched my heart. There, is that what you wanted to hear?"

"Holmes," I continued, "that is exactly what I wanted to hear you say. You're not that cold, steely, heartless soul who cares for no one but himself. There is a compassionate individual in there somewhere and it's something that you should cherish. God forgive me, but it makes you seem human!"

The look on my friend's face was priceless. Holmes didn't know where to look, what to do, what to say. The man was truly lost for words.

"See here, Watson," he whispered with great intensity, "I may have softened a bit, but it was only because I began to feel guilty for having placed that young girl in harm's way. When I saw her being paraded in the cavern, bound and gagged, having recently been covered by a funeral shroud, I felt ill. All I could think of was Clara Miller's heart being broken by the careless actions of two strangers. Watson, for one of the few times in my life, I feared for what might happen to all of us. And, at that moment, I would have sold my soul to the devil to know that Aggie Miller was safe at home with her mother."

With that having been spoken, I thought I saw some tears beginning to form. While I had long wanted to finally experience some display of care and concern in this brave man's steely demeanor, I hadn't suspected that my prompting would lead to such heartfelt reaction.

"Watson, I must apologize for my weakness," he said sternly, 'but this you will know, never again will I allow my good intentions to override that which I know to be the correct thing to do. I'll never allow myself to put a child in jeopardy. Never again!"

After that heart-wrenching admission, Holmes struck a match to his briar and left the compartment. He apparently needed to remove himself from the situation and gather himself. Sensing how much that emotional outburst must have affected him, I shook my head, issuing a severe personal rebuke, "Watson," I whispered, "you fool. Why in the world would you pressure your best friend with those concerns?"

Soon, Holmes returned from his brief absence, much more like the Holmes I was accustomed to seeing, "Well, Watson, I have to ask you what you thought about the disposition of the booty that the thugs had discovered. Were you satisfied with the ruling?"

"For the most part, I agreed with the local commissioner's decision," I responded, "but I'm sure there will be some individuals who will challenge how the coins and silver were dispensed."

I continued, "Of course the decision to remand the silver bullion to the English government will be disputed by Spain, but since it had been hidden on British territory during that great battle, clearly it qualifies as spoils of war. I'm sure Spain will try to overturn the ruling, but I don't think they have a chance in hell of changing the outcome."

Holmes shook his head in agreement, but he quickly offered, "Yes, Watson, I am in complete accord with you on that point. Still, one never knows what might happen should a future hearing come to fruition. What about the Roman coins that were found in Kents Cavern?"

"That ruling, I'll admit, was not to my liking," I elaborated, "Holmes, I feel that Mr. Powe should have received a share of that treasure. Just imagine, those coins had been in that cave for centuries! Only the Premonstratensian monks at Torre Abbey, and other branches of that religious order, would have had any knowledge of the existence of the Roman coins. Additionally, the recovered booty wasn't on the grounds of the Abbey anyway. If I were Powe, I would file a legal challenge to have a portion of the gold found on his property awarded to him. It's terribly unjust to have the entire amount placed in the coffers of Torquay."

Holmes only replied, "I can see your point, Watson, but we'll have to leave those decisions for others to make. We can only hope that when all of the litigation has been completed, all parties will be satisfied."

My traveling companion's last remark was quickly followed by a loud, shrill whistle, signaling our locomotive's progress through another small hamlet along the way. Soon, we would be arriving at our London terminus, bringing another one of our adventures to a successful end.

Afterword

Thursday, March 15th, 1928

    I recently was reviewing all of the adventures in which my good friend and companion, Mr. Sherlock Holmes, and me, had experienced. When I had finished compiling my tales, I had to say that I was profoundly pleased by my findings. Now, it's not that I'm basking in self-praise for the outstanding body of work that I have contributed to world literature. No, although some fans of our tales have been known to claim as much, that was never my purpose.

    Certainly, we've been through our share of successes and I should add, the occasional failure. That cannot be denied, but such is life. Now, you might wonder, what is the point that I am trying to make?

    Actually, it became more of a reflection of the people whose lives have become inextricably connected with Holmes and me by virtue of our shared experiences. In these tales, we have come to know the best and worst of mankind, separating the wheat from the chaff as we helped people with some of life's trials and tribulations. In most cases, we have been successful in our efforts, and in doing so, we've enjoyed strong friendships, alliances and attendent financial gain.

    After all, our clients were privileged to have come to know and appreciate the skills of the world's finest consulting detective.

    At any rate, while leafing through our case files, I fondly remembered our meeting with a most curious young girl from Torquay. Her name at the time was Aggie Miller. That was many years ago, but both Holmes and I remember her well. She became involved in one of our most interesting cases involving multiple murders, the pursuit of long lost treasures and some spectral events that were of great interest to citizens of her lovely home town.

During our visit to that coastal community, Holmes and I were treated to one of the most exuberant, clever, multi-talented individuals that we've ever encountered. As we worked to solve the mysteries in that lovely Devonshire region, which I've named *Treachery in Torquay*, Aggie's tenacity and intelligence were most memorable. We came to know and appreciate her family and other members of the peaceful Torquay community whose world was being altered forever by a series of senseless murders. It was 1905 when we were called to help a family whose lives were being threatened.

Of particular interest to me was the talk that Holmes and I later had about this young girl and her future. While I've identified her by her childhood name, most of you, dear readers, may know her by her more famous moniker! You see, Aggie Miller, the inquisitive, gifted youngster that helped us with that Torquay case, grew up to become the famous mystery author, Agatha Christie!

Mrs. Christie was most kind in her praise of the stories penned by yours truly, Dr. John Watson. Indeed, she was kind enough to state that my published adventures had a profound effect on her. So much, she said, that she decided to embark on a career of mystery writing.

For that acknowledgment, I am truly thankful. I am proud that my humble efforts may have in some way influenced her life decision to become a writer. I might add, that from my experiences in reading her work, she has succeeded brilliantly!

Dr. John Watson, MD

Acknowledgments:

Torre Abbey was constructed as a working Premonstratensian Abbey. Years ago, when the monastery order moved from that site, it eventually fell into the hands of a famous Torquay family, the Cary family. I have attempted to keep certain aspects of those historical facts as a part of my story. Action takes place in many sections of the Torquay countryside: Kents Cavern, Daddyhole, Ashfield, and the famous Imperial Hotel.

While my work is purely fictional, I thought it might be interesting to blend actual places with actual depictions of fictitious members of the Cary family, taking care to portray those members in only the most positive light.

To that end, any resemblance to actual events or persons, living or dead is coincidental. I would also like to express my appreciation to the Conan Doyle Estate and Agatha Christie, Ltd. for use of their characters.

I wish to thank my lovely wife, Gloria, and the rest of my family and close friends for their support during this project. Their patience and understanding during the composition of this novel was integral to the successful completion of my work.

This is my second pastiche involving Sir Arthur Conan Doyle's brilliant characters and I sincerely hope that my efforts may serve to enhance the enjoyment of fellow Sherlockians!

I would also like to thank the following organizations, authors, agencies and others listed below for their use and permissions:

The Conan Doyle Estate

Agatha Christie. Ltd.

The Bedside Companion to Sherlock Holmes (Riley & McAllister)

Torquay, The Charm and History of its Neighborhood (John Presland)

A Short Description of Torre Abbey (Hugh R. Watkin)

Wikipedia: Agatha Christie

Daddyhole: (An Article by local historian Dr. Kevin Dixon)

Graphics Credits:

page 68, Imperial Hotel, adventures-of-the-blackgang.tumblr.com

page 196, Torre Abbey, Hugh R. Watkins

page 213, Ashfield, 20i30.blogspot.com

page 226, Daddyhole JSBlog-Journal of a Southern Bookreader

page 237, Kents Caverns, www.kents-cavern.co.uk

page 287, Spanish Barn, geograph.org uk

I am particularly appreciative for the contributions of my team of editors who have done an excellent job in assisting me in this endeavor.

Gloria Lawler

Joseph M. Lawler

Elaine Kuffa

Megan Kuffa

Ted Merli, Jr.

Also from MX Publishing

MX Publishing is the world's largest specialist Sherlock Holmes publisher, with over a hundred titles and fifty authors creating the latest in Sherlock Holmes fiction and non-fiction.

From traditional short stories and novels to travel guides and quiz books, MX Publishing cater for all Holmes fans.

The collection includes leading titles such as _Benedict Cumberbatch In Transition_ and _The Norwood Author_ which won the 2011 Howlett Award (Sherlock Holmes Book of the Year).

MX Publishing also has one of the largest communities of Holmes fans on Facebook with regular contributions from dozens of authors.

www.mxpublishing.com

Also from MX Publishing

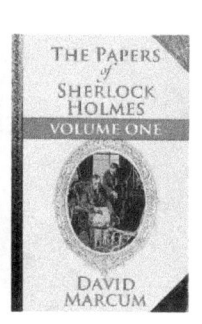

Our bestselling books are our short story collections;

'Lost Stories of Sherlock Holmes', 'The Outstanding Mysteries of Sherlock Holmes', The Papers of Sherlock Holmes Volume 1 and 2, 'Untold Adventures of Sherlock Holmes' (and the sequel 'Studies in Legacy) and 'Sherlock Holmes in Pursuit', 'The Cotswold Werewolf and Other Stories of Sherlock Holmes' – and many more……

www.mxpublishing.com

Also from MX Publishing

"Phil Growick's, 'The Secret Journal of Dr Watson', is an adventure which takes place in the latter part of Holmes and Watson's lives. They are entrusted by HM Government (although not officially) and the King no less to undertake a rescue mission to save the Romanovs, Russia's Royal family from a grisly end at the hand of the Bolsheviks. There is a wealth of detail in the story but not so much as would detract us from the enjoyment of the story. Espionage, counter-espionage, the ace of spies himself, double-agents, double-crossers...all these flit across the pages in a realistic and exciting way. All the characters are extremely well-drawn and Mr Growick, most importantly, does not falter with a very good ear for Holmesian dialogue indeed. Highly recommended. A five-star effort."
The Baker Street Society

www.mxpublishing.com

Also from MX Publishing

The Missing Authors Series

Sherlock Holmes and The Adventure of The Grinning Cat
Sherlock Holmes and The Nautilus Adventure
Sherlock Holmes and The Round Table Adventure

"Joseph Svec, III is brilliant in entwining two endearing and enduring classics of literature, blending the factual with the fantastical; the playful with the pensive; and the mischievous with the mysterious. We shall, all of us young and old, benefit with a cup of tea, a tranquil afternoon, and a copy of Sherlock Holmes, The Adventure of the Grinning Cat."
Amador County Holmes Hounds Sherlockian Society

www.mxpublishing.com

Also from MX Publishing

The American Literati Series

The Final Page of Baker Street
The Baron of Brede Place
Seventeen Minutes To Baker Street

"The really amazing thing about this book is the author's ability to call up the 'essence' of both the Baker Street 'digs' of Holmes and Watson as well as that of the 'mean streets' of Marlowe's Los Angeles. Although none of the action takes place in either place, Holmes and Watson share a sense of camaraderie and self-confidence in facing threats and problems that also pervades many of the later tales in the Canon. Following their conversations and banter is a return to Edwardian England and its certainties and hope for the future. This is definitely the world before The Great War."
Philip K Jones

www.mxpublishing.com

Also from MX Publishing

The Detective and The Woman Series

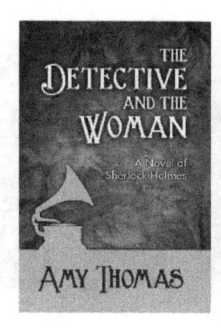

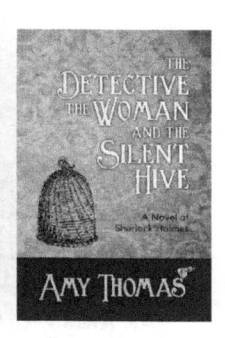

The Detective and The Woman
The Detective, The Woman and The Winking Tree
The Detective, The Woman and The Silent Hive

"The book is entertaining, puzzling and a lot of fun. I believe the author has hit on the only type of long-term relationship possible for Sherlock Holmes and Irene Adler. The details of the narrative only add force to the romantic defects we expect in both of them and their growth and development are truly marvelous to watch. This is not a love story. Instead, it is a coming-of-age tale starring two of our favorite characters."
Philip K Jones

www.mxpublishing.com

Also from MX Publishing

The Sherlock Holmes and Enoch Hale Series

The Amateur Executioner
The Poisoned Penman
The Egyptian Curse

"The Amateur Executioner: Enoch Hale Meets Sherlock Holmes", the first collaboration between Dan Andriacco and Kieran McMullen, concerns the possibility of a Fenian attack in London. Hale, a native Bostonian, is a reporter for London's Central News Syndicate - where, in 1920, Horace Harker is still a familiar figure, though far from revered. "The Amateur Executioner" takes us into an ambiguous and murky world where right and wrong aren't always distinguishable. I look forward to reading more about Enoch Hale."
Sherlock Holmes Society of London

www.mxpublishing.com

Also from MX Publishing

Sherlock Holmes novellas in verse

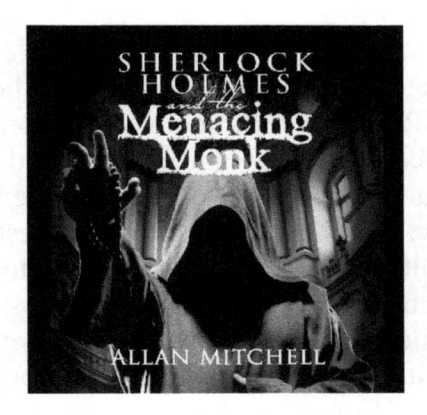

All four novellas have been released also in audio format with narration by Steve White

Sherlock Holmes and The Menacing Moors
Sherlock Holmes and The Menacing Metropolis
Sherlock Holmes and The Menacing Melbournian
Sherlock Holmes and The Menacing Monk

"The story is really good and the Herculean effort it must have been to write it all in verse—well, my hat is off to you, Mr. Allan Mitchell! I wouldn't dream of seeing such work get less than five plus stars from me..." **The Raven**

Also from MX Publishing

THE VATICAN CAMEOS
A SHERLOCK HOLMES ADVENTURE

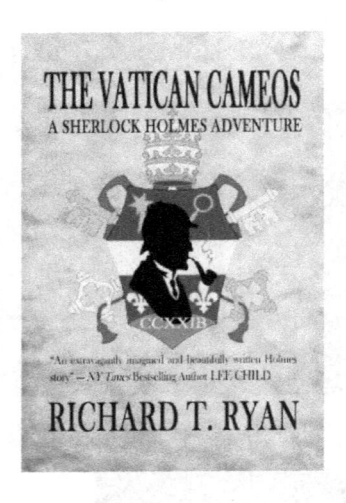

RICHARD T. RYAN

When the papal apartments are burgled in 1901, Sherlock Holmes is summoned to Rome by Pope Leo XII. After learning from the pontiff that several priceless cameos that could prove compromising to the church, and perhaps determine the future of the newly unified Italy, have been stolen, Holmes is asked to recover them. In a parallel story, Michelangelo, the toast of Rome in 1501 after the unveiling of his Pieta, is commissioned by Pope Alexander VI, the last of the Borgia pontiffs, with creating the cameos that will bedevil Holmes and the papacy four centuries later. For fans of Conan Doyle's immortal detective, the game is always afoot. However, the great detective has never encountered an adversary quite like the one with whom he crosses swords in "The Vatican Cameos.."

"An extravagantly imagined and beautifully written Holmes story"
(**Lee Child**, NY Times Bestselling author, Jack Reacher series)

Also from MX Publishing

The Conan Doyle Notes (The Hunt For Jack The Ripper) "Holmesians have long speculated on the fact that the Ripper murders aren't mentioned in the canon, though the obvious reason is undoubtedly the correct one: even if Conan Doyle had suspected the killer's identity he'd never have considered mentioning it in the context of a fictional entertainment. Ms Madsen's novel equates his silence with that of the dog in the night-time, assuming that Conan Doyle did know who the Ripper was but chose not to say – which, of course, implies that good old standby, the government cover-up. It seems unlikely to me that the Ripper was anyone famous or distinguished, but fiction is not fact, and "The Conan Doyle Notes" is a gripping tale, with an intelligent, courageous and very likable protagonist in DD McGil."
The Sherlock Holmes Society of London

www.mxpublishing.com

Also from MX Publishing

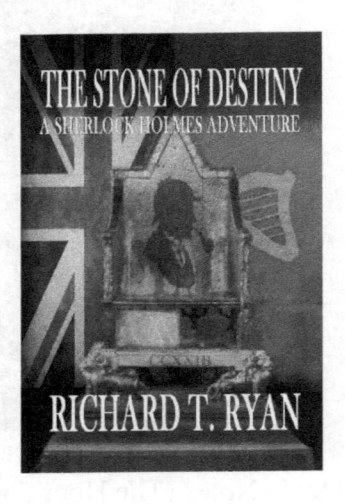

During the elaborate funeral for Queen Victoria, a group of Irish separatists breaks into Westminster Abbey and steals the Coronation Stone, on which every monarch of England has been crowned since the 14th century. After learning of the theft from Mycroft, Sherlock Holmes is tasked with recovering the stone and returning it to England. In pursuit of the many-named stone, which has a rich and colorful history, Holmes and Watson travel to Ireland in disguise as they try to infiltrate the Irish Republican Brotherhood, the group they believe responsible for the theft. The story features a number of historical characters, including a very young Michael Collins, who would go on to play a prominent role in Irish history; John Theodore Tussaud, the grandson of Madame Tussaud; and George Bradley, the dean of Westminster at the time of the theft. There are also references to a number of other Victorian luminaries, including Joseph Lister and Frederick Treves.

Lightning Source UK Ltd.
Milton Keynes UK
UKHW011835221122
412659UK00011B/1523

9 781787 053014